# WITHOUT
# A
# TRACE

# BOOKS BY PEGGY WEBB

# PEGGY WEBB

# WITHOUT A TRACE

bookouture

Published by Bookouture in 2024

An imprint of Storyfire Ltd.
Carmelite House
50 Victoria Embankment
London EC4Y 0DZ

www.bookouture.com



ISBN: 978-1-83525-398-4
eBook ISBN: 978-1-83525-397-7

*To Marte Mason Bock Johnstone, friend extraordinaire who loves reading books as much as I love writing them. With deepest gratitude.*

# PROLOGUE

## HONEY ISLAND SWAMP, LOUISIANA

There she was. Her hair lush. Her face exactly what he wanted.

The girl was alone. Such easy pickings.

He slid along under cover of the trees, a shadow, unseen. Anticipation made his eyes glow like the terrifying Rougarou of Creole legend, the wolf-like creature who stalked his prey in the swamp at night. He was larger than life. Untouchable. Invincible.

Finding a spot that put her in perfect range, he settled in to wait.

She turned and stared toward his hiding place. He hadn't moved, hadn't made a sound. Did she have a sixth sense?

His dart gun held just enough lethal injection to knock her out until he could get her to his special place. The burlap bag was waiting to transport her there like so many dead animals. And then the fun would begin. He raised the gun and aimed.

Still, she stared, her body poised as if for flight. Did she know this was her day to die?

# ONE

## ASSISI, ITALY

*"Find me. Save me..."*

The whisper curled through Assisi like smoke, twisting along the narrow streets of the medieval Italian town, borne on the soft night air that stirred cypress trees, rising above ancient walls and the olive groves beyond. The cry for help went unnoticed by mothers and fathers, sons and daughters sleeping in the giant shadows cast by Mt. Subasio and the Basilica de San Francesco.

But in the heart of the historic town, in a studio flat of pink stone walls and arches so old they had their own story to tell, the whisper came clearly to Annie Logan as she lay on her wrought iron bed, transported to another place by her dreams. Mists swirled around her. She saw massive trees, their roots jutting up from slow-moving water, green with algae. Overhanging branches half-hidden by a curtain of Spanish moss held secrets so dark they shuddered her soul.

"Where are you?" Annie's dream-self asked as she wandered through the swamp, searching.

*"Find me."* The voice was male, deep, and heavily accented.

His whisper echoed through Annie, strangely alluring, tugging at her as if a silver cord bound them.

She struggled against the connection. "Who are you?"

Silence answered her, prolonged, heavy with fear. Suddenly... from the distance... a woman screamed... followed by his voice calling to her once more. "*Help me.*"

Annie's terror was so palpable she jerked awake, her heart hammering, her mouth dry. The luminous dial on her old-fashioned bedside clock showed midnight, the witching hour. This dark dream from the bayous of her mother's childhood usually came to her at midnight, the details vivid, the message clear. *Danger.*

She grabbed her cell phone and punched in her sister's number. It would still be early evening in the States. Jen, the oldest of the three Logan sisters, answered in her usual authoritative, straight-to-the-point way.

"Annie? If you're calling to tell me you've had a dream predicting disaster for our family again, I'm going to run through Gulf Breeze screaming."

"I don't know..." Annie murmured.

She put her cell on FaceTime just to have the reassurance of seeing her beloved sister, so like their mother with her wild mane of black curls, dark eyes that see your soul, and the regal bearing of a queen. Jen was sitting in a lounge chair in the pool room of her posh home in Gulf Breeze, Florida, as vibrant and filled with determination as she had been in the spring, when Annie last saw her. Of the three Logan sisters, Jen had always been the one to hold them together. She had even taken over the role of mothering after their own mercurial mother, Delilah Broussard Logan, had died in a car crash that also killed their jovial Irish father, Patrick Logan.

"Tell me what you see." Jen was drinking tea from her favorite cup. A ritual for her—for all of them really. Water sparkled behind her as her teenagers frolicked in the indoor pool. The sound of a waterfall cascading into the pool soothed Annie's soul.

"A man keeps calling to me for help, and there's always a woman screaming." Did the scream sound like her own, or was she letting fear take over? The dream was still so real, she shivered. "This is the third time I've had the same dream this month, and they're getting stronger each time. The man is definitely in a swamp. I sense such a strong connection with him, I think he's close to our mother's people."

The bayous of south Louisiana around New Orleans had not only spawned the larger-than-life Delilah Broussard, but also the mystical gifts she had passed along to her three daughters—foretelling dreams to Annie, warnings through scent to Rachel, and alarms from nature's creatures to Jen. Steeped in the Creole legends and myths of her French and African ancestors, Delilah had passed through their lives like smoke, the mystery of her saturating everything they did and believed, coloring their future so that neither Jen nor Rachel nor Annie could ever escape the past she kept shrouded in darkness.

Jen's face was calm as she sipped her tea. "Did you see danger to yourself or to any of our family?"

That was a definite yes, Annie thought. The sense of personal menace was so strong, Annie found herself constantly looking over her shoulder. Fear eroded her confidence. She felt vulnerable and scared, emotions that were foreign to her.

Annie replayed her dream warnings, the danger hidden in mist and the whisper of a voice that pierced her heart. "I don't see danger to you or Rachel or your children, but the sense of foreboding feels personal. Do we have any living Broussard relatives?"

"I don't know, and I don't want to know. And neither should *you.*"

"These dreams are drawing me toward the bayou. I think I should go to New Orleans and try to locate Mom's people."

"No!" Jen cried. "Stay as far away from that place as you can. Those vicious least terns I saw on the beach before Tommy and Marianne were kidnapped are back, and it feels like the warning is for you." As Jen launched into one of her long-winded lectures, Annie relived their terror when her niece and nephew were taken. "Concentrate on your art, and live a good life. Delilah kept the past from us for a reason. Don't try to open that Pandora's box. I don't want to have to worry about my baby sister. You hear me?"

"Loud and clear."

"But you're going anyway. I can hear it in your voice and see the stubbornness in your face."

"I haven't decided yet."

She'd fallen in love with New Orleans on her brief visit there last spring. After her stay with Jen, her agent decided to book an art lecture for her at Tulane before she flew back to Italy. *Speaking at the university will be great PR for you when I book showings of your watercolors in America,* she'd told her.

Annie had not yet agreed to art shows in the States. But lately, she had felt a tug that had nothing to do with her dreams. She felt restless, unfinished somehow, as if an essential part of her was missing and could only be found back home.

She was torn between taking her sister's advice and following her urge to discover the secrets her mother had buried in the bayou.

"I'm deciding for you," Jen said. "This family has had enough drama to last a lifetime. *Don't* go courting more."

Over the past year, Rachel had been kidnapped by a local madman and Jen's children had been taken in the night, events so terrifying, Annie had thought she might lose both her sisters as well. Still, from the time she was nine and started having prescient dreams, she'd never ignored them. Even then, almost twenty years ago, she had known the dreams were more than the normal way a mind processes the day's events. They had been Technicolor predictions of things to come, the warnings so clear they left no doubt in her mind that they were real.

"I make no promises."

"Listen, Annie. Gran's not as young as she used to be, and the drive from Colorado to Gulf Breeze last spring took a toll on her. Benjamin and I are flying out to the ranch with the children for Thanksgiving break. It's sort of a second honeymoon for us, and the twins are wild about the idea of seeing their cousins and riding horses. All of us together will be a handful. Don't add any more trouble to her plate."

"I can't *believe* you said that. Victoria Logan would snort at the idea she's getting old." Her fierce grandmother would do more than snort; she'd be stomping mad. Annie started giggling at the idea, and couldn't stop. Her sister joined in, and soon the two of them were burning up international call-time with their fits of glee. Finally, she wiped her face with the edge of her sheet. "I'm glad you and Benjamin are doing so well."

"We're better than ever. A crisis can bring out the best or the worst in people. And the aftermath is as unpredictable as nature."

All Annie's senses went on alert. "Wait, what are you not telling me? What have *you* seen?"

"The great blues are back, circling and casting their giant shadows."

The great blue heron was a large coastal bird, standing four feet high and boasting a wingspan of seven feet. Last spring when Annie had been in Gulf Breeze, they had plagued Jen by circling at her bedroom window with warnings of danger that had nearly destroyed her family.

Suddenly chilled, Annie pulled the covers closer. "Who was the message for?"

"The herons are coming to my office this time, but only when my new patient is with me. She's a tall, auburn-haired beauty like you, except she doesn't have your ocean eyes.

They're brown instead of blue-green." Jen paused to tell her son Tommy to stop splashing his sister. "The warnings are for *you*, Annie. I've suspected it for a week, but now I know. Promise me you won't do anything rash."

"I'm impulsive, but never rash."

"That's debatable..."

Annie smiled. Jen was a psychologist—Dr. Turner to her patients—and fond of probing the mind. Everything was debatable with her. "All right. I'm not going to hop on a plane to New Orleans. At least not yet. I have an art show here tonight."

"Good. If the Broussards wanted to have anything to do with us, they'd have made themselves known years ago. They're either a snooty bunch or have a lot to hide."

Annie didn't believe a word of it. Their mother was the one who severed contact with her family and kept them hidden. Maybe the Broussards had tried to get in touch, but Delilah discouraged it, and Gran wouldn't allow it.

She could ask, of course, but Gran might or might not tell her. She was not just stubborn; she was ornery. Her response would depend on her mood.

After they said their goodbyes, Annie tried to sleep, but her rest was fitful. Though the stranger no longer called to her, she kept hearing a weird sort of creaking song in her dreams that could only come from the throat of a swamp creature. Before dawn, she gave up on sleep and did a quick internet search on the wetlands around New Orleans.

According to one article, in winter the swamps come alive with the chorus of three types of winter-breeding frogs.

*Frogs!* They even had interesting names—the chorus frog, the spring peeper, and the Southern leopard frog. The idea of hearing them in person intrigued her so much she imagined sitting in a boat in the middle of the green water of her dreams, sketching them. Why not? She had done watercolors of Italy for so many years, she felt as if her art might soon grow stale.

*If I go, Jen will kill me.* Annie's laughter blended with the sound of cathedral bells as she brewed coffee and gathered her sketch pad and art supplies. What she needed was a quiet day on the Piazza del Commune, centering herself as an artist and pampering herself with the lemon gelato that had almost become an obsession with her.

But maybe Jen was right. She would be foolish to leave the place she loved to go in search of trouble.

Annie gathered art supplies and donned a wide-brimmed hat with a turquoise ribbon that matched her eyes. Suddenly, a cold wind swept over her, as if someone had tapped her on the shoulder.

*Help me!*

The whisper chilled her to the bone. It was the same voice from her dreams, the message as clear as if it were written on her walls.

Someone in the bayou was waiting for her, but evil *also* waited in the mist, its shadow pulling her into a past that could prove deadly.

# TWO

## PIAZZA DEL COMMUNE

Annie's multi-colored gypsy skirt swept over the cobblestones as she strolled to the plaza and spread her belongings on a table that gave her the best view of the people and the city around her. Her outdoor office, she called it.

She'd chosen a shaded spot. She pulled off her hat so her hair tumbled around her shoulders in dark waves that glinted with hints of reds. It was the kind of balmy day that could almost make her forget her sister's warnings and her own disturbing dreams. As usual, she checked her emails, texts, and social media accounts on her cell phone before she started her work. They were not her favorite things to do, but were necessary to maintaining a career, even as an artist.

She deleted the usual junk, then read one from her agent, wishing her good luck on her showing at the gallery this evening. Her lone text was from Jen, reminding her that nothing good could come from meddling in their mother's past.

Annie put quick posts on social media, the usual snapshots with *I'm here, and this is what I'm doing,* and then scrolled through comments on her most recent post inviting friends to attend her showing at the gallery in Assisi tonight. One response immediately popped out.

I see you and I know what you did. I will make you pay.

An awful premonition swept over her. *Someone's watching me.* Everything that had happened to her two sisters came flooding back, the terror of almost losing them. And all of it had started because someone evil was near.

Trying to tamp down her fear, she glanced around the plaza as if the person who posted might be out there somewhere, trying to uncover some dastardly deed from the past that she didn't even remember. *Where are you? Who are you?* She hugged herself to hold back her shivers.

Finally, satisfied she had no watcher, she did a quick search of the sender, a man who called himself John Davidson. He was not in her friends list, and his account appeared to be a fake. All his posts were generic and recent, with no comments, and he had only two followers.

She deleted his post, a simple act that might have ended the matter except for Annie's gift. A waking dream flashed through her mind, water everywhere... and death. Its lightning strike left her unable to breathe.

It took several minutes and every bit of her Logan courage to pick up her pencil and sketch pad. But she still couldn't shake the feeling that a hurricane of horror was slowly building... and it was headed straight towards her.

At midday, she fortified herself with a lemon gelato, then continued her sketch—three nuns in full habit from the order known as the Poor Clares of Perpetual Adoration. Suddenly, the feeling of being watched became so strong she knew she was in the crosshairs of something out there, someone whose selfish intent sent chills through her.

Across the plaza, a swarthy man with a generic baseball cap

hiding his upper face sat alone at his table, staring straight toward her. Was it a stalker? An obsessed fan? Both familiarity and danger pulsed around him. Did she know him?

Without warning, he aimed his cell phone at her and began to walk aggressively in her direction. Fear whispered through her, followed by indignation. Whatever happened to asking if he could take her picture? Whatever happened to courtesy? Respect?

She rose from her chair, her blood pumping so furiously she could almost hear the beat of her heart. The man moved closer —threatening, bold—as if he had the right, as if she were some kind of public property he owned.

*Make yourself big enough to scare a bear.*

She stretched herself up to her full five feet, nine inches. "What do you want?"

He didn't answer, just moved irrevocably toward her, his cell phone still aimed and recording, his face dripping with sweat. Anticipation? Anxiety?

"Don't come any closer!" She jerked up the only weapon she had and raised it above her head. "I know five ways to kill a man with this pencil."

Annie stared the man down, pencil poised to do major damage. She knew how to weaponize it, too. Her beloved brother-in-law, Rachel's first husband, had taught her self-defense, before he had become a fallen soldier himself.

Doubt bloomed across her stalker's face. He stopped between two tables and lowered his cell phone. The four couples at the tables shrank back, their expressions stony.

Heads turned to watch the stand-off, but nobody intervened. Nobody wanted to get involved.

There was a horrible moment when she thought her bluff might not work. Annie's fear ratcheted up. If this man was her online stalker, he had vowed to make her pay. But for what?

"Back off! *Now!*" She made herself sound mean and ugly, a

woman who meant what she said. To disguise the fact that she was shaking inside, she stormed toward him, waving her arms. "Leave me *alone*."

Thankfully, the man spun around and hurried off in the direction of the Hotel Giotto, though not before he called her a string of names so unflattering that a mother standing at the gelato stand bent to cover her toddler's ears.

Still shaking, Annie sank into her chair, her desire to sketch gone. Had the man in the piazza been a manifestation of her dream? Was he the man who threatened her online? Or had he merely been an overzealous fan who spewed out his venom at her for spoiling his rude invasion of her privacy?

An artist's muse will vanish in a twinkling when threats and chaos appear. Hers had probably leaped continents and oceans to cower somewhere in the frozen Tundra.

Still, she tucked her fear and the warnings into a corner of her mind, refusing to let the man ruin her day. Dismissing him as an overzealous fan, she packed up her supplies and walked to the Basilica di Santa Chiara in the heart of the city. The cathedral was vast and peaceful, a perfect place to vanish in plain sight. She chose a pew in a corner at the back of the nave, and closed her eyes to meditate. Finally, she found her quiet center and returned slowly to her flat.

A letter waited in her box. Her spirits lifted when she saw the return address. New Orleans, Louisiana, USA. She only had time for a quick read and a light evening meal of pears and cheese before she had to dress for her art show.

The letter was from Antonia "Toni" Delgado, the woman who had almost destroyed Jen's life and then, ironically, had become a best friend to Annie with one simple act of grace and kindness. In the aftermath of the nightmare in Gulf Breeze last spring, Toni wrote to all of them—Jen and her husband, Gran, and even Annie—sincere, heartfelt letters of apology where not one word rang false. The rest of the family accepted the apology and moved on. But for Annie, it was the beginning of a friendship that grew stronger with each phone call and letter.

Toni's latest was little more than a handwritten note, but it felt like an omen.

*Annie, my new job at the New Orleans DA's office is a dream come true, and I have a new apartment in the Vieux Carre (French Quarter) that I can see myself living in forever, growing old alongside an even older but adoring husband and lots of great-grandchildren. You HAVE TO COME! You can no longer say I don't have a place to put you. Get your gorgeous self on a plane and have an old-fashioned American Thanksgiving with me. Call and say yes. XO Toni*

*P.S. I LOVE that we have a proper correspondence with letters and photos we can store in a box to show our children!*

She would definitely call Toni, but what would she say? Yes or no?

# THREE

## GALLERIA LE LOGGIE

That evening, murmurs of *bella artista* followed Annie through the cobblestone streets. Stars shot sparks of fire through her auburn hair, and moonlight turned her white wrap and signature white dress to silver as her skirt and cape floated around her.

She was head and shoulders taller than the locals. Add her four-inch stilettos, and she topped six feet. People turned to watch as she walked toward the Galleria Le Logge where her latest watercolor collection would be featured this evening: A Study of Sunflowers, swirls and bursts of yellow glowing against backgrounds of azure sky, silver moonlight, stark stone walls, mists of fog and rain, the primitive carts of street vendors, a country kitchen table, a handwoven basket in the arms of a child —all appealing in her trademark detail and finely tuned colors, similar to the naturalist James Audubon but with a technique all her own.

Inside the venue, Rocco Salvatore, the balding owner of undetermined age who managed to be both dapper and portly, had displayed her work under lights and placed massive bouquets of her favorite white calla lilies on tables filled with Italian delicacies and fine wine. Though Annie usually wove her way through a crowd, tonight she chose to remain near her favorite painting in the center of the gallery, her back turned to the wall so no one could surprise her from behind.

Rocco noticed and headed her way. "You aren't mingling tonight. Is something amiss?"

"Everything is perfect," Annie said, smiling. Though she was still shaken from the morning's events, she smiled to show she meant the compliment. "It has been a long day. I thought I'd let the crowd come to me."

"Perfect." His smile showed dazzling teeth, a little too large for his mouth and blatantly false. "You anchor, I'll mingle." He scooted off toward the refreshment table.

The crowd flocked to her, and she took the time to chat and answer their questions about her work. With her natural charm and her ease with the art lovers, no one would have guessed the elegant artist was not fully present.

Her mind was still on the horrible incident in the piazza. Digging deep for the fearlessness that had allowed her to live alone for years in a foreign country and thrive, she dragged her mind off her problems and focused on answering questions about her art.

Suddenly, Annie's senses went on full alert. The crowd had shifted her away from the wall, and someone was approaching her from behind. When a hand closed around her arm, she whirled, her heart hammering.

A tall man with blazing black eyes and white hair held her in a vise grip. She swallowed back a scream, and told herself she was in a room filled with art patrons and the security Rocco always hired for events. What could happen?

"Annie, you are very beautiful." His gaze was predatory, his voice too silky, too intimate.

Cold shivers went through her, and she took a step back.

Thankfully, he released her arm. "I'm sorry... I don't recall your name."

"You don't know me. I buy your work for a client in Mandeville, Louisiana."

*Near Mom's childhood home.* Annie caught the flash of sun on green water, knife blade on a bare throat. A waking dream. A nightmare that pelted her with fear. Was this man somehow connected?

Still keeping his identity hidden, the stranger gestured toward her watercolor of the Hermitage of the Cells, tucked among the slopes of Mt. Subasio and shrouded in fog, a dark brooding piece that matched the way he made her feel.

Fortunately, Rocco came to close the sale, and escorted the strange man off while Annie chatted with departing guests. When Rocco returned, the gallery was empty except for the two of them and a few lingering guests.

"Annie, the show is a sell-out. Tell your hard-nosed American agent to put me at the top of the list for your next art show. Whenever you're ready. I'll clear the calendar."

Bea Lowenstein would be by flattered at the hard-nosed tag. She *was* stubborn, and credited her success to toughness. She worked hard to keep her reputation that way.

"I'll tell her." Annie linked her arm through his and stood by the door to thank each guest for coming.

Being accessible was a big part of any artist's life, and one Annie usually enjoyed. Her whole childhood, she'd been schooled by the best, Victoria Logan, who was always the center of any ranching circle she traveled throughout the state of Colorado, and her mother, Delilah, the toast of every lover of jazz throughout the world who had the privilege of hearing her sing in her brief career in music. Tonight, though, had been an exercise in patience, if not a full-blown trial of her ability to present a serene façade to the public while the scared little girl inside her wanted to run screaming back to the safety of Colorado and a grandmother who would die to protect her.

As Annie left the gallery, the town was still alive with tourists. Assisi was a major religious pilgrimage site, and they poured in and out of shops and restaurants and thronged along the meandering streets to catch a glimpse of the lighted Basilica de San Francesco with its massive bell tower under moonlight. Still cautious from her disturbing encounter at the piazza and her fright at the gallery, she pulled up the hood of her cape and strode toward a small, quiet café, her glance frequently sweeping the crowd for suspicious characters.

Unable to shake the feeling that someone was watching her, she mulled over defensive moves. If she needed a weapon, her strappy silver stilettos would do. She could sink the heel deep enough to make someone think twice about attacking Annie Logan.

The shop bell over the door tinkled as she entered the café. She scanned the area for watchers, then found a table in the back. Fortunately, nobody paid attention as she sat with her back against the wall. A young waitress took her order for hot chocolate, and when she was out of earshot, Annie placed a call to her agent's personal number.

Bea answered on the first ring, her voice raspy from the cigarettes she smoked. The tinkle of ice against glass indicated she was enjoying a bedtime drink, probably while wearing her outrageous lime green robe printed with cabbage roses. "Annie, I hope this is good news about the gallery show this evening."

"It was great." She passed along Rocco Salvatore's request, and told Bea about the stalker in the Piazza del Commune.

"That's unacceptable. Did you report him?"

"No. I thought he was just an overzealous fan." Annie startled at a commotion near the door, and whirled in that direction. But it was only a couple of rowdy teenagers.

"File a report. You can't be too careful these days."

"I'll do that tomorrow. Are you sitting down, Bea?"

"What? There's more bad news?"

"I hope it's good. I'm heading to New Orleans for a few weeks. Can you book a gallery showing?"

Annie had a favorite collection she had been reluctant to sell. She called it Meditation—cathedrals with vaulted arches and ancient frescoes, small stucco churches with a single bell tower, both primitive and ostentatious naves, hidden gardens, and quiet retreats all over Italy. Letting them go seemed a small price to pay for finding her mother's family.

"I'd be happy dancing, but sourpuss is my middle name. If I can get a small gallery to take you on such short notice, I can coordinate blanket publicity that will pull in the holiday crowd. It's doable."

"Thanks, Bea."

"It's my job. What time is it over there?"

"After midnight."

"Go home. Get some sleep. I'll be back in touch... And, Annie, take care of yourself."

"Thanks, Bea. You, too."

But instead of leaving, Annie ordered another hot chocolate. Since her dark bayou dreams started, sleep had been elusive. Add the threatening comment on her social media, plus the stalker in the piazza, and she felt like Alice who had tumbled down the rabbit hole. Anything could happen next. Even the most bizarre and unimaginable things possible.

Being an artist who felt every emotion was enough to set her apart as different. Add her technicolor dream warnings and the public personae that made her easy to track, and she might as well be walking around with a target on her back.

By the time she headed home, the temperature had dropped, thunder rolled, and clouds blotted out the stars, giving the night an ominous feel. Though she knew November in Assisi was notorious for frequent showers and thunderstorms, she couldn't shake the feeling that the approaching rain was a precursor of worse to come, that something unknown was gathering force to destroy her. The first drops began to fall just as she reached her flat.

It was two in the morning. Past the witching hour of foretelling dreams, which had been her intent. She washed her face, put on silk pajamas, and propped herself on pillows to read Toni's letter once more, just in case she had missed something. Her friend had enclosed a photo of the view from her New Orleans' residence on the third floor of the Upper Pontalba Apartments—Jackson Square, lush greenery, artists and musicians lining the sidewalks, glimpses of intriguing shops and restaurants that would sell the shrimp po' boys Delilah had talked about but never tried to recreate in her kitchen on the ranch in Colorado.

The photo seemed to come alive in Annie's mind, beckon to her, whisper to her. Satisfied she'd made the right decision, she tucked it back into the envelope with Toni's note, then snapped off the light and snuggled under her covers, hoping for a dreamless sleep.

The dreamworld of mysterious bayous and dark secrets didn't come to her softly, as it always had, with mists and swirling green water and a deep male whisper for help. It slammed through her, a deluge of furious, foaming red that soaked her hair, her pajamas, her skin. It roared through her with screams that pierced the night, high-pitched and terrifying. A woman begged for her life even as her butchered body turned the bayou into a river of blood.

The dark water sucked the young woman under, while ribbons of scarlet poured from her wounds and twined around her. The bayou went quiet. Not a sound could be heard, not even a peep from the singing frogs. The moon vanished and stars disappeared, as if a giant hand had snatched them from the sky.

Annie's dream-self wept at the poignance of Nature mourning the death of a beautiful woman who died far too young. The silence was so deep, it seemed to announce the end of the word. And then, suddenly, the stillness shattered and the dark water spit her out again. She floated, face-up, her eyes staring sightless at the sky.

The dead girl's face was Annie's.

# FOUR

## NEW ORLEANS, LOUISIANA

Toni navigated the streets as if she had been born in New Orleans instead of New Jersey. Because of her pants and jacket, the baseball cap atop her pixie haircut, and the daredevil, tomboyish way she handled her bicycle, you might have mistaken the figure pedaling toward Jackson Square for a teenage boy if you didn't notice her dark eyes with impossibly long lashes or the vivid slash of red on her lips.

Make no mistake about it, Antonia "Toni" Gloria Delgado was all fiery Sicilian woman and proud of it. Cross her at your peril. Underestimate her intelligence at your own risk. And never, ever come to her table with a puny appetite. She won't invite you back if you don't eat heartily of the abundant meals she prepares in her kitchen using the recipes passed down from her ancestors in the home country.

She was a woman on fire, and she was reinventing herself.

One of the things she loved best about her new job as an attorney at the DA's office in New Orleans was the laid-back casual vibe of the city. The ambience, plus the proximity of her office to her apartment in the French Quarter, confirmed that her move from Gulf Breeze had been smart. She was an easy fifteen-minute bike ride from work, a bit longer in the late afternoons when people began to pour from their offices and congregate in shops and restaurants around the square.

Artists and street musicians gathered there to display paintings and play the blues that sprang from the cotton fields of the Mississippi Delta and found its full voice in the sassy trumpets, growling trombones, and moaning saxophones of the hard-luck, broken-hearted jazz musicians who gravitated toward the Crescent City where pirates once roamed.

The lively commotion was a balm to her heart. Though she cherished her independence, she missed her big, affectionate, and lively family in New Jersey.

Toni heard the music before she saw the square, the haunting melody that could only come from the silver trumpet of one man. The blue notes ripped her heart in half then promised to put it back together again. Would it? she wondered. Would she even dare let it try?

"Definitely not."

People turned to see who she was talking to. Let them look. She was done caring what other people thought, especially guys with heartthrob looks and a sad story to tell.

He was on his usual corner facing the historic St. Louis Cathedral, his trumpet pressed to his lips as he watched for her red bicycle and her baseball cap. His name was Brick, of all things. A darker version of the handsome actor Paul Newman in Tennessee Williams' *Cat on a Hot Tin Roof*. Brick Beaufort, the prodigal son of some big-wig Louisiana senator and plantation owner who disdained music and despaired that his youngest son chose the rocky, uncertain career path of a musician.

That part of Brick's story, she knew. The rest of his history was hidden in the depths of his dark midnight eyes. And she intended to keep it that way.

He waved her to a stop. "Hey, Jersey!"

"Hey, yourself." She brought her bike to a halt.

He had adopted the nickname on her first day in New Orleans, that brutally hot day this past summer when she stopped to listen to his jazz. They struck up an easy conversation, which had led her to inquire about the best place a single female attorney could live in the French Quarter. She told him she favored a place with character, security, and a great view.

*Well, Jersey,* he'd said, *look across the street and you'll see your new home.*

She thought her baseball cap from Jersey Joe's Diner earned her nickname, but he said, no, it was her charming accent. She had the clipped New Jersey speech of her hometown combined with a soft blurring of her vowels from her unfortunate stint of living in Gulf Breeze, Florida. *Unfortunate* because of her brief departure from her principles, her common sense, and her upbringing to chase after Jen Logan Turner's husband, Benjamin.

She didn't plan to repeat that foolish episode with anybody. Even a man as drop-dead handsome as Brick. Already, she was thinking of a fresh way to say no without hurting his feelings when he issued another invitation for beignets and café au lait, dinner, a stroll along the river, or whatever else his creative mind could conceive.

"They found a young woman murdered in Honey Island Swamp today," he said, surprising her.

"That's heartbreaking. The taking of another human life is always a terrible thing." Toni's heart twisted. No matter how much of it she saw in her work, she always felt as if a piece of her own humanity had been chipped away when she heard the chilling news of murder.

She remembered every broken and bloody victim she'd ever defended, and she wanted to scream. She remembered Jen's terror last spring when she was being poisoned and hounded, and she wanted to cry.

"I just wanted to warn you to be careful," Brick said.

"I will."

Honey Island Swamp was in St. Tammany Parish and under the jurisdiction of the St. Tammany Parish Sheriff's Department. Still, its proximity to New Orleans made the news of murder disturbing, especially if someone was targeting young women. She hoped it didn't make national news, or her grandmother Mimi would be on the phone telling her to pack her bag immediately and get back home so the large Delgado family—all of them boisterous and opinionated—could look after her. As if she were eight years old instead of twenty-eight.

"You still have my phone number?" He shaded his face against the bloom of lights that suddenly came on all along the shops and restaurants around the square.

"I do."

"If you need me, just call." His grin was both ironic and charming. "And I'll come running."

"Thanks." The way he looked at her made her think of that one puppy in the pound that made it hard to walk away. She was on the verge of telling him to go out and find himself a nice, uncomplicated young woman and settle down to raise lots of kids when she thought better of it. Just because she was working to fix her own life didn't mean she should be standing here trying to fix his. She didn't know if he needed fixing. It was just a gut feeling.

She waved goodbye then coasted across the street to lock her bike in the rack before she let herself into her own apartment.

"Honey, I'm home!" she yelled.

Nobody answered. Of course, they didn't. She did a whirling dance around the polished wooden floors and lush rugs anyway, just for the joy of being alive. Then she changed into loose-fitting sweats and cooked her favorite comfort dish, pasta with a homemade basil pesto she made from the fresh herbs and pine nuts she'd bought at the local market, and the cold pressed olive oil Mimi got at the Italian market back home in New Jersey then sent to her so she wouldn't *starve to death down there among the mosquitoes and the snakes.* Her grandmother's description of south Louisiana.

Toni settled onto her sofa with dinner and switched on her TV. The murder of a young woman in St. Tammany Parish dominated the six o'clock news. *Who would do such a horrible thing?* Heartsick, Toni leaned in to watch the broadcast live from Honey Island Swamp, one of the many bayous in south Louisiana. This one was so close to New Orleans the horror might as well have taken place right outside Toni's front door.

Linda Holloway, the reporter, stood near a rustic store with a view of the bayou beyond. "We're on the scene where the body of a young woman was pulled from the swamp. Her murder was brutal. Bloody. Horrific. I've never witnessed anything like it. It was not a killing; it was a butchering."

Her appetite gone, Toni pushed her plate aside and was headed to her kitchen when images of the swamp filled the TV screen. It looked creepy to her, exactly the kind of place to leave a body if you wanted it to be eaten by the bottom-dwellers in the murky water before anybody ever found it.

Frightened and furious at the senseless killing, her peaceful evening now in tatters, Toni grabbed the TV remote to press *off* when a photo of the victim flashed on the screen.

*Annie?*

Toni's knees buckled, and she crumpled to the sofa, the remote clattering to the floor while the beautiful woman on the screen stared back her.

*Oh, Annie! Please! It can't be you!*

# FIVE

Frozen in horror, Toni stared at the image. The long mahogany hair with just enough curl to look gorgeous instead of bushy, the expressive eyes, the amazing face. The victim was wearing a locket with a carved rose design on top.

"Oh, Annie..." Toni bent double, sobbing, while Linda Holloway described the murder scene. "The killer struck like a shadow, unseen and deadly, leaving behind a beautiful victim with claw marks down her right arm."

*Claw marks?*

Toni jerked upright, horrified. A closer look at the TV screen showed the victim's eyes were brown. A wave of relief washed over her. Still, the resemblance to Annie was eerie.

She glanced at the slick magazine on her coffee table, *New Orleans Lifestyle*. The arts editor had done a feature on Annie when she came to New Orleans last spring to speak at Tulane. The cover photo perfectly captured her magical presence. One look and you felt as if your heart had been turned inside out, as if she had cast a spell on you with her turquoise eyes, as mesmerizing and changeable as the sea, as if something essential in you had shifted and you might never recover. One conversation and you knew her soft, feminine exterior masked keen intelligence and uncommon bravery.

A detractor had once labeled her a Bengal tigress parading as a Persian kitten. Annie never pretended, but if you threatened her or anyone she loved, she *was* a tigress—fierce, wildly independent, amazingly beautiful, and so mysterious you could spend a lifetime getting to know her and still end up viewing her as a puzzle you never solved.

Toni, herself, was a testament to the mystical power of Annie Logan. When Toni left Gulf Breeze, she had severed all ties with Benjamin, the object of her misplaced affections, and his wife Jen; but she couldn't do the same with Jen's sister. Her friendship with Annie was proof that the universe could bring the best to you in unexpected ways if you were brave enough to let it.

She tore her attention from the magazine and back to Linda Holloway. She was a well-known television personality in New Orleans, tall and painfully thin. Her short blond bob ruffled in the wind as she talked.

Toni shivered as if the breeze were blowing across her. The murder was so gruesome, so shocking, she double-checked her lock on her apartment door then snapped off the lights as if the darkness could keep a killer from finding her.

"Janine Porter, a twenty-year-old art student at Tulane in New Orleans, was part of a tour group here yesterday. With us is her friend and fellow student, Cam Westman." The reporter turned toward a distraught young man wearing a college football jacket. "Cam, can you tell us where you were when she disappeared?"

"At this little hole-in-the-wall bait shop and trading post getting sandwiches and souvenir tee shirts and stuff. Janine said she was going to the restroom, and that was the last time I ever saw her."

While the reporter explained that there had been no sounds

of a scuffle, the camera panned to an unpainted shack with a Pete's Place sign, gas pumps, and a primitive front porch. A panoramic view showed the entrance to a single toilet at the back with a door opening toward a path that curved around the store. A patch of grass separated it from a parking lot. Trees and overgrowth looming in the background created an air of menace.

The reporter added, "Indoor surveillance footage shows Janine picking up the key at five o'clock yesterday afternoon from the owner, Pete Thibodeaux." A stocky, almost-handsome man stood beside the reporter. His thick dark hair announced him to be middle-aged, but his beard made him look older. "Pete, you are the last known person to see Janine alive. What happened after you gave her the key?"

He spat a stream of tobacco then wiped his chin with the back of his hand. "I was busy and didn't notice anything till this strapping young feller yelled, 'Where's Janine?' I went out back and found the toilet still locked. I pounded on it and yelled, but she never answered. That's when I started searching and found the key in the grass not far from the door."

The bayou lay beyond—so peaceful under the burning sun you'd never suspect evil waited there—while Linda's voiceover said, "The killer came and went, dark and evil. Now a young girl is gone. And no one knows where the Shadow will strike next."

*That poor girl's family must be devastated.* Toni wiped a few tears then carried her plate back into her kitchen. She was putting the leftovers in a take-out box for tomorrow's lunch when her cell phone rang.

"Annie!" She put her cell on FaceTime just to reassure herself that her friend was still alive instead of dead at the bottom of a bayou. "Did you get my letter and the photos?"

"I did. Your apartment looks fantastic, I can't wait to see it."

Annie was standing on her balcony in silk pajamas, blue,

which emphasized her eyes. Beyond her the full moon was so spectacular, Toni felt as if she were in Italy with her.

"Does that mean you're finally coming to see me in New Orleans?" Toni, a great lover of theater and music, struck a dramatic pose, swooning over her kitchen cabinet, hand on her forehead. "You'd better say yes, or I'll die of eating an unwashed grape!"

Annie laughed at her ridiculous imitation of Blanche DuBois in playwright Tennessee Williams' famous work, *A Streetcar Named Desire.* Set in New Orleans, of course. The streetcar was still there.

"Yes, Miss Blanche, but it's going to be a multi-purpose visit, and I'll be staying a few weeks, maybe longer. If I can stay with you a couple of days so we can catch up, I'll book a hotel for the rest of my visit."

"You will not! I won't hear of it. My domestic Italian heart has been longing to have somebody to cook for. You're more than welcome here as long as you want to stay. This is a huge apartment, three bedrooms. We'll have to make an appointment to see each other." Toni popped a pod of chicory coffee into her machine and set her favorite mug under the spout. "Tell me what's going on."

"My agent has booked a show for me in New Orleans, and she always makes sure the venue goes overboard with publicity. Posters will be popping up in so many places you'll get sick of seeing me."

"I will not. I'll be bragging." Toni hadn't realized the six o'clock news had depressed her so much until Annie's bell-like laughter lifted her up again. She grabbed her cup and took a sip of the dark brew famous to the area. "What are you doing up so late?"

"My dreams."

She knew—and was intrigued by—the unusual talent. But when Annie began to describe her dreams in detail, Toni felt as if she had entered the Twilight Zone. The bizarre similarity between Annie's dreams and the murder in Honey Island Swamp shocked her so much, she had to sit down.

"Are you okay?" Annie asked. She was moving about the small balcony like a caged tigress, blue silk swirling around her, moonlight turning the red in her hair to flame. The dream had been harder on her than she was telling.

"You're not going to believe this. Someone murdered a young woman in the bayou. The media is calling the killer the *Shadow*."

"That's so horrible!" Annie looked visibly shaken. "How did it happen?"

Toni told her the details, but left out any mention of her resemblance to the victim. Surely it was just a coincidence? And she had no intention of spoiling her friend's trip to New Orleans with wild speculations.

Annie moved from the balcony and inside a softly lit apartment filled with her art, the watercolors both spectacular and soothing. "Toni, I'm not surprised, and I think I'm somehow connected."

"What are you saying? You think somebody's trying to *murder* you?" Fear seized her once more, but common sense told her the killer would probably be in handcuffs before Annie arrived. Law enforcement was impressive in the New Orleans area.

*Wait. Just wait...*

Annie was quiet for so long, Toni's lawyer instincts warned her that she was about to hear a sanitized version of what her friend really thought. She had come to expect that from her clients who felt threatened. Secrecy was one of the protective instincts.

"It's possible," Annie finally said. "I don't know. I'm trying to find out if any of my mother's people are still living, and I believe murder is pointing to their specific location. Are there any people of Creole descent still living in Honey Island Swamp?"

"Yes. I've never been there, but they do boat tours to show off the vanishing culture as well as the wildlife in the bayou."

"Mom's family is so far off the radar I haven't discovered anything on the internet, not even on social media. It's going to take groundwork from somebody in the area."

Toni loved the stories Annie had told her about her childhood on the ranch, but she also knew that her friend's mother had never revealed a single bit of information about her Creole family. "I have the resources and the curiosity to do the digging. Tell me what you want."

"Anything you can find on the Broussard family—names, addresses, occupations."

"This is right up my alley. I'll even do a background check. So, when are you arriving?"

"Next Wednesday. We'll have Thanksgiving together! I'm already packing some of my watercolor canvases to ship to the gallery."

"This is exciting!" Toni would get to cook a feast, set a fancy table. *Entertain!* "Which gallery?"

"Green Oak. The owner is a sculptor, Paul Chenevert. He's probably French Creole. His surname means someone who lives by the green oak."

"I know that gallery. I've been there a couple of times. It's in the historic Fauborg Marigny district. There are lots of really old Creole cottages there, too, and a great market that sells all kinds of food, including Creole."

"Perfect, I love places rich with history. What's the gallery owner like?"

"I don't know." Toni had heard from some of the unattached female lawyers in her office that he was a handsome widower. Not that it mattered to her. She wasn't looking. "From what I hear, he rarely comes to the gallery, but the manager is nice.

Evangeline Aguillard. She's young, friendly, and *really* pretty. Tall, too."

Toni felt a ridiculous flash of envy for tall women who would never be labeled cute or petite or even, heaven forbid, *little dumpling,* which one of her uncles had once called her. In a very sweet way, of course. Without any ill intention. Still, she sometimes wondered what it would be like to have every eye turn her way when she walked into a room.

"That's great to hear," Annie said. "As soon as I get my airline ticket, I'll email travel plans. See you next week!"

Toni was so excited she didn't know what to do first: start planning a Thanksgiving banquet or start searching for the Broussards. Both were equally appealing to her.

*Food first,* her mother and her grandmother always said. *A full stomach makes everything easier.*

She grabbed her notepad and wrote *Thanksgiving turkey,* but all she could see was the face of the dead girl. All could think of was a killer so elusive he'd been dubbed the Shadow.

By coming to New Orleans, was Annie walking straight into the path of someone who wanted her dead?

She was coming, and she would destroy everything he loved.

The Swamp Witch had predicted it years ago. *She will come again. Nothing will stop her. She will destroy everything you love, and you will die alone, a bitter, broken man.* The old woman's voice echoed through his mind as he glided his boat through the water, searching, ever vigilant.

His nemesis had been here once, and she was coming again. He had to stop her. But first, he would make her pay. The price would be dear. Everything he had suffered because of her, she would suffer *twice* as much.

He had already set his plan in motion. A satisfied smile curved his lips as he remembered the blade slicing through the girl's perfect skin, the claws raking her arm, the way she had screamed, the surprised look on her face when she died. Like a sacrificial lamb. Her blood covering the water.

They called it murder. The fools! Janine Porter was merely a pawn in his game, convenient and expendable. Her death was a warning shot, the price *she* had to pay.

Had *she* seen it yet? Had she realized it was the first part of her punishment?

His mind replayed a tape of Linda Holloway's hysterical reporting. Did those fools think the Porter girl's body had been *discovered*? He meant for them to find her. Otherwise, he would have pitched her overboard for the alligators. He knew how to carve the meat for their next meal.

He navigated among the cypress knees, unseen by any living thing except the night birds and swamp creatures whose eyes glowed from the overhanging branches of the trees and the velvet-like algae atop the water. Their gazes were predatory, hungry. Any one of them would strike without warning, snuff out his life in an instant with their venom, their teeth, their stingers, their claws—all the weapons they'd been born with. He identified with them. Was one of them. And proud of it.

Mist rose from the water, cooled by the night air and the approach of winter. Under cover of darkness and fog, he was nothing more than an unrecognizable hulk. He could be the Honey Island Swamp Monster of local legend or the more fearsome Rougarou of Creole legend that transformed at night from a man to a vicious predator who prowled the bayous looking for victims to tear apart with his wolf-like teeth and eagle-like talons.

Both legends suited his purpose. In the morning, he would spread the word that he had spotted the Rougarou while he tended the traps he'd set for mink and river otter and the lines he'd set in the water to catch fish. His fish haul would feed him and his neighbors, too. Any extra would be sold at the trading post, along with the mink and otter hides.

What was a man if he couldn't take pride in supporting his family, telling a good story, dancing a good jig, being a great hunter, fisherman, and lover?

He finished off the sleek otters with a hammer-blow to the head and stuffed them into his burlap bag. He was going to have a good haul. There were still traps to tend and hours till daylight. He was at the top of his game. He let out a howl that echoed through the swamp, then imagined the terror of anyone in the shacks along the bayou awakened by the unearthly sound.

He threw back his head and laughed. Even the sound of his wicked glee would strike terror into the soul of anyone listening.

"I'm coming for you!" He beat his chest and howled like a wolf. It echoed through the swamp.

Was she nearby? Did she hear?

He was master of the bayou. He owned the night.

Nothing could beat him, not even his nemesis—the girl.

# SEVEN

## NEW ORLEANS, FRENCH QUARTER

As the plane touched down on the runway, Annie could hardly believe she was in New Orleans. Her sisters hadn't wanted her to come. When she told them about the trip, they both had a fit, as her Southern mother used to say. Her memories of the phone conversations with them were still vivid.

"You're courting trouble." Jen had been on FaceTime, storming around her kitchen in Gulf Breeze and waving a spatula like a weapon. "Don't you dare go to New Orleans and make me have to come over there and bail you out."

"Just think about it, Jen. I'll be back in the States, and I can see you and Rachel again."

"I'm not buying that. You're just looking for trouble."

Rachel had been much more particular in her warning. While Annie waited for the plane to taxi to a stop, she recalled their phone conversation, word for word.

"You can't go!" Rachel was in the office at the ranch, her black curls tamed into a messy bun, a stack of papers from the third graders she taught lying in front of her on the big desk that had belonged to their grandfather. "Jen and I think it's a terrible idea. Probably even dangerous."

"I can't cancel the show."

"Yes, you can. For Pete's sake, Annie! They're *killing* young women over there in that swamp close to New Orleans."

Unfortunately, the sensational nature of the crime had caused it to make national news. But Annie knew her middle sister well. The news was not what drove her to call. Though Rachel wished she'd never been born with a gift, she understood its significance and never ignored the warnings.

"You've had a sign, haven't you?" Annie said.

Rachel's heart-shaped face flushed. "I wish I could say I hadn't."

"You might as well tell me about it. I won't stop until I know."

"I woke up this morning smelling apricots. There were none in my kitchen, and they certainly weren't hanging from birch trees in the dead of winter in the Rockies." Rachel paused, the danger of scent so real she struggled to shake it off. "I finally remembered that the oleander blossom has a fragrance very similar to apricots, and it's the official flower of New Orleans. It's a deadly plant. A killer. The scent was a clear warning of danger. So, please, stay away from that city!"

"I can take care of myself, Rachel. Stop worrying. Just have fun with Jen and her family over the holidays."

Annie saw the moment Rachel gave in. Her new husband, Hank Carson, walked into the office, followed by her two children and their aging dog. Hank kissed her on top of the head then leaned into the FaceTime frame to smile at Annie, his blue eyes and ruggedly handsome face a perfect complement to Rachel's dark-eyed beauty. Their love for each other was clear to see.

"I wish you were joining us for Thanksgiving." He slid his arm around Rachel and flashed another easy smile.

"Maybe next year, Hank." She liked her new brother-in-law. He was a pilot who had served in the military alongside

Rachel's first husband, Max; a trusted comrade, sworn to protect Rachel if the need ever arose. Annie was thrilled for her sister, and decided to tack a visit to the ranch onto the end of her trip.

Rachel blew her a kiss. "Annie, don't you *dare* get yourself into trouble in the bayou. Cross your heart."

She was already in trouble, but she crossed her heart, anyway. Fortunately, Rachel never added *and hope to die.* Since the death of her first husband in the killing fields of Afghanistan, she avoided the word in all its variations.

The plane taxied to a stop, and a general feeling of relief swept through the travelers. *We made it.*

Would Annie make it through this journey? There was nothing normal about it. She and her sisters all knew the possible consequences of her visit. If she discovered the truth about their mother, Delilah's legacy could be torn apart. Even more sobering, all the warnings were clear. And Annie, herself, might not survive.

As the seatbelt sign flashed that it was safe to grab her carry-on and deplane, Annie decided there was no normal, not with a world populated by people as different as snowflakes. Though they were all formed the same way, it was impossible to duplicate the same intricate design.

She slung her bag over her shoulder and wheeled her carry-on through the airport. Heads began to turn her way.

*Is it my height? My long stride? The Italian silk scarf billowing like a blue cloud behind me? My hat?*

Annie soon discovered why. Posters of New Orleans' attractions lined the walls. Among them were posters from Green Oak Gallery, announcing the art show of the famous watercolorist from Italy. Her photo stared back at her from every corridor.

She was glad to arrive at baggage claim and lose herself in

the hustle and bustle. A petite, dark-eyed dynamo with sassy red lipstick and a new pixie cut waved and shouted at her.

"Annie! Over here!" Toni wore jeans and a simple white shirt with a bright green blazer, a great departure from the provocative outfits she'd worn when she was legal assistant to Jen's husband in Florida. She exuded such a laidback vibe, she seemed almost like a different person. A happier version of the woman Annie had seen last spring.

She strode over and leaned down to hug her. "I was going to take an Uber."

Toni burst out laughing. "No way could I let that happen. Mimi would never stop lecturing me about my bad manners."

They grabbed Annie's bags off the carousel and made their way to Toni's car.

"Hang onto your hat." Toni popped on a pair of sunglasses with rhinestones in the frames. "I don't drive much in New Orleans. Mostly, my car stays in the garage and I use my bicycle."

She barreled through the city. Buildings, street signs and posters featuring Annie's art show became one big blur.

At a changing light, a Saab roared from a side street, threatening to broadside Toni's car. She leaned into the horn while Annie caught a terrifying glimpse of the driver. Swarthy skin, face shadowed by a baseball cap. Her encounter in the piazza came flooding back—the fear, the sense of being watched and under siege, the terror of her dreams.

"Toni, did you recognize that man?"

"No. Why?"

"He looked like an overly aggressive fan who pestered me in Assisi."

"Do I need to turn around and get his license plate number?"

Annie could picture the chase, Toni speeding to beat red lights and ending up at the police precinct paying a big fine.

"No. He's just a nuisance. That's all."

*But is he more?*

Annie's dreams never lied. Something dark and menacing hovered around her, had followed her across an ocean. Her gift bombarded her in flashes—dark eyes watching, whispers on the wind, and green water, *always* water. Her waking dream transformed her watcher from annoying to threatening... to deadly.



Toni's apartment in the French Quarter was a haven from the commotion and a wonder of mid-nineteenth-century architecture. She led Annie through her home, pointing out the sconces modeled after gas lanterns, the crown moldings from original designs, and the ceiling medallions designed by none other than the Baroness Pontalba.

The guest bedroom that would be Annie's had the same 1840s feel but with the addition of contemporary furniture and modern conveniences and comfort. After she stowed her bags, she changed into her jeans and her favorite blue Italian leather jacket, then she and Toni walked to the original Café du Monde at the French Market across from Jackson Square for their famous beignets and café au lait.

Unable to shake the sight of the driver in the Saab and the feeling that trouble had followed her halfway around the world, Annie scanned the crowd. With families gathering at home to celebrate Thanksgiving, it was small.

They found a table outside with a great view of the mighty Mississippi, and settled into chairs to enjoy the doughnut treat with its powdered sugar coating and the strong chicory coffee laced heavily with cream. The song of the river drifted around them as it rolled toward the Gulf of Mexico, unhampered by narrowing channels or jutting intrusions of land.

There was something about a river that always worked magic on Annie. "I could become addicted to this." She wiped the powdered sugar from her fingers and relaxed. She was in a city known for its charm. "Have you found anything on my Broussard relatives?"

"I found one. His name is Angel Broussard, and his address is in the Marigny, which is not surprising."

"That's great! Does he have a phone number?"

"None listed. But he does have a car. I found him in the Department of Motor Vehicles. The interesting thing is that his history at the DMV goes a long way back. He's not young."

"That explains why I could never find him in a computer search. I'd like to try to see him today. And the art gallery, too, if we have time."

"We do." Toni dusted sugar off her hands and pushed her empty plate aside. "The gallery will be open until nine tonight unless they've closed early for Thanksgiving. The Marigny district is just across Esplanade. We can walk there, or we can rent you a bicycle and ride."

"What fun! Let's ride."

"Where to first?"

"The gallery."

Biking around Jackson Square, swirling with color and art and music reminiscent of Creole jazz musicians, Annie felt the exhilaration of being in the City of Romance. With the wind in her hair, the sun on her face, and her friend finally at her side, she tried to forget the dark dreams that had led her there.

But her gift wouldn't let her. There were whispers in the wind, shadows beyond the swirling colors, flashes of a steel blade, and the voice still calling to her from the bayou. *Help me.*

And hovering over it all was an unknown killer called the Shadow.

# EIGHT

## NEW ORLEANS, THE FAUBOURG MARIGNY

Annie immediately fell in love with the Faubourg Marigny. Entering the district was like stepping back into the early nineteenth century. Once a plantation developed by Creole landowner Bernard de Marigny, its rich history was told in the ancient oaks lining Elysian Fields Avenue where the Creole jazz musician Ferdinand LaMothe, better known as Jelly Roll Morton, once sneaked off from his upright Creole grandmother to play piano in the red light district of the infamous Storyville, home to the fallen women she would never have allowed in her house. As they cycled, Toni told her that locals simply called it the Marigny.

Green Oak Gallery nestled underneath a live oak tree dripping with Spanish moss. Ivy climbed up the building's ancient red brick walls, and colored prisms shot rainbows from every window.

Annie parked her bike in the rack out front. "If the owner has the same kind of charm as his gallery, I'm in trouble."

"Let's find out." Toni grabbed her arm, and they hurried inside.

When they opened the front door, they set off chimes that

played the first two lines of "Ol' Man River," the famous song from the musical *Show Boat* by Jerome Kern and Oscar Hammerstein. The chimes wove a spell that stopped Annie in her tracks and transported her back to a time of hoop skirts, silk bonnets, and a magical calliope pumping out music as a paddle wheeler steamed its way down the Mississippi.

"I'm enchanted," Annie said. "Why didn't you tell me about this?"

"I wanted to surprise you. And I wanted to see that look on your face."

A lovely young woman with dark eyes and wavy dark hair approached them, her face lighting in a genuine smile that was both gracious and charming. Her white sweater emphasized her olive skin.

"Welcome to Green Oak. I'm Evangeline Aguillard, and you *have* to be Annie Logan. I'm thrilled to meet you! Your work is just *stunning*." She called to a petite young woman with a close cap of wispy blond hair who was working on a display. "Lacy, take care of the front while I talk with our visiting artist."

Lacy's smile was broad and friendly. "Sure thing."

Evangeline led them toward her office, chattering on about the merits of Annie's work and their many clients who would be excited for a chance to buy it. Pushing aside the papers and books Annie recognized as creative clutter, she motioned toward comfortable plush velvet chairs and offered coffee.

"Thanks, but we just came from the Café du Monde," Toni told her, and Annie added, "This is a really lovely gallery. Is Paul Chenevert here?"

"I'm sorry, he's not. He's usually at his home here in the Marigny or his cottage on Honey Island Swamp. Working." Angeline nodded toward a sculpture carved from the wood of a cypress tree, an eagle with outspread wings. "That's one of his sculptures."

"It's incredible," Annie murmured. The sculpture was so realistic, she expected to see it take flight.

"He'll be pleased to hear that. He values the opinion of other artists." Evangeline made a note on the pad in front of her. "I'll be sure to pass the compliment along... and to tell him you were here. Shall I have him call you?"

"That's not necessary. I always like to check in with a gallery before a showing, so the owner knows I've arrived." Though the gallery already had her number, Annie slid a card across the desk to Evangeline. "I'm available if either of you need to get in touch with me."

"This is wonderful. I'm so excited to be working with you." Evangeline handed her card to Annie, the bracelets on her right arm catching the light. One was a bangle set with random rhinestones, and the other a unique silver cuff with a raised fleur-de-lis design. The silver was hand-hammered. An artisan piece. Annie's sister Jen would love it. "We're closing early today and won't be open tomorrow," Evangeline added, "but don't hesitate to call if you have any questions or suggestions."

"Thanks," Annie told her. "But I can assure you I won't interrupt your Thanksgiving holiday."

Evangeline erupted in a full-bodied laugh. "You'll have to excuse my giddiness. I'm leaving in a few minutes to meet a boyfriend who is an absolute *hunk*! I've only been dating him for a couple of weeks, but I'm hoping this evening will go so well that any calls tomorrow would be awkward, to say the least."

In the easy way of kindred spirits in the Deep South who have just met, Annie and Toni both wished Evangeline good luck with her date, and sincerely meant it. Then they left the gallery in search of Angel Broussard.

.   .   .

The Broussard cottage was painted sky blue with lavender trim. Two well-worn, cane-bottomed rocking chairs sat on the front porch, and a welcome mat was spread in front of his door. The curtains were drawn over the windows, and a light burned behind the one to the right of the door.

Both apprehension and anticipation flooded through Annie. Was she soon going to be face-to-face with one of her mother's relatives? Or was a simple knock on the door going to lead her down a path she wished she had never taken?

"I hope the welcome mat is a good sign," she said quietly.

Toni was quick to pick up on her anxiety. "I'm here with you, whatever happens."

"I know."

"Do you want me to ring the doorbell?"

Annie nodded, and the sound of the bell echoed through the house. The house remained silent, no sound of approaching footsteps, no sound of voices.

She caught a glimpse of motion out of the corner of her eye, and turned to see an ancient and bent woman in print dress, a red scarf, and a blue checked apron shuffle onto the front porch of the yellow house across the street. Her rose-colored shutters were trimmed with pink, and her door was purple. The cottage looked like a cupcake, as did all the Creole cottages on the street. Seeing this part of her heritage was a revelation. Was it any wonder Annie grew up loving color?

"Maybe he's hard of hearing?" Toni asked as she rang the bell again. She followed that with a series of loud knocks.

A knot of tension settled in the pit of Annie's stomach. She glanced upward to the small window that indicated the Broussard cottage might have a second floor. Was that movement behind the curtain? Had the owner seen them and decided to hide until they went away?

She couldn't bring herself to touch the doorbell. "Try one more time," she told Toni.

A quavering voice came from behind them. "He's not home."

They turned to see that the woman from across the street had crept up on them and was standing near the doorstep, staring with faded blue eyes sunken into a face as wrinkled as a peach pit.

It seemed to Annie that the ancient woman was staring straight into her soul. "Do you know where he is?" she asked.

"Gone back to the swamp." The old lady clamped her mouth tight, as if she wished she'd never spoken.

"Which swamp?" Toni walked toward the woman, and she took a step back.

"I'm not telling you anything. I don't know you."

There was something unsettling about the old woman, but Annie also felt sorry for her. "I'm Annie Logan. My mother was Creole and grew up in this area. Her name is Delilah Broussard, and I was hoping to learn more about her family as well as the culture. Can you help me?"

The old lady mulled over the question before she finally spoke. "Angel will tell his own story in his own way."

Annie sensed the woman knew far more than she was telling. She called up patience from the sun, vanishing over the horizon to await the night, leaving behind a display of colors she could never hope to duplicate on canvas; endurance from the oak and magnolia trees, whose massive girth and gnarled branches spoke of centuries of history they had witnessed; and compassion from the earth that nourished them.

"I'm certain he appreciates how discreet you are," Annie said. "If you can tell me when he'll be home, I'd love to come back so he can tell me his story."

"I don't know. He comes and he goes."

"When he returns, do you mind telling him that I stopped by to see him and would like to talk?" She gave the woman her business card that also featured a small photo in the corner. If

Angel was related to her, maybe he would see the resemblance to Delilah. "He can get in touch with me at this number."

"If I live long enough, I'll give it to him. There's killings here every day. Anybody could be next."

With that ominous warning, the strange woman shuffled back across the street, leaving behind a blue fog—suspicion, uncertainty, chaos—that was only visible to Annie. Without ever turning to look back, the old woman went through her front door, taking her untold stories with her.

Part of Annie's gift from her mother was in what she could only describe as waking dreams, an uncanny ability to read people and places by the history that had attached itself to them. Was Angel's neighbor dying, or was she referring to the recent murder in Honey Island Swamp? What did she know that she wasn't telling?

"I'm sorry we didn't learn more," Toni said.

"Delilah hid her history for so many years, it will be impossible for me to uncover it in one day. Thanks to you, I've seen this little house."

The cottage belonging to Angel Broussard whispered its own story of hard work, hard times, and heartbreak, interspersed with music, laughter, and joy. Though Annie strained to discover a kinship with Angel, to hear echoes of her mother crooning songs of the soul, those stories remained a mystery to her.

"There are some great locally owned restaurants here that serve the best shrimp po' boys in New Orleans," Toni said. "Lots of them have jazz bands playing, especially on Frenchman's Street. Are you up for dinner and entertainment in the Marigny?"

"Sounds perfect."

But with the air turning blue and Annie's mother whispering warnings from the grave, Annie knew things were far from perfect.

. . .

By the time they got back to the Upper Pontalba Apartments in the French Quarter, it was almost midnight, and the end of a very long day for Annie. She said goodnight to Toni and settled into her room with her laptop. She sent a quick email to let her agent know that both she and her watercolors had arrived in New Orleans, and she'd already met the manager of the art gallery.

Habit had her checking her social media accounts. John Davidson had left another comment.

You should never have come back. You'll be sorry.

This was no kook; it was a stalker, following her activities, making threats. Vibrating with fear and fury, she deleted his comment.

How did her stalker know she was in New Orleans? She searched the room, jerking open closet doors and curtains, as if she might find him hiding there. But all she found was the story of this ancient building sighing its heartbreak from the floorboards and the walls.

Still, Annie felt violated, helpless. She fought against the apprehension that wanted to overtake her, make her weak. How do you push back against someone who hides behind a fake account on social media? She was always careful to keep personal information off her own accounts, but her schedule and her movements were easy to track. She was a public figure with a website. There was no way to maintain complete privacy.

Still, her art show was weeks away. Did he actually know she was in New Orleans, or was it just a lucky guess? Annie clicked onto Toni's Facebook account, and there it was, posted yesterday.

Can't wait for my friend Annie to arrive. Happy dancing!

It didn't take a genius to discover the only Annie on Toni's Friends list was Annie Logan. Social media was a double-edged sword.

She put John Davidson's disturbing message out of her mind and climbed into bed, hoping for a good night's sleep. But her prescient dreams had followed her across the ocean. The male voice that had whispered to her in Italy, now called urgently to her in New Orleans.

*"Help me. Save me."*

Mists swirled around her dream-self as she raced through the swamp. "Why are you calling me? Show yourself."

Annie glimpsed him through the cypress trees. A shadow, a study in black and shades of gray, his face hidden. He was tall, and his hair was as dark as raven's wing. He was moving fast, rapidly disappearing from view.

"Wait... Who are you?"

Something popped, like a door slamming, and starlight flooded a slender female figure with long hair. Suddenly, a scream pierced her dreams, a woman, begging for her life.

The bayou bloomed red with blood.

# NINE

## HONEY ISLAND SWAMP | THE KAYAKER

Early morning mists swirled around the man in the kayak in the backwaters of the Peal River that fed into the bayou. He was glad to be on the water alone, glad to use the excursion as an excuse to avoid a Thanksgiving meal with a family who didn't understand him.

A snapping turtle slid into the water with a plop, and a lone red fox on shore stood in the wide-legged stance of a wild predator protecting his prey. His eyes gleamed in the early morning light, challenging.

As the kayaker paddled over for a closer look, the fox slunk away, and the water around him transformed from green to brackish brown. The color of rust. Or blood.

His paddle struck resistance. When he pulled it out of the water, a hand floated to the surface, followed by an arm, a shoulder, and a woman's face. Once, it had been lovely.

He said a prayer for her as she stared at the sky, her eyes sightless. Her dark hair floated around her like seaweed. Her feet and legs rested on the shore, bent as if poised for flight, as if they still held the muscle memory of running, even after they had turned stiff and blue.

Death was cruel. Even to the beautiful.
Hidden by the mist, the Shadow watched.

# TEN

## FRENCH QUARTER

When she woke up the next morning, Annie threw on her favorite cozy blue sweats, pulled her hair into a ponytail, and followed the smell of coffee and buttery cinnamon buns to the kitchen.

Toni was perched on a bar stool, cradling her coffee cup, her playful side showing in her sweatshirt featuring Mickey Mouse and her house shoes sporting Mickey's face and a set of mouse ears. "Grab a cup. Did you sleep well?"

"I did." Annie's conscience pricked her, but she didn't want to spoil Thanksgiving by talking about her stalker and her dreams of murder. She nabbed a honey bun. "I'm going to enjoy spending the day with you, just us girlfriends, hanging out."

It was a relief to spend the morning talking and laughing and cooking, if you could call Toni's feast of Creole, Italian, and French dishes mere cooking.

"That's a mind-boggling array of food." Annie reached over to sample a sausage ball Toni had just taken from the oven.

"Every meal should be a celebration, *especially* Thanksgiving." She handed Annie another ball.

"What can I do to help?"

"Hand me the crushed red pepper from the spice rack, and then stir that pot of sauce."

"You're just like Gran." Annie handed her the spice then started stirring. "She would never let me do anything except stir a pot or set the table."

"I consider that a compliment. Victoria's unpretentious and spunky."

"Just like you!"

When they finally carried the dishes to Toni's vintage sideboard, their laughter trailed behind them. They ate in her formal dining room at a table set with linen, gleaming with silver cutlery, and dappled with rainbows from the prisms on the chandelier. They topped their leisurely meal off with white chocolate bread pudding that Annie declared to be so decadent she would be useless for the rest of the day.

"Oh, no, you won't," Toni said. "We're going to change clothes and bike all over the French Quarter and along the river. You'll be *begging* for the leftovers when we get back home."

The day went by in a flash. As Annie took in the sights and scents of a city that had preserved its rich French and Spanish history, she envisioned it all on watercolor canvases filled with layers of color.

When they pedalled back to the square, Toni remarked, "I thought my friend who plays trumpet might be on here this afternoon. I was going to introduce you."

"I'm intrigued. Is he someone special?"

"He's a nice guy, that's all." Toni shrugged. "But who knows what the future holds?"

Evening was already approaching, but it didn't settle quietly in the French Quarter. It came in like a parade with lights, music, and laughter. "The city that never sleeps," Toni added. "Do you want to sample the night life?"

"Another time, maybe. Let's have leftovers. You cooked enough to feed a small army."

Annie's latest dream was still with her, and the overwhelming sense of disaster waiting just around the corner. All the signs pointed to it, not just her dreams, but Jen's great blues and Rachel's scent of oleander.

Annie glanced at the ornate wrought iron balconies on the buildings around the square, expecting to see oleander spilling over the sides of clay pots. But the last glow of sun showed no hint of the white oleander that had plagued her sister Jen last spring and now wove its scent around Rachel. Violas and pansies spilled from pots, and the buds of winter-blooming camellias showed tints of pink and red that would soon turn the square into a living garden.

A shadowy figure appeared in the alley across the street, stopping briefly to stare, face hidden by a cap pulled low. It vanished so quickly Annie might have believed she imagined it except for the chills that swept through her. Someone was watching. Had been watching since she arrived in New Orleans. She was relieved when she and Toni were inside the apartment. They went straight to the cozy kitchen, heated their food, and carried their plates back to the comfortable sofa in the den so they could catch up with news of the outside world.

An ad for Annie's art show at Green Oak Gallery flashed across the TV screen, and Toni cheered. "I wish Mimi could see me now, entertaining a world-renowned artist."

"Call her and tell her, if you want to. Put her on FaceTime, and I'll say hi."

Toni grabbed her cell phone, but just as she was about to punch in her grandmother's number, a tall, thin reporter with a bayou in the background said, "Another young woman was found murdered this morning in Honey Island Swamp."

Annie felt sick to her stomach. Her dream visions swamped

her, the mist rising around her as if it had come into Toni's living room.

She barely saw the banner along the bottom of the screen identifying the reporter as Linda Holloway. "With me now is the kayaker who found her." A man of uncommon good looks stood beside her.

"That's my friend, Brick Beaufort." Toni turned up the volume. "That must have been awful for him."

Annie listened with growing horror as Brick told of his discovery. Her latest dream was playing out in the details. Multiple stab wounds. The water red with blood. The victim young, female.

When the victim's photo flashed onto the screen, Annie froze. She could be seeing her own face, the same long, wavy hair, except darker without any red, the same expressive eyes except clear blue without any hint of green, the symmetrical features that had long been considered the standard for beauty.

"The victim was identified as Sylvie Bergeron Hopkins, of Birmingham, Alabama. Her aunt, Julie Bergeron, is here with me." The reporter turned toward a distraught, middle-aged woman with a topknot of dark, curly hair. "Can you tell us what happened?"

"I picked Sylvie up at Pete's Place for Thanksgiving." The woman teared up, losing control.

"Take your time, Julie." The reporter's voice dripped with sympathy, but it appeared stage-managed.

Julie Bergeron dabbed at her face with a tissue she took from the pocket of a print dress, her bright pink fingernails on full display. "We went to bed last night about ten o'clock. When I got up this morning, she had just vanished."

The camera panned to a closeup of the reporter. "The victim was taken sometime during the night. There were no signs of forced entry. The only sound came from the screen door popping when Sylvie apparently went outside to watch the stars."

While the reporter talked, the panoramic view showed the bayou beyond, its pristine beauty alluring, and yet somehow forbidding.

"Some say it's the Honey Swamp Monster or the Rougarou of Creole legend, but most locals believe this new threat to young women in this small enclave is the Shadow. Once again, he has left his claw marks on the victim's right arm. If you have information that might lead to the perpetrator, please call the number on your screen."

"*Claw marks?*" Shivering, Toni switched off the TV. "I just can't watch any more of that. It's too awful."

"I saw this in my dreams last night." Annie struggled to regain control over her own terrible premonitions as she pushed her plate aside and tucked her feet under her. "Toni, you never told me what the other victim looked like."

"I didn't want to sound a false alarm. I thought the killer might be caught before you got here. Honestly, I didn't know what to do."

She looked so distraught, Annie leaned over to hug her. "It's all right," she whispered.

"No. It's not." Toni ran her hands through her cropped hair. "I'm in the DA's office. I know better than to overlook the smallest clue."

"She looked like me, didn't she?"

"She did." Toni wiped her hands across her face, trying to regain control of her emotions. "I thought it was coincidence, and I still do. Do you know of any reason someone in Louisiana would be killing women who look like you when it's common knowledge you live in Italy?"

"I have an online stalker." She told Toni about her Facebook follower who called himself John Davidson.

"*Good grief!* Why didn't you tell me?"

"Like you, I didn't want to raise a false alarm. And I wanted to believe he was a harmless fan with an unhealthy obsession. But I can't ignore the warnings from my dreams... and all these murders. Someone or *something* is tracking me... and it's pure evil."

"Maybe we should hire a bodyguard for you," Toni said, and Annie waved away the suggestion as if it were a pesky fly. "I'm serious! I don't want to lose you. Not after we had to go through such a nightmare just to be friends."

"Bodyguards are for mega-celebrities. Movie stars and famous singers. Thank goodness, most people on the street don't even recognize me."

"*He* does. I'd like to root this John Davidson out and turn a few of my Delgado cousins loose on him. He'd think twice about harassing another woman... Annie, a bodyguard makes sense."

"I'm not ready for that. So far, the stalker hasn't done anything except infuriate me and make me more cautious."

Finally, Toni agreed. "Okay. You win. For now. But it's only because you're taller."

Annie swatted her with a napkin, and they finished the evening with girl talk and laughter.

Annie's laughter died after she said goodnight and returned to her room. There was another comment waiting on social media from John Davidson. She stared at it, paralyzed as her blood turned to ice.

Are you sorry yet? Only you can make it end.

# ELEVEN

Friday morning ushered in one of those sunny, mild days that could make you think it was still summer, instead of the end of November. The murders in Honey Island Swamp seemed as far removed from New Orleans as Toni's childhood home in New Jersey.

Toni did a few stretches, then dressed for comfort in jeans and a tee shirt, and hurried into her favorite part of the apartment, her kitchen. Her pleasure at a successful holiday meal and an upcoming weekend of perfect weather died when Annie came into the kitchen. Though she looked like a model in designer jeans and a white poet's shirt, she was obviously distressed.

"I saved this for you." When Annie opened her laptop and pointed out the threatening comment, cold fingers crawled down Toni's spine. "I have a strong feeling that '*only you can make it end*' is referring to Sylvie's murder," Annie added, "and maybe the other victim, too."

"Let's sit down and talk about it." Pushing her own apprehension aside, Toni carried two cups of coffee to the kitchen table. "Killers do these bizarre things, like target a certain type of victim. I've seen it in my work. But online stalkers get their kicks scaring people. We have nothing that connects John Davidson with the swamp murders."

"Then you don't think I should go to the police with this?"

"Personally, I'd like to see this John Davidson behind bars. But from a legal standpoint, this is not evidence of a crime, and nobody can even prove that it's relevant. Hide the comment so it'll still be there if this coward ever slips up and posts something that *can* be used."

Annie perked up as her hands flew over the keyboard. "Done. If that coward thinks he can intimidate me, he's sadly mistaken."

"All hail to the Queen of Fierce." Toni gave her a high five. "Now, let's forget about him. We're going to bicycle to my favorite place for breakfast, Horn's on Dauphine in the Marigny, and then I'm going to show you as much of New Orleans as possible before I have to be back at work on Monday. I guarantee you a splendid day!"

"Sounds great. I'll take it."

Their spirits were high as they grabbed their jackets, loaded their backpacks, and headed out for the day's adventures. "Eating at Horn's is an experience," Toni told her. "You're going to love it, I promise."

As Toni had expected, the line of tourists and locals waiting to eat at Horn's had snaked out the front door and scattered among the slatted benches on the front porch. The renovated building had kept its ancient charm. She found a bench for them, and they were reading the day's specials on a large chalkboard on the porch when Annie's cell phone rang.

"I'd better see who this is." Annie glanced at the screen. "That's strange. It's Evangeline. I thought she was visiting a new boyfriend."

"So did I," Toni said. "I wonder what's up?"

"We'll find out." Annie took the call. "Evangeline! I hope your holiday went well." Something shifted across her face as she listened, as if a ghost had tapped her on the shoulder. Then she touched the screen to her put cell on speaker.

Toni heard a deep, heavily accented male voice. "Evangeline told me you're here to do an art show at the gallery where she works, and I asked her to call so I could talk to you."

"Do I know you?" Annie asked. She had turned so pale, Toni opened a water bottle from her backpack and handed it to her.

"Your name tipped me off, but when I saw your picture on the business card you gave my girlfriend, I knew it was really you. Are you Delilah Broussard's daughter?"

"Yes. And who are you?"

"I'm Lucien Morel, your twin brother."


Within hours, Annie was on the road out of New Orleans.

She kept telling herself to breathe. It seemed impossible that six little words could snatch you out of everything you believed to be true and cast you into unknown territory so murky and unreal you hardly even knew who you were anymore. And yet, here she was, staring out the passenger side window of Toni's car as they left the city and raced toward Honey Island Swamp, looking exactly the same as she had yesterday, but feeling like somebody else entirely. Someone who had shared her mother's womb with another person she never knew existed.

*Can it possibly be true? What if he's lying?*

Annie *had* to find out, no matter what.

Toni had said the drive to the bayou would take forty minutes. It felt like an eternity.

Still, it would be worth every agonizing minute to finally

find the man who had called to her from her dreams. She had recognized his voice the minute she heard it on the phone. A stranger who claimed to be her brother. How could her mother leave a child behind? Why had she never spoken of him?

"Are you sure you want to do this?" Toni asked as she ripped through the countryside with reckless abandon, driving as if she were in a race at the Grand Prix. "We're headed straight toward a serial killer. For all we know, this guy calling himself your twin could be the one murdering those women."

"I don't believe Evangeline would be that easy to fool." Annie remembered Evangeline's self-confidence and her easy manner. To manage a gallery, she *had* to understand people.

"She told us she's known him for a mere two weeks." Toni navigated a sharp turn on what seemed to be two wheels.

"I only saw you a few times last spring," Annie reminded her, "and yet here we are. Racing toward disaster like Watson and Sherlock Holmes."

"Lucy Ricardo and Ethel Mertz might be more like it." Toni swerved to avoid an armadillo in the road. "I can pick a lock if I have to and bluff with the best of them, but I'm no match for a killer. I'm just a tough-talking Sicilian my Uncle Al used to call Little Dumpling."

"Little *Dumpling*?"

"Oh, yeah. Just to show you how much I *don't* fit that description, I'm going to teach you how to pick a lock."

"*Good*. Every artist needs a vice."

It felt wonderful to have a light moment amidst the barrage of shocking news, even for only a moment. Annie was grateful for Toni's company. Though she had said she could rent a car and meet Lucien and Evangeline by herself, Toni had not only insisted on driving her there, but she'd also packed a backpack and a cooler full of food. "I'm not leaving you in the bayou by yourself," she'd said. "Especially with a target on your back."

That could be true. It occurred to Annie that if she and

Toni disappeared in the swamp, neither of their families would know where they were. She considered calling Jen to let her know, but a big streak of independence and fierceness stopped her. Wasn't every new day an unknown? It was up to her to write her own story on the day, to live free and unfettered by fear, to seize each moment and color it with the vibrancy and abandon she brought to her art.

*No,* she would not be running to her grandmother or her sisters until she had some answers. Lucien Morel could be a liar and a con artist. Though Delilah Broussard had been mercurial and secretive, Annie would keep the memory of their mother intact.

At least until she could discover the truth.

# TWELVE

## PEARL RIVER



Lucian Morel was a man torn in two.

He had longed for his twin his entire life. Yet, every time he hitched a ride to the library in Pearl River, the small city bordering the swamp, he knew he risked exposing his activities to his dad, Jacques Morel, who cut a wide swath well beyond the bayou. He was a magnet, attracting people, extracting information from them, using, and then discarding them as if they were no more than mosquitoes buzzing around his head.

Currently, Jacques was dating the library director, Helen Whitaker, a spinster. A strange match.

Helen saw Lucien when he settled his tall frame into a library chair, removed his cap, and ran his hand through thick black hair, worn longish and curling around the collar of his chambray shirt. She made a beeline his way, her fuzzy, unnatural red hair bobbing as she walked. She was a plain middle-aged woman, bordering on homely.

*But had she guessed his secrets? Would she tell?*

"Lucien, dear boy, what brings you here?"

He doubled the wattage of his smile. Like father, like son. He was not beyond using charm and exaggerating the lilt in his Creole accent to manipulate. "The usual. Do you have anything new on architecture?"

"The new *Deep South Architecture* magazine just came in." She beamed at him as if she had personally published the magazine. "Right this way."

He'd always wanted to be an architect, to make a name for himself creating buildings that looked as if they sprang from the natural setting around them. But reading books and magazines about architecture was a cover for his real purpose.

He slid behind the stacks, connected to the library's Wifi, and powered up his cell phone's search engine. He wasn't about to open his activities to public scrutiny with online social media. Fortunately, his sister was famous and had her own website, complete with a page of public appearances.

And there she was. Annie Logan. A sound made him look up. There, too, was Miss Whitaker, lurking around the stacks, spying.

"Do you need something, Miss Whitaker?"

"No." She put her hand over her heart as if she'd had a bad fright. "Oh, no. I'm just... tidying up back here."

She scuttled off, and Lucien glanced back at Annie's website.

She was coming to New Orleans. Even before he knew of her, he'd been filled with a strange longing, as if the best part of himself were missing. He'd had dreams of her, visions of seeing her in the mist.

He was going to see her, or die trying.

But what would be the cost?


As Lucien anchored his boat at the dock in Honey Island Swamp and helped Evangeline up the stairs that led to Pete's

Place, he was all too aware that he would be adding fuel to the fire of vicious gossip circulating the swamp. Though Pete Thibodeaux was the one being questioned about the recent murders, some of the people he would encounter today were whispering that he was the one butchering women in the bayou. Women who looked very much like Annie Logan.

The locals' love/hate relationship with his father was finally coming home to roost. And he was the target.

A dark rage rose in him. Lately, he was finding it harder to control it. His hard-scrabble life was slowly corroding him from the inside out, like acid he'd swallowed and couldn't spit out.

Evangeline smiled at him, beautiful angel that she was. The white sweater she loved to wear enhanced that image, as did the gleam of her silver bracelets when she put her hand on his arm. "It's going to be okay, Lucien."

"I'm glad you're here with me." She was exactly the support system he needed now. It had been genius to invite her to spend Thanksgiving with him.

Her compassion and her intuitive ability to understand his deepest feelings had attracted him the evening he met her. His friend Boone Fontenot had driven him to the party of a mutual friend in the Marigny. The fact that Evangeline looked so much like the sister he longed to know had sealed her fate.

It had been the kind of party he and Boone always gravitated toward—piles of boiled shrimp and plenty of beer, a CD playing zydeco, everybody dancing and laughing. For a while he could forget that he was a man who had lost half his soul.

Many years ago, when he was just a boy, Delphine, the woman they called the Swamp Witch, had whispered to him, *Be vigilant. Your soul will return to you. Twice.*

Evangeline was the first return of his tattered soul. As he sat beside her on one of the wooden benches on Pete Thibodeaux's porch, searching for the first sign of Annie Logan, he knew his twin would be the second return of his soul, the final piece that would allow him to be done with the past and get on with his life.

"Lucien, look! There she is." Evangeline's excitement was contagious.

Annie stepped from the car, looking breathtaking. He catalogued every inch of her; expensive clothing, right down to the boots, her high cheekbones, so like his, the curve of her mouth, almost a mirror image of his. The universe righted itself. He could see clearly for the first time since the day he was born, half of a whole. Suddenly, everything seemed possible, even a future beyond the grind of bayou living his father had mapped out for him. Hunting and fishing, swapping exaggerated stories of dancing prowess and love conquests. Isolated by a culture and a dying way of life that reduced them to a tourist attraction in a mosquito-infested swamp.

Annie was tall, like him, her skin stamped a dusky golden tone by their French/African Creole mother. She walked with confidence, not with her great beauty, but with a fierce inner spirit that shone from eyes the color of the sea. Eyes that perfectly matched his own.

Her hair was dark and thick, and fell in in waves around her face, a Morel family trait. What surprised him was the hint of red in Annie's hair. Did their mother have that same tint in her hair? The few photographs he'd seen online didn't show the small details about Delilah clearly, and he was eager to learn more.

For now, he was content to watch as Annie and her friend made their way toward the porch. He and Annie were fraternal twins, not identical in every way but alike in so many details it was obvious they were related. The high cheekbones, the lean body, the height. She stood out in the crowd. The people he'd grown up with, and even people he didn't know, swiveled to watch her.

"That's Toni Delgado with her," Evangeline pointed out.

"A big personality in a small package. She's a lawyer, and a bit formidable. I wouldn't want to cross her."

"I don't intend to cross anybody."

Annie's friend was small, with movements as quick as a cricket and big eyes as sharp as an owl. He was immediately drawn to her. She gave off a vibe as natural and comforting as the earth. Still, anxiety spiraled through him.

"Everything is going to be great." Evangeline put her hand over his. "Annie looks at ease."

"She's not. I can tell by her eyes." Her also felt her uncertainty in his soul. She was like him, putting on a good front.

Annie entered the porch, stopped a few feet from him and stared, the look on her face a perfect mirror of his. He felt as if he had stuck his finger into an electrical outlet. Years of longing coalesced into a single moment on a crisp November day when he was finally face-to-face with his twin.

"You must be Lucien." Annie's voice was musical, appealing. There was no hint of the Creole in it, or even of the West where she grew up. "Morel, did you say?"

"Yes. Jacques Morel is my father. And yours."

Her chin inched up a notch. Denial. And why not? He'd had an entire life to know their father, but she was just getting started.

Annie introduced her friend then glanced at the people milling around them. Pete Thibodeaux always had a crowd at his place, both locals and tourists. One of them was the librarian from Pearl River. As she passed by, she paused to smile at Lucien then scurried into the store like a little red mouse. He could see how ordinary, unassuming people like her would reassure his sister.

"Do you mind if we talk here?" she asked.

"Not at all."

"I want Toni with me, and Evangeline, too."

"Of course." He wanted her at ease. Women were always

more receptive when they felt safe. "I have nothing to say that I mind them hearing, but let's find a spot with more privacy from the crowd."

"Sounds good," she agreed.

He led them off the porch to a picnic table underneath an enormous magnolia tree, still in viewing distance of the crowd on the porch but far enough away so that their conversation wouldn't be overheard, and they would be out of range of Pete's surveillance cameras. He'd had quite enough of them.

When they were seated, he told Annie, "Why don't you go first? I know you must have questions."

"Why do you believe I'm your twin sister?"

"When I was old enough to understand, our father told me that you're my twin, and that my real mother is Delilah Broussard."

Annie drew back as if she'd just touched her hand to a hot stove. "That can't be true."

"But it *is*. Think about it. Didn't she come here often?"

"My mother always traveled alone to see her family, and would often stay long periods of time, but I have a hard time believing she was your mother. And I *know* Jacques Morel is not my father."

"Before we were born, Delilah came to the bayou and stayed almost nine months. We were conceived shortly after she got here."

Shock and disbelief registered on her face. "That's not possible..."

"It is. She and Dad were children together, grew up together in the swamp. They were sweethearts for a long time before she married Patrick Logan."

Annie was quiet for so long a dragonfly landed on her shoulder. According to folklore, the dragonfly is a symbol of good luck and a weigher of souls. Though Lucien was perfectly at ease in the world outside the small enclave in the bayou, he had been steeped in the legends and the culture of his people. With two Creole parents, he had the soul of a mystic.

The dragonfly gave him a glimpse of the future he'd always wanted; college and a degree in architecture that would take him away from the swamp and into a city where his ancestry would not set him apart. At the same time, the place he longed to escape gave him the finely tuned sensibilities to feel the dragonfly taking the measure of his soul. Would it find him lacking? Or would it find him strong and ready to become who he was intended to be, no matter what it took?

"This is all too much." Annie stood up, and the dragonfly lifted toward the sky.

Was she going to leave? His dismay matched the darkening sky. Clouds had begun to gather, and the air was cooling. He could smell the rain that would soon come.

"It's getting late, Lucien." Evangeline reached for his hand. "Why don't we all walk to that cute little café down the road for lunch?"

"Great idea," Toni said. "I'm starving. Let's take my car."

All eyes turned toward Annie. When she nodded *yes,* the first raindrops fell on Lucien's head. A baptism or an omen?

"We'll meet you at the car." He grabbed Evangeline's hand, and they sprinted toward his boat to get her rain parka.

The rain picked up speed, pelting Lucien with an urgency that set off one of those strange premonitions he'd been having since he was a small child. He was being warned of terrible things to come, events he couldn't see or even guess.

Happenings so horrible the thought shivered his soul.

# THIRTEEN

## THE SHADOW

No one noticed him in the rain. No one saw him watching the tableau playing out at Pete's Place.

*Fools, all of them.*

Didn't they know *he* was in charge? Didn't they yet understand they were merely pawns in his game?

He felt himself coiling with tension, getting ready to strike. His nemesis was far too self-confident. *She* needed to be taught another lesson. And he knew just how to do it.

*Kill someone she loves.*

## FOURTEEN

*Someone's watching.*

Annie glanced around, shivering. A chill came with the rain hammering Pete's Place, and impressions so strong she couldn't ignore them. There was evil in the air. It had a taste, a smell, both as familiar and terrifying to her as the moment last spring when she'd arrived in Gulf Breeze to find her sister Jen covered in blood.

She was eager to leave this place and to hear what else Lucien Morel had to say.

"I should have brought an umbrella." Toni hustled to keep up with Annie's long stride as they hurried to the car.

"It's just a shower, Toni. I don't mind getting a little wet." The smell of evil intensified. Annie glanced around the parking lot to see if she could spot a dusky-skinned man in a baseball cap. It was deserted. The crowd that had milled around earlier had either dashed into Pete's Place to get out of the rain or had hopped into their boats and cars to head home.

"What did you think of Lucien?" Annie added.

"It's possible the two of you are related. I see the resemblance. DNA for same-parent testing is about forty percent inaccurate, but it might be worth your while."

"There's a whole lot more I need to know about him before I'd be ready to take that step." Annie wondered how Rachel and Jen would react to news of a brother. "Did you see that massive knife in a sheath strapped onto his hip?"

"Yes, but I don't know whether I think it was scary or sexy."

Annie and Toni separated and went around opposite sides of the car to open the doors. They leaped back, their screams so loud they could be heard all the way to the end of the pier.

There on the front seat of the car was a coiled rattlesnake. Annie's terror went up the charts. Her upbringing in the Colorado Rockies had taught her the perils of one of Nature's deadliest killing machines. At the sight of them, the snake reared its vicious head and shook its rattlers. It was the sound of death.

Their continued screams brought people running, but Annie was past seeing. She was lost in a fog of waking dreams. Impressions bombarded her. The feeling of impending doom. The stench of death. Two people. One dark, the other vague. The snake dumped from a crude sack, waiting to sink his deadly venom.

"Annie!" A hand jerked her away from the car. Lucien. Terrified. "Get back!" A blade flashed in his hand. With one swipe he cut off the snake's head. "Don't touch it. It can still bite."

Pandemonium erupted all around the car. People pressing forward to have a look. More screams, shouts, questions.

"How did it get there?"

"Where did it come from?"

"I didn't see anybody out here. Did you?"

Exclamations and dire predictions.

"Mercy me!"

"It's an omen."

"It's voodoo."

Annie was still shaking, but her fog had lifted, carried off by the rain and the life force pulsing from the crowd around her. One of them was a timid-looking woman with soggy red hair standing next to her, her eyes big and bright with fear. Or was it excitement?

"You poor dear." She patted Annie's arm, and a little jolt went through her.

"Um, do I know you?"

"If you've ever been to Pearl River, you do. I'm Helen Whitaker, the director of the library there. Are you all right? Did it bite you?"

"No. I'm fine." Annie felt far from fine, but if she told this perfect stranger what she was really thinking, it would set her hair on fire.

"Rattlesnakes are nasty things. You should be more careful, dear." With that cryptic warning, she hurried off, clutching her purse tightly under her arm.

"Ma'am?" Annie was startled to see a large swarthy man next to her. She hadn't even noticed his arrival. "I'm Pete Thibodeaux. It's hard for snakes to get into these newer model cars all by themselves, and they don't go in without a reason. Do you want me to call the law?"

"They're not likely to find any fingerprints." Toni rounded the car, shivering from fear and the cold rain. She stationed herself by Annie and slid into her lawyer persona. "Both of us touched the door handles. Our prints would smear anything that was there. And this rain is not helping. Annie, what do you think?"

"How would somebody get into a keyless car?"

"RFID readers," Toni said. "It takes two people. One at the car, one close to my key fob. It's easier to do than you would think. Just takes seconds." She turned to Pete. "Mr.

Thibodeaux, make the call. The law might not catch whoever did this, but at least we'll have a report on file."

The rain pelted them harder, and the curious began to scatter.

"Why don't you two ladies wait inside?" Pete offered his arm, and led Annie away. Soaked and shaken, she was only too happy to get out of the rain and away from the awful sight in the car.

Evangeline went into the store with them, but Lucien stayed behind, saying he would oversee disposing of the snake and cleaning up Toni's car.

Soothed by the warmth inside, Annie checked out her surroundings. Pete's Place was a revelation to her, a combination of old-fashioned general store, country eatery, and male-dominated trading post. And yet, it seemed to be brooding, as if the place, itself, were a living thing. Another time she would have taken the time to explore, but the taint of danger was still in the air, and deputies from the St. Tammany Parish Sheriff's Department would soon be there.

Pete Thibodeaux ushered the three women into his office. A harried looking, plus-sized woman he introduced as his wife, Erma, hurried in with coffee. She did a double take when she saw Annie, then quickly hurried from the room. But not before she shot Annie a strange look that set off alarms.

Curiosity? Jealousy? A warning?

After his wife left, Pete hovered around Annie, anxious. "Are you okay, ma'am?"

"Yes, thank you."

"You sure remind me somebody I used to know." All her senses went on alert. "Her name was Delilah Broussard."

"She was my mother. How did you know her?"

"We were sweethearts, but that was a very long time ago."

Pete had an off-beat, vagabond appeal that would have attracted her mother. "Mom's past is a mystery to me." Annie warmed her hands against her coffee cup. "Did she ever date Jacques Morel?"

His boom of mirth was a refreshing change from the earlier bedlam. "Delilah went with him to a dance once, but she preferred substance over bluster. Jacques was a ladies' man, irresistible to everybody... except *her*."

Was that the truth or his version of it? Annie decided to probe deeper. "Did you ever see her when she came back to the bayou after she married my dad?"

"She'd stop by the store a few times to chat. She talked mostly about her daughters. Rachel and Jen, I believe." He studied her. "I heard somebody calling you Annie. Right?"

"Yes. I'm the youngest." She smiled as if her very identity was not in question. She had no intention of becoming the latest topic of gossip in the bayou. "Did Mom also see Jacques while she was here?"

"She ran into him at the store once—I'd say about thirty years ago—but that's all I know." He chuckled. "If you want to run into somebody, come to Pete's Place. It's something of a landmark here in the bayou."

There was a tap on the office door, followed by a male voice. "St. Tammany Sheriff's Department."

The presence of law enforcement made the threat to Annie all too real. Her sisters' warnings and her own dark dreams were unfolding like a horror show in slow motion.

Something unthinkable lurked in the moss-draped bayou. And Annie knew she was the target.

# FIFTEEN

Waiting outside in the rain, Lucien wanted nothing to do with the cops. Thankfully, a snake in the car in the middle of a swamp was not an earth-shattering occurrence, and they didn't bother to come out and take his statement about how he killed it.

Fifteen minutes after the two St. Tammany Sheriff's deputies arrived, they came out of Pete's Place and drove off. Shortly afterward, the women came out, Annie and Toni unflappable, but Evangeline, shaken.

He looped around her waist. "Are you okay?"

"I will be as soon as we get out of here. Annie or Toni could have so easily been killed. Let's get lunch and try to forget that snake."

They climbed into Toni's car and headed to get lunch.

The sign on the front of a shack painted blue simply said LORNA'S EATS. Awnings on the open windows kept out all but the fiercest rains.

The inside was as plain as the outside. Straight-backed chairs and simple wooden tables covered with blue checked oilcloths grouped around a buffet. The owner, Lorna Jensen, had attempted a touch of sophistication by putting a Mason jar holding a plastic sunflower in the middle of each table. As far as Lucien was concerned, she could have left them off. People around here cared about the basics. Living in the swamp taught them the difference between necessities and useless frills.

The crowd was sparse, only two middle-aged couples and one teenager occupied two of the tables along a wall near the entrance to the kitchen.

Two empty booths stood in a secluded corner underneath a bank of windows kept open almost year-round for the view and the ambience. No tablecloth. No plastic centerpiece. Just a pair of large glass shakers labeled SALT and PEPPER near the wall and a single candle in a pottery dish plopped into the middle of the table.

They slid into the booth, and Evangeline's face lit up. "A candle! How romantic! Let's light it."

Lucien flicked his cigarette lighter, and the tiny glow shot sparks off Evangeline's bracelets, a silver cuff and a bangle with rhinestones. A sudden blinding light shot from the rhinestones, a lightning bolt to his heart. Danger was everywhere, and he was helpless, unable to identify the source.

Across the table, his twin noticed his agitation and stared at him, ocean eyes to ocean eyes. Did Annie see what he saw? Were their minds as similar as their faces?

A waitress with a pencil holding up a tight, gray bun enclosed within a hairnet ambled over to take their order. They all opted for the buffet—fried catfish and hushpuppies. Slaw and baked beans on the side. Two kinds of dessert. Bread pudding and chocolate brownies.

For a while, they concentrated on their food. The silence was uncomfortable, highly charged. Too much had been left unsaid. Too much hung in the balance.

Annie was the first to break the silence. "The year I was born, my mother returned from the swamp with me. But I know

Patrick is my father, and I know she would never have left a child behind."

Lucien was relieved to finally have his say. "Dad said Delilah didn't want me. She said I would destroy her family." Annie was still not convinced. It showed all over her face. "Dad let the world believe my mother died in childbirth over in Baton Rouge. When I was five, he told me the identity of my real mother so I would understand that I am one hundred percent Creole. Then he made me promise I would never speak of you or Delilah again—and that I would never try to find either of you."

Lucien thought how easy it had been to make the promise as a child. His dad was his whole world. He'd had no idea of how the loss of someone he didn't even know would eventually become a bottomless chasm that threatened to swallow him whole.

"How do you know Jacques Morel was telling the truth? Delilah was mysterious and moody, but she loved me unconditionally."

"Did she ever mention me?" he asked.

"No, never."

"Then, she was not being truthful with you."

Annie's stubbornness didn't surprise him. It was a match for his own. The two of them would have been a formidable team against the wily charms of their father.

"How can I know you're telling the truth?" she asked him. "And why *now*? After all these years?"

"When you live in a swamp cut off from the outside world, you depend on those close to you. I was fifteen before I broke my vow to my father and first tried to find you. He said he would disown me if I tried that again. For a teenager, the idea of being cut adrift was unacceptable."

He was done keeping her a secret. The snake incident had ensured Annie would be the talk of the bayou. He knew both couples in the restaurant, too. After today, word would spread like wildfire. His father would know what he had done, and he had no idea what the consequences would be. Jacques Morel wasn't known for his soft heart and easy ways.

So be it. Lucien was ready for him. If Jacques pushed him too far, he was finally going to meet his match.

Annie studied him over the rim of her glass. "Why didn't Jacques want you to find me? If he is really my father, it seems he would want me to be part of his life, too."

"We never needed anybody else, and I think he felt betrayed by Delilah, too." Annie stiffened with resistance. So be it. Life is hard. Jacques made sure he learned that lesson. "When I was small, there were whispers that Delilah was my mother, but he squelched them. People around here don't want to cross him. Eventually, they forgot and moved on."

But Lucien never had. And he never would. "Dad and I have always been a team," he added, "two against the world."

"What about Delilah's relatives? Do you know them?"

It was strange that she didn't use their names. Had Delilah kept them a secret, too?

"Our grandfather tried to see me when I was almost three. I don't know what Dad told him, but he never came again. Through the years, I've spotted him at various places, but both of us kept our distance."

An alertness came over his sister. It showed in both her face and her posture, a sense of waiting, of longing.

Sorrow swept through him. "Our grandfather is Angel Broussard. You don't know him, do you?"

"I know the name. Nothing more. Do you know where he lives?"

"I do. If you like, I can take you there."

The waitress came back to hand over their check and disappear with their empty plates. "Why now?" Annie asked. "After all the years and your father's threats, why did you call me?"

"All my life I've had visions of you, and a sixth sense that you are the other half of me," he said. "And I simply had to find you."

Shock bloomed across her face, and uncertainty. The rain had finally stopped, and she stared out the open windows as if she might find answers in the hundred-year-old bald cypress trees and the green water beyond. She searched for so long that she seemed to be reading the very history the bayou held in its dark depths and secret hideaways.

"Do you have any proof other than your word that you are my twin?" she said.

He reached into his pocket and pulled out a silver charm bracelet. It was small, made for a delicate wrist, much like Annie's. It held three heart-shaped charms. He dropped it into her palm and watched her face transform as she read the names on the charms. Rachel, Jennifer, and Patrick. Her two sisters and the man she believed to be her father.

She closed her fist around it. "Where did you get this?"

"From the midwife who brought us into the world, Delphine Thierry. She was known in the bayou as the Swamp Witch. She brought it to me when I was seven. She said it was proof of who I am and a secret I should keep. She also said you would return to me."

"I'd like to talk to her," Annie said. "Where is she now?"

"She disappeared shortly after she gave me the charm bracelet. Legend has it, she was snatched out of her house by a hurricane and left behind everything she owned, even the clothes off her back."

Annie went still, and Evangeline reached for his hand, her face soft in the glow of candlelight. The sounds of the swamp seemed magnified—the song the water made as it meandered among cypress knees, the symphony of hundreds of birds attracted by the lush wetlands, the drumbeat of a croaking bullfrog, and the distant bellow of an alligator. There was comfort in the familiar.

A tiny seed of hope began to grow among the layers of Lucien's anger and despair. Still, years of living in a swamp where danger lurked around every tree stump and eddy in the water, he understood the art of waiting.

"I'm going to reserve judgement about that until I learn more," Annie said. "I'd like to talk with my grandfather."

"Fair enough. Toni can leave her car at Pete's. People visiting the swamp do it all the time."

Everything felt surreal as they left the restaurant and parked her car at Pete's place. Lucien helped them carry their belongings to his boat. He felt as if his entire life had been pointing to this one moment. Standing on the pier in the swamp where he and his sister had been born.

The moment felt predestined, almost sacred, but a sudden vision of Annie in the swamp, screaming, chilled him to the bone.

Who was after her, and why?

# SIXTEEN

In all the years Annie had wondered about her Broussard family, she never imagined she'd be in south Louisiana, climbing into a boat with a stranger who believed himself to be her twin, one who looked so eerily like her she felt as if she'd been split in two.

She studied his dark curly hair, the chiseled planes of his face, his impressive height—everything people remarked about her, duplicated in him. And his *eyes*! Her own unusual blue-green eyes shot through with a starburst of gold around the iris, staring back at her.

She pulled her gaze away. She didn't know anything about him except what he had told her. Delilah gave her a mystical gift, but the down-to-earth grandmother who had raised her taught practical matters.

*Never jump to conclusions.*

As Lucien's boat skimmed over the water, Annie's dream world sprang to life, complete with the algae-covered water and the chorus of frogs. It was a relief to tear her mind off Lucien's claims and focus on the fascinating world around her. As the boat wove around the otherworldly cypress knees rising from the water, the overhanging branches of massive trees moved in the disturbed air, whispering of generations of her ancestors living close to the land. Echoes of loving and fighting, struggling and overcoming, poured through her in the musical cadence of the Creole.

Curtains of Spanish moss hanging from the trees began to sway, their movements wild and erratic, out of proportion to the small disturbance of wind as their boat passed by. Nature's warning of danger.

Annie was suddenly aware of Lucien's reaction; the way his nostrils flared, his eyes widened. Was he reading the signs, too? She hugged herself, as if she could hold the disturbing thought inside.

Small houses on stilts appeared unexpectedly, scattered loosely along the riverbank.

"An enclave of our people," Lucien explained, and Annie was glad to get her mind off yet another similarity between them.

Deep inside the swamp, the landscape was so primitive and pristine it appeared untouched by human hand. Then a grouping of old houseboats gave lie to the theory. They were half-hidden among the thick cypress and gum trees, and had fish nets hanging over their railings. Lucien described them as fish camps. Though most of the ancient wetland habitat was state protected, some of it was not, which allowed the original inhabitants to preserve their old ways of life.

It turned out that he was not only a lover of nature, but of history. He answered all her questions about the bayou and added his own commentary. His voice was rich with Creole cadences and deep with a timbre that could only mean one thing.

"Do you sing?" Annie asked him, and his unexpected burst

of laughter sent frogs leaping off their perches, the undersides of their long legs white and vulnerable as they splashed into the water.

"I do, but not in public."

"He should. He has great baritone." Evangeline's happiness showed in her face and in the way she looked at Lucien. "I've heard him singing in the shower."

Her confession caused a general hilarity that made the trip seem easy, and even fun. Annie was glad for the respite from the web of darkness that had been closing around her.

*So this is what it's like to have a brother.*

The thought came out of nowhere, and yet she knew all was not as it seemed. She understood herself well enough to pay attention to the small things others might label random chance or a meaningless fluke.

Lucien's emotions billowed out behind him like flags, happiness mixed with regret, a poignant longing for something beyond his grasp intermingled with an incomprehensible rage. The mixture was powerful, almost toxic.

Annie struggled out of the fog of her waking vision to join in the conversation. Toni, who loved opera, was engaged in a lively discussion that covered everything from Beethoven to Puccini to Wagner. To an outsider looking on, the four of them could be lifelong friends on a holiday outing.

But to the locals searching for the best fishing spot and navigating their boats toward the hidden coves where they had set their traps for mink and river otter, the three strange women in the boat were viewed with the natural suspicion that comes from growing up with fears of the dreaded Rougarou and the spells cast by the Swamp Witch.

They knew how to survive danger from the familiar, but the unknown threw them into a frenzy of speculation and outright hostility.

Their alarm clawed at Annie like a small, pesky animal. She fought to set that aside, too. "How far to Grandfather's house?" she asked Lucien.

"It's just around the bend."

Impressions bombarded her. An old man with white hair and bent head, his face filled with the despair of loss. The image made her heart hurt. "Does anyone else live in the house with him?"

"As far as I know, he lives alone."

Talk faded into the background as they drew closer. Mist rose from the cooling water, and her grandfather's history continued drifting around her. Music intertwined with grief. The scent of oleander mixed with sawdust. Angel's hands, once strong and supple, now spotted and gnarled with age, still held the muscle memory that knew the art of molding raw material into something beautiful.

Excitement sizzled through her. She shifted toward the one person who could answer her questions. "Lucien, is my grandfather a sculptor?"

"No. But he worked with his hands. He was a fine carpenter. The furniture he made was so perfect in design and detail, it was sold in the best stores in New Orleans. Some say he made a fortune."

"His cottage in the Marigny doesn't reflect that," she said.

"Neither does his house here, but he owns an impressive amount of land." He guided the boat across the cypress knees and into a narrow channel. "You'll soon see."

Angel Broussard lived in modest raised Louisiana cottage set well back from the water and almost hidden in the thick grove of live oak trees, draped with Spanish moss. Red maple, gum, and magnolia trees fanned out around the immaculate house and grounds, creating a wide cocoon of privacy and the impression of elegance and fading Southern gentility. A long pier led from a shell path in front of Angel's property to the boat dock where Lucien cast anchor beside a small blue boat with an outboard motor.

"I think I should speak to my grandfather alone first," Annie said. She knew it wouldn't be easy, for either of them. Her mother's secrets had built a wall between them. Did he even know about her?

"I agree. Take your time. Shout if you need me. I can hear you from here." He got out of the boat and helped her onto the dock. "Good luck."

The walk along the pier and up the well-worn shell path took her to a wrought iron fence with a gate anchored by posts topped with ornately carved pineapples. The symbol of welcome. Taking that as a good sign, she lifted the latch and entered a well-tended garden, bursting with winter blooms. Salvia and sedum vied for space with butterfly bushes, marigolds, and zinnias. But the showpieces were the large pink camellias and the banks of angel trumpets dripping with bell-shaped yellow flowers.

The bursts of color triggered her imagination. She could sit in this garden for hours and be content, slashing watercolors onto canvas.

She was about to climb the steps to the porch and ring the bell when a stooped man with a map of wrinkles on his weathered face and a headful of silver curls rounded the corner of the house. Thunderstruck, they stared at each other. She could see her mother in his high cheekbones, his dark eyes, and the wild riot of his hair.

"I didn't mean to startle you," she said. "My name is Annie Logan."

Tears trickled down his face and meandered in the deep grooves etched there by time. "Is it *possible*? After all these years?" His heavy accent and musical cadence spoke of his

French Creole heritage. "I thought you were Delilah, come back to me."

"I'm your granddaughter, the youngest of three."

They moved toward each other with the inevitability of tides pulled by the moon.

"Let me look at you," he said, and she bent down so he could cup her cheeks and study her. "It's true." He pointed a finger toward the sky painted rose gold by a setting sun. "Nina, she has come back. I will not die alone in my old age."

Was he senile? Did he still think she was Delilah? Her heart broke a bit at the thought, and she felt the ache all the way to her toes.

"I'm so glad I found you," she said, smiling to reassure him. "Is it okay if I call you Grandfather?"

"You think me soft in the head?" Chuckling, he circled a crooked finger around his white hair. "I held you in my arms before your mother left with you. The Swamp Witch brought you. Before she vanished, she told me Delilah's third daughter would return to me. Come, let's go inside before dark catches us."

Annie explained that her friend Toni was waiting in a boat with their backpacks and a hamper filled with food. He insisted they stay with him. "For as long as you can," he added. "I have many questions."

"So do I." She promised they would stay at least for the weekend, then added, "Lucien Morel brought us here."

"*Ba!*" He shook his fist at the sky. "He can stay dead to me. I want nothing to do with him."

What had happened between them to cause such an outburst? It neither confirmed nor denied Lucien's claims. There would be no more family reunions today. As she hurried back to the dock to fetch Toni, she felt transformed, a woman who didn't know how much she had needed her Broussard grandfather until she found him.

One miracle was enough. At least for now.

Annie was nearing the boat when the algae on the lake turned from a velvet-like shade of green to something dark and fearsome.

Her joy slowly drained away, leaving behind the awful certainty that her troubles were just beginning.

## SEVENTEEN

Annie shoved aside her dismay as she and Toni carried their belongings to Angel's home on the bayou.

The inside of the house was a revelation. Her Broussard family history was told by the framed photographs on the wall. Her grandmother, Nina, looked like an exotic princess in her colorful dress and turban. She was a Creole of African heritage with regal bearing, beautiful cheekbones, and full lips she had passed along to her only child, Delilah. Angel's love for her showed in the way he described her kindness, her skill with a needle and healing herbs, and the rich coloratura voice her daughter had inherited.

Photographs of Delilah tracked her from the day she was born until the day she married. Annie found it curious and telling that there were no photos after that. There was nothing on the wall to even hint that Delilah had another life and a growing family in Colorado.

There were no pictures of aunts, uncles, and cousins, either.

"I love the photos," Annie told him. "Do you have more in an album?"

"No. I was an only child, and so was Nina. She died two

years before you were born. The only blessing I can see from her death is that she never lived to see our Delilah die in a car wreck." After all these years, Angel's voice still dripped with pain. "She had only two regrets in this life. Her first was that we could have no more children after our daughter was born. Her second was that she never got to see your sisters, Jen and Rachel."

Annie's own sense of loss was visceral. She struggled to control a growing outrage at the mother she had always loved and even idolized. All that talent and the amazing gift of knowing she had passed on had skewed Annie's perception. The huge oil painting of Delilah that dominated the hallway of the ranch house where she and her sisters grew up had elevated her to the status of royalty, above reproach.

The grandfather clock in the corner of the front room chimed six, and Angel led them into a large, old-fashioned kitchen.

Toni's face lit up. "This is amazing! It looks like Julia Child might have cooked in here." She started unwrapping dishes from the cooler and spreading them on the red gingham cloth that covered an oak table with ornate carvings on the legs. "Did you make this table, Mr. Broussard?"

"I did. I made all the wooden furniture in this house."

"It's beautiful. I can't wait to tell my grandmother in New Jersey." Toni ran her hands over the delicate carvings, her appreciation for its beauty visceral. One of the many reasons she and Annie were kindred souls.

When Annie sat down at the same table where her mother had once taken her meals, she was overwhelmed with a need to understand her past. "Grandfather, why didn't you and Nina ever try to see my sisters?"

Toni nudged her. "No more serious talk, Annie." She passed the honey-baked ham she had brought. "Discussing problems at meals is bad for your digestion. Mimi says pleasant talk at the dinner table will help you sleep well and grow old without ulcers." She grinned. "I'm living proof. Not a single ulcer."

Although she wanted to hear more, it felt good to return to normalcy, and even better to see her grandfather's face light up as he joined in the fun.

"I haven't heard laughter like that since Nina died," he said.

"Now that Annie's back, those days are over," Toni told him. "She's just as beautiful on the inside as she is on the outside. You'll never be without love and laughter again."

Annie mouthed *thank you,* and counted her blessings. Not only had she seen beyond what Toni called her *brief departure from common sense,* but she had also seen straight into her generous heart. Theirs was a friendship that would grow stronger through the years.

After dinner, Angel built a fire, and they all settled into comfortable chairs around the brick fireplace in the front room. At his request, Annie told him about her sisters and their children. His hunger to hear stories about his daughter's family far outweighed her need to discover the truth about her mother's past.

She answered his questions until the fire had burned into embers, and then he led them upstairs to a small bedroom with twin beds. Photos of Delilah and framed playbills from the places she had performed decorated an entire wall. Ornate perfume bottles still littered a small dressing table that also held a brush where a strand of her long dark hair was tangled in the bristles.

"This was your mother's room. We always thought we'd have another daughter to share it with her." Angel choked up a bit then pulled himself together, opened a cedar chest, brought out two patchwork quilts, and handed them to Annie. "There's more in the chest if you need them. Nights in the bayou can get cold this time of year."

He bid them goodnight, and his footsteps echoed on the polished oak floors as he left the room.

Toni sank onto one of the twin beds, and kicked off her shoes. "I *adore* him! He's plainspoken and sincere, much like Mimi."

"He's all that and more. I'm thrilled I found him." So many conflicting emotions swirled through Annie, it was almost impossible to contain them. "I don't know what I feel about Lucien."

"He's very handsome and looks so much like you, I was shocked. He also has your magnetism, but he seems like a complicated man."

"Exactly. But to be fair, he kept secrets for *years* that would eat anybody else alive." Annie suddenly felt his pain as if it were her own. She handed Toni one of the quilts then busied herself spreading the other one on her bed.

"When are you going to tell your sisters?"

"Not yet. Jen and Rachel will be upset when they find out I'm in the swamp where those dead girls were discovered. And I still haven't learned everything I need to know about the summer my mother came here and returned to Colorado on Valentine's Day with a new baby in tow."

Sounds drifted through the window, the swamp coming alive at night. The symphony of frogs, amplified by the heavy night air, was joined by the eerie call of a screech owl.

"Listen to that." Annie sat on the edge of her bed, relieved to shift topics and grateful to hear nothing except the ordinary sounds of Nature. "Wouldn't you love to be floating along in a boat, wearing night vision goggles so you could see it all?" She could picture it, her sketch pad in her hand, a big hat shading the page.

"I'd like to fish in the broad daylight, but I don't want to be anywhere near that place in the dark. It sounds creepy out there. It *is* creepy out there. Do you hear that big alligator bellowing?"

"I do. It's fascinating."

"It's dangerous. Especially with a serial killer on the loose and that fool stalking you. Did he leave more comments... Oh, wait, do we even have Wifi?"

"We do. I think you were in the bathroom when Grandfather told me. We're on the edge of the swamp close to a little town called Pearl River." Annie powered up her laptop and scanned her social media. "There's nothing. Maybe John Davidson got discouraged that I didn't respond, and has moved on to somebody else."

"I doubt it. There's to logic in a sicko like that." Toni unzipped her backpack. "I hope you learn everything you need to know tomorrow so you can leave with me on Sunday and put this mystery behind you."

"I don't think that's likely."

"Well, I do." Toni opened her own laptop and began typing. "If we'd known where your grandfather lived, we could have driven all the way."

"The good news is that my online stalker won't know, either."

"Unless he's local?"

"Even if he is, I don't think the stalker will do more than try to scare me. Most people who hide behind anonymity are cowards."

"Yep." Toni nodded and kept on typing.

But what if they were both wrong? Annie couldn't ignore all the signs and warnings. What if her online stalker was here, all along? Or, what if he was also the aggressive man in the Piazza del Commune? What if his obsession had led him to follow her to America?

She shivered, thinking of the man she'd seen following them in the car from the airport. Toni would have some insight on the matter, but she was now bent over her keyboard, her brow furrowed in concentration.

"I'll be quiet while you work," Annie said.

"I'm not working. I'm doing research on Lucien and Jacques Morel so I can uncover your past as fast as I can and get us out of this killing field."

A vision slammed Annie with the force of a sledgehammer. Mist, everywhere, and dark figure lurking inside, watching. "Toni, what if my online stalker *is* the Shadow?"

# EIGHTEEN

## THE SHADOW

Her name was on the lips of everyone who had seen her at Pete's Place. *Annie Logan.* The artist. News of her spread like wildfire through the swamp. It was whispered on the wind. It drifted through the fog, wove through the treetops, and even invaded dreams.

*Delilah's daughter...* The resemblance was striking, unmistakable.

And now she was here. Within his grasp.

Still, he had to be careful. Two killings had the law crawling all over the swamps. The FBI was now involved. Surveillance video inside Pete's Place identified men who had interacted with the dead girls, and they were being hauled in for questioning.

*Fools.* Didn't they know better than to get caught on camera? He'd been skirting around it for years.

The fog of suspicion fell heaviest on Pete's head. Rumors sent the curious flocking to the trading post to see the suspect. The cautious passed by his dock and went ten miles out of their way to avoid doing business with him.

That harridan from New Orleans chortled on the TV daily,

whipping everybody in her audience into a frenzy. She knew nothing about swamp life, and understood it even less.

The locals lived with omens and charms and dark legends that gave their children nightmares. What the outside world said about one of their own meant nothing to them. If necessary, they would swear to his innocence and would break the law to hide him.

The swamp was filled with places where a man could vanish—out-of-the way spots where trees and bushes and vines were so entangled sunlight couldn't get through; hidden groves where both the curious and the believers practiced dark rituals involving snake handling, orgies, and mindless ecstasy; shanties protected by swamp creatures so deadly they could kill with one strike.

The Shadow knew how to move with the fog, to blend with the darkness, to show the world a mere illusion of himself. By the time he was finished, he would be a legend. Didn't he deserve that kind of notoriety after all he'd suffered? The loneliness, the isolation, the ever-present feeling that the life he could have lived had been stolen from him.

And all because of *her*.

If things had turned out differently, the whole world could have been his. He intended to rectify that. No matter how many people he had to kill.

Before all this was over, *she* would suffer. Take from him, and he would take back. She was the one who would die alone. Not him.

He whipped his gun out of the holster and blew the head off a deadly viper slithering toward his boat.

The woman with him applauded. She thought it was romantic to be on the water in the moonlight.

"My hero," she whispered, and leaned to kiss him. She tasted like peaches flavored with evil.

Little did she know. He could shoot her through the heart

with the same lack of remorse. She would be just another bloody carcass floating in the swamp.

But not yet. She was still useful to him.

He guided his boat into the secluded inlet and cast anchor, gleeful at the task ahead.

Wouldn't *she* be surprised in the morning? If he didn't have someone in the boat with him, he'd hide in the dark just to see the look on *her* face.

# NINETEEN



ANGEL'S BAYOU COTTAGE

Toni was still bent over her laptop, thinking about putting on her pajamas and climbing into the little twin bed when a loud sound echoed through the night. Chills ripped through her and she jerked upright. "Was that a gunshot?"

"I wouldn't be surprised." Annie seemed totally unfazed at the idea of somebody creeping around in the dark firing shots. "People around here carry guns. Many of them put food on their tables by hunting, plus they live in the middle of a bayou filled with predators."

"You've got that right. And one of them is two-legged." Toni got up and marched toward the window to close the gap in the curtains. "The killer could be out there spying on us right now."

"We're on the second floor. Nobody can see in."

"I've been climbing trees all my life. If I can do it, anybody can." She gave the curtains another yank, marched back to the bed, and jerked up her laptop. "You need to be more cautious, Annie. Sometimes I think you might be too brave for your own good."

"I'm not. I just don't want to go around looking over my shoulder. Did you find anything yet?"

When Annie walked over and sat down on the bed beside her, Toni hated to admit how much better she felt. She was used to a large family. There was always a sibling or a cousin around to make the world feel like a better place.

Toni scrolled to the article she'd seen about Jacques Morel. "Lucien and Jacques are not on social media unless they're online using an alias, but I did find this small article about Jacques. It appears to have first been in a newspaper in Slidell, Louisiana, before you were born."

The article was titled HERO SAVES SWAMP WITCH. It was accompanied by a black and white photo that showed a good-looking man with dark hair and a chiseled body emerging from a fire, carrying a tiny woman wearing a turban.

They both leaned forward to read the article.

Jacques Morel, a well-known hunter and fisherman from Honey Island Swamp, rushed into a burning cottage in Slidell last night to save Delphine Thierry. The cottage is owned by Mrs. Rosalie Edmunds.

Mrs. Edmunds was hosting a party for a close group of friends who had come to have their palms read. All the younger women escaped without harm, but Miss Thierry, the woman known as the Swamp Witch, was trapped underneath a crossbeam that had fallen from the ceiling.

Morel is hailed as a hero by the citizens of Slidell, as well as his friends and neighbors in Honey Island Swamp. "He's the local Robin Hood," one bayou resident said. "He shares everything he has with those less fortunate."

"You can't believe everything you read," Annie said.

"Maybe Jacques Morel is not a hero, but the guy did come out of a burning building with a woman thrown over his shoulder? Pictures don't lie. If he turns out to be your father, it looks like he's not so bad."

"He's *not* my father."

As Annie walked to her own bed and slid under the covers, Toni didn't comment. Friends were supportive, not argumentative. She closed her laptop and turned off the light. "'Night," she said. "Sweet dreams."

"Sleep well, my friend."

"I will. After all, tomorrow's another day." Toni imitated Scarlett O'Hara's deep Southern drawl, though New Jersey was about as different from the culture in *Gone with the Wind* as you could get. Her silliness made Annie laugh, which had been her intent all along.

Toni snuggled under the covers, wishing it would be that easy to make the horror of those dead girls in the bayou go away. Here she was, right in the midst of all that killing.

Who would be next? What if it was her or Annie?

When Annie woke up in her mother's childhood room, she was filled with elation. How many years had she wondered about her Broussard family?

The scent of strong coffee drew Annie from her bed. Though she hadn't yet adjusted to the time difference, she was accustomed to keeping odd hours. She was fully alert as she threw on jeans and a white shirt then tiptoed out of the room and down the stairs.

"Annie?" her grandfather called to her from the kitchen. "Is that you?"

"It is!"

"Fetch the *Bayou Weekly* off the front porch. I forgot to get it. It'll be on the door mat."

"Okay." Early morning sunlight fell across the walls of the den, highlighting Delilah's photographs. It was a vivid reminder to Annie of everything she had to lose by digging up the past.

The thin weekly newspaper lay on the welcome mat in

front of the door just as her grandfather had said. She picked it up then covered her mouth to muffle a scream. Underneath the paper lay a dead crow, the heart pieced by a bullet, the neck twisted at a macabre angle. A bloody note was attached to one leg.

*Get out before someone else dies.*

Was someone *watching* her now? If the killer could leave this note on the *doorstep* without being seen, what was to keep him from entering the house undetected and butchering them all?

Terrified and sick to her stomach, Annie hung onto the doorframe to keep from bolting.

How had her stalker found her so easily in this isolated spot? No one knew she was here except Lucien and Evangeline. Had they talked? Had someone at Pete's Place seen them leave together and followed in a boat?

Horrified that she had brought this evil to her grandfather's door, she searched in every direction. Nothing presented itself except early morning in the bayou—the still air, a hint of pink in the sky, the green smell of water, and the earthy scent of the jungle-like forest around her.

Holding the dead crow by one wing, she hurried across the front yard and heaved it as far as she could over the fence. She heard a small plop as feathers and blood and bone landed out of sight, somewhere in the tangle of underbrush.

Then a disturbing thought pushed through. The crow and the note were physical evidence that someone was after her. Was it her online stalker? The man from the piazza? Or could it possibly be the Shadow?

Just how many people was she dealing with?

. . .

When Annie went back inside, Angel was standing at the stove beside an old-fashioned percolator. The small TV on the wall above a corner desk was playing an advertisement for kayaks. He beamed when she walked into the kitchen.

She kissed him on the cheek then set the newspaper on top of a small desk in the corner and went to the sink to scrub her hands.

"Coffee is in the pot, cream's in the refrigerator, and the sugar bowl is on the table." He sliced through a stack of bacon and threw the pieces into a large cast iron skillet, his motions efficient and certain. He reminded her of Gran, who preferred iron skillets to anything that was lighter weight; easier to clean, and probably more efficient.

She was still shaking when she poured cream into her coffee, and the second-guessing started again. Should she go back and search for the note? The idea of stuffing the bloody thing in her pocket made her shiver. It was evidence, but of what?

She took a sip of the good strong brew, trying to calm herself. Her stalker would win only if she let him.

"This coffee is delicious." Did Angel detect the fear that was still in her voice? She took a couple of deep breaths before soldiering on. "Can I help you prepare breakfast? I'm pretty good with biscuits."

"Nothing would please me more." He handed her a faded blue apron that was hanging on a hook beside the back door, then began laying out the dough bowl and cutting board and biscuit fixings. "The apron belonged to my Nina. She's smiling down now, watching you make biscuits in her kitchen."

As Annie lined up the ingredients on the cooking island, she pictured the woman she'd seen in the photograph smiling at her, murmuring endearments and encouragement in a voice as rich and sweet as dark native honey. She wished her sisters were here to share the moment with her.

Bacon popped and sizzled on the stove behind her while she measured flour, baking powder, and salt into the bowl and began to cut in the butter. "I'd love to know more about my mother."

"What do you want to know?"

Her grandfather was a man who appreciated boldness. The stories that clung to him and his house told her so. The walls pulsed with fierceness and courage.

She poured buttermilk into her bowl and began to knead the dough. "Why did she keep us from you?"

"She hated me for opposing her marriage to your father. She came back to the bayou to visit me out of respect, nothing more."

As she listened, Annie thought about relationships, how fragile they were, how easily torn apart by the small things. It saddened her that neither her grandfather nor her mother had been willing to reach out with a mending needle and stitch themselves back together.

"Why did you oppose the marriage? My dad was a great man and a successful, well-respected rancher."

"Nina called me pig-headed and tried to talk me out of it. But that red-headed Irishman was as different from our Creole people as a man could possibly be."

She couldn't help but smile. Red-headed, Patrick Logan was, and Irish through and through.

"Dad was sociable and easy-going, a wonderful husband and father. He never had trouble fitting in with anybody."

"Maybe I misjudged him back then, but I knew my daughter. She would never be happy on a ranch in the Rockies where she'd be trapped all winter by ice and snow. Isolated. She enjoyed a mild climate and big crowds. She had a career she loved. He took her away from all that." He paused to stir the bacon. "Was she happy?"

Annie pictured her mother playing with her and her sisters

in the attic, letting them play dress-up in her old costumes, laughing at their attempts to sing the ballads she had once made popular. She saw her smiling, weaving crowns of four-leaf clovers for them in the pasture where cattle grazed. She saw her galloping across the hills on her favorite Appaloosa stallion, her hair and her laughter streaming behind her like a kite.

But then there were the dark moods when she holed up in her room and wouldn't come out, the sudden disappearances their dad explained as *one of your mother's little vacations to see family*. The long absences. The secrets.

Annie turned to see her grandfather watching her, his face a study in pain and regret.

"Sometimes she was very happy. She adored Dad, and I know she loved me and my sisters. But she was often sad. I never knew why... until now."

"Because of what I did."

"It was much more than that." She studied her grandfather as she talked. "According to Lucien Morel, he's my twin, and my mother abandoned him."

"I wouldn't believe anything I was told by a Morel!"

Angel's face went from uncertainty to stubbornness to rage. The very walls vibrated with it, screaming a family history so dark Annie *knew* that what she discovered would have the power to destroy her.

TWENTY

Mist seemed to gather inside the kitchen, rising from the floor and tangling around Annie's legs, snakelike and alarming. Lucien was there, half hidden by fog. Despair floated above him, as sharp and destructive as a rattlesnake's teeth.

This was not mirage but a waking dream. What was it telling her? That he shared their mother's dark moods? Or was it more, something more sinister? Annie peered through the mist, but the past and present were so closely intertwined the dream-message eluded her. As it floated off in the lifting fog, she found herself solidly planted in the kitchen, her mind reeling, her hands sticky with biscuit dough.

There was her grandfather, as stubborn as a post, still determined to block all talk of Delilah's past with the Morels.

Annie jutted out her jaw. She could be just as stubborn. "Lucien said Mom and Jacques were sweethearts before she met Dad."

"*Bah*. He tried to court her, but she knew he was a bad seed. She wouldn't look at him twice. She fancied herself in love with Pete Thibodeaux, and some boy I forget. Every boy in the swamp was after my Delilah. Not a single one of them was worthy of a hair on her head."

Her grandfather would surely know, and even Pete Thibodeaux mentioned Delilah's aversion to Jacques. And yet, wasn't it the nature of rebellious teens to sneak around and do things they didn't want their parents to know? Maybe her mother had known her father would oppose Jacques exactly the way he later opposed the man she married.

"Tell me about the day I was born." She wasn't about to give up until she knew the truth. "Did my mother give birth to one child or two?"

"I don't know." Angel got the cagey look of a little boy pretending he never took the chocolate chip cookies, though his hand was clearly still in the cookie jar.

"How is that possible? She was *here*."

"She was in the bayou, but not with me. She stayed here with me about three months, and then suddenly she packed up her bags and left. Later, I found out she was staying with the Swamp Witch, but I didn't go after her." Tears gathered in his eyes. "I wish now I had. If Nina had been alive, I would have."

Mention of the Swamp Witch triggered Annie again. Suddenly, she was bombarded with impressions; a tiny, wizened woman in a red turban, surrounded by trees so thick the sunlight couldn't find a way through. Fog swirled around her and a strange, haunting chant that was almost like music. When you listened closely, though, the chanting turned into a plaintive wailing, sorrow mixed with terror of the unknown future unfolding, phantomlike, in front of you.

This vision dissolved with no more effort than a soap bubble breaking apart, leaving behind the slightest iridescent haze in the air to show it had once been there.

"Why would my mother go to the Swamp Witch? Are you related?"

"*Bah*. I spit on her!" Her grandfather's jaw hardened so it looked like the blade of a hatchet. "Even if I was related to Delphine Thierry, I wouldn't claim it. She tampered with people's minds. I don't believe in all that mumbo jumbo. But Nina did. She and Delphine were close friends. Delilah saw her as a sort of aunt."

Disappointment almost overwhelmed Annie. The strength and rawness of her own emotions shocked her. Had she been hoping her grandfather would know Delphine's secrets? That he would say that he knew Lucien was her twin? Or that he wasn't?

She'd always had enough confidence for two, and now she was split in half. Her mind rejected Lucien's claims while her heart kept tugging her toward him.

"When Delphine brought me to you before my mother left the swamp, did she mention a twin or tell you anything that happened the day I was born?"

"No. She only said you were Delilah's child." Angel looked as if he had aged ten years since she first came into the kitchen.

"I know this is hard for you, Grandfather. It's hard for me, too. Please understand that I have to know about Lucien, just as I had to know about you."

When he turned his back to take bacon out of the skillet, she thought she had pushed him too far. If he wouldn't tell her everything he knew, and Delphine was gone, who would reveal her mother's secrets? The one thing Delilah had said about her family was that the Creoles in the bayou were clannish and suspicious of outsiders.

In the den beyond the kitchen, the grandfather clock chimed the hour. The house seemed to sigh and whisper, spilling its hidden stories in a language that Annie didn't yet understand. She glimpsed shadows, a silhouette of her mother running her hands over the growing mound of her belly that she would soon be unable to hide, the fear that seized her, the uncertainty. She felt a rush of wind as the door opened, saw the stars, heard the crunch of leaves as Delilah stole away in the dark.

Annie hurt for the frightened woman her mother had been. But what had scared her so? That she was pregnant by Patrick Logan or by a man who was not her husband? The big question was *why*. Why would a woman who loved her husband and two daughters have an affair with another man?

Her grandfather turned from the stove and came over to wrap his arms around her.

"Dear child." He held her at arm's length so she could see the sincerity in his face. "If I knew whether Lucien Morel was your brother, I would tell you. There were rumors about the boy. I even tried to see him when he was a toddler. I thought, if he belongs to Delilah, I'll know."

"Did you know?"

"His eyes... They broke my heart, and yet, I couldn't be sure. Delilah had kept everything from me, even her pregnancy. Then the Swamp Witch hid her. I knew nothing until Delphine brought you here, and there was no mention of Lucien. But even not knowing the truth, I wanted to be part of the boy's life."

"Why?"

"Jacques Morel is a monster, unfit to raise a child, especially one who might be of Broussard blood. It was just me, alone in this big house. I thought I might make a difference in the boy's life."

"What happened?"

"Morel told me he'd kill me if I ever came near him or the boy again. He said if I ever mentioned the boy's name in connection with Delilah, he'd burn my house down and make sure I was in it first. He's evil. I spit upon him!"

Everything in her recoiled. Despite the evidence Lucien had presented, this cruel man her grandfather described couldn't possibly be her father.

"My mother came back here many times while I was growing up. If Jacques is so bad, why didn't she try to take Lucien back?"

"After you were born, she refused to set foot in the bayou. When she came to visit, we always stayed in the house off the Vieux Carre in the Marigny."

"I need to talk to Jacques Morel."

"He's dangerous, *ma chérie*. Don't keep pursuing this."

"I have to know."

Her grandfather bowed his head and made a motion in the air. It was the sign of the cross.

Humbled and contrite, she reached to hug him. "Don't worry about it, Grandfather. Let's have a wonderful day together. I want to see your workshop and spend time in your gardens, sketching. And I know Toni wants to go fishing."

She could see the effort it took for him to cast off his worries and embrace the moment. It was heartbreaking to watch, and yet beautiful.

"First, let's get those biscuits of yours in the oven." His smile was warm and appealing, so like Delilah's that Annie almost lost her breath.

Her better angels whispered in her ear. *Be like Angel. Seize the moment.* "Let's do it. I could eat them all, I'm so hungry."

Suddenly, a grainy video shot across the TV screen, accompanied by Linda Holloway's breathless reporting. "As police broaden their net for the person responsible for killing Janine Porter and Sylvie Bergeron Hopkins, they continue searching video footage from Pete's Place, recorded when both girls were there."

Annie hadn't seen photos of the first victim, but she recognized the second from the news report she'd seen at Toni's apartment. The victim's aunt moved into view on the video, and then walked out of the frame with her niece, arm in arm. Probably heading home for the holidays.

The man walking behind them was none other than Lucien Morel. Annie lost all taste for biscuits.

Suspicion and fear settled into the pit of her stomach. Was the man who claimed to be her brother capable of murdering young women in the swamp?

# TWENTY-ONE



This was not the way Paul Chenevert wanted to spend a Saturday morning. He sat in a hard chair in the interview room with two deputies at the St. Tammany Parish Sheriff's Department office. Detective Sargeant Joe Keane—young, eager, a recent hire from New Orleans—leaned against the wall, while Sheriff Harold Debeau took a seat opposite Paul.

Debeau had a jaw like a shovel, a headful of gray hair, and a gravelly voice. "This is just a formality, Chenevert. We're questioning everybody on the video footage from Pete's Place when the two female victims were there. Were you there?"

"I was. Both times. I spoke to each of them." No use denying it. The evidence would be on the tapes.

"What was your conversation about?"

"I didn't have a conversation with either girl. Janine Porter asked me the location of the toilet, and Sylvie Bergeron Hopkins asked if I had a light for her cigarette. She said she'd left hers at home."

"What else did you talk about?"

"Nothing. They both asked a question, and I answered out

of politeness. Nothing else was said. We went our separate ways."

"What was your relationship with the victims?"

"I didn't know either girl."

The sheriff didn't need to know that he'd seen Janine in his art gallery a time or two. What was the point? He barely remembered her being there, and they had never even spoken to each other until that day in Pete's Place.

It was time to ditch his habit of politely accommodating everybody with a need before it got him into more trouble than he could handle. Chivalry went out of style with the Dark Ages.


It was a relief for Paul to get back to his studio in his Honey Island Swamp home. Sunlight poured through the skylights and the bank of windows, illuminating his row of gleaming tools, his sculptures and works in progress, his worktables. As he worked, sawdust swirled in motes of light, the smell of it transporting him into the heart of Nature where he had carefully selected his wood—big sections of fallen cypress, chunks of cedar and red gum, blocks of solid oak. The wood came alive in his hands, warm and smooth to the touch, its heart pulsing in his palms as he carved away the excess to release the woodland creature trapped inside. It was a hawk. Meant to spread its wings and soar.

As the hawk's head began to emerge, he lost himself in the work, became nothing more than a goggled, masked, and aproned vessel for his art. Sawdust thickened the air and shavings fell to the floor of his workshop, collecting on his shoes, his pants, and along his bare forearms, deeply tanned from hours in the sun photographing the birds and animals, the fish and reptiles, the insects and arachnids he would later bring to life as sculptures.

When his cell phone rang, it was nothing more than a pesky

mosquito, buzzing around his head. Whoever was calling would give up and go away. Most people didn't bother. He was always in his workshop or lost in the books and music that weighed down every shelf in his den.

This caller persisted. Something about the call triggered his curiosity. He discarded goggles and mask then pulled his cell from his pocket. It was Evangeline, his gallery manager.

"Paul, I hope I'm not interrupting your work?"

A call almost always interrupted his work, but he hadn't yet become the kind of curmudgeonly hermit who had discarded all manners. Almost. But not quite.

"Not at all. But it looks like business is interfering with your holiday."

Her laughter could mean she was happy, or it could mean she was too embarrassed to show her true feelings. In his opinion, she had let herself get involved too deeply with Lucien Morel before she took the time to find out who he really was. The man was an enigma, prone to showing the world a façade while rarely revealing his own feelings.

Not that his opinion on Evangeline's personal life mattered. He supposed Lucien was a decent enough guy. As far as Paul knew, he'd never been in trouble with the law. But lately there had been talk about Lucien's temper. There were even rumors that he might be responsible for the killings in Honey Island Swamp, though it was based more on the locals' love of the talk than any sort of hard evidence.

He pulled his mind back to his mostly one-sided conversation with Evangeline.

"Actually," she said, "I called to let you know that Annie Logan is here. In Honey Island Swamp."

That wasn't surprising. "Lots of tourists come here."

"She's not on tour. She's visiting the grandfather she's never met, Angel Broussard."

Now that was interesting. None of Angel's family had come

to visit in the eight years Paul had lived here. If you called vanishing into your work in order to forget the life you once had *living.*

Evangeline was waiting for him to make some sort of reply, but he had none. A man who couldn't untangle his own guilt about killing his wife and infant daughter had no business making any comments about an old man reuniting with his granddaughter. He could still hear the crunch of metal as the car he was driving skidded into the bridge railing that crushed his family.

"Since Annie came to the gallery to see you, I thought you might want to drop by and pay her a visit." She sighed, as if dealing with him was on par with pulling splinters out of her hand.

"Umm hmm." He knew he was difficult. Moody and taciturn. And that was a generous description. Most of his neighbors, both here and in the Marginy, called him antisocial. He was only approachable and moderately friendly with the clients and artists in his gallery, and that was a façade, impossible to maintain for more than a couple of hours.

"She's right next door." Evangeline breathed out in a little whoosh as if she had no energy left to deal with him anymore.

"She has my number. I'm sure she'll call if she needs me."

*Chenevert, try to act human, just this once.*

His conscience had been acting up lately, getting cheeky. He summoned up his latent and mostly missing manners.

"I appreciate you telling me," he added.

"Really? I think it would be great if you'd drop by to see her… to make her feel welcome. She's a long way from home. And she's a very nice person. Besides, beautiful."

Paul chuckled. *Was Evangeline matchmaking?* It wouldn't be the first time. "I'll drop by."

"When? I don't know if she'll be here longer than this weekend."

"How does today sound to you?"

"Just perfect. I think you're going to really like her. I mean, *really!*"

Her excitement was palpable. She was a great employee and a genuinely good person. Would it hurt him to encourage her in what was now obviously an effort to pair him up with Annie Logan?

"If she's anything like her art, I'm sure I will. Thanks for letting me know."

He had no intention of going. Of course, he didn't. Getting mixed up in other people's business had put him on the hot seat with the St. Tammany Parish Sheriff.

He donned mask and goggles again then picked up a blade and chisel and tried to concentrate on the section of wood that would become the hawk's beak. But all he could see was the cottage next door, tucked among the lace curtains of Spanish moss—and a silver-haired gentleman who would have been far less lonely if Paul had taken the time to look up from his own problems and see those of his neighbor.

He flung his apron, mask, and goggles aside, splashed water over his face to remove any traces of sawdust, and headed toward the long path in the lush tangle of vines and bushes and trees that led from his five-acre property to the cottage show-place on the twenty-five-acre estate owned by Angel Broussard.


Angel and Toni had gone fishing, and Annie had the cottage and gardens all to herself. Her joy at painting was tainted by fear that her stalker might be somewhere out there in the jungle-like growth watching her.

As her hands flew over her sketchpad, she tried to forget about the dead crow she'd tossed over the fence. Birds and wetlands creatures whose names she didn't yet know serenaded her from the evergreens and deciduous trees across the fence.

Beyond the garden gate, she glimpsed the long pier and the deep green water.

The day had grown increasingly warm. She balanced her sketchpad and pencil on her knees, then rolled up the sleeves of her white shirt and gathered her hair in a ponytail with a red scrunchie she usually wore around her wrist as a backup plan. She had always loved the sun on her face, and she lifted it to feel the soothing warmth.

"Hello." The unfamiliar male voice shot her out of the kitchen chair she'd dragged into the garden. *Had he found her?*

She whipped her head around to the source and saw a tall, devilishly handsome man with shaggy blond hair, piercing blue eyes, and a rakish smile. About her age, she'd guess. His jeans hung in a cavalier manner around lean hips, and his blue chambray shirt was sprinkled with something that appeared to be sawdust.

He stood well inside the garden gate, no more than ten feet from her. How did he sneak up on her like that? And for what purpose?

If he were up to no good, the only large weapon she had was the wooden ladderback chair she'd just vacated. Angel had made it, and she could attest to its sturdiness. But would it knock him out?

"I didn't mean to startle you," he said, his face an unreadable mask. He looked altogether like a pirate. Or perhaps a serial killer whose offbeat appeal would camouflage his intent for months or even years before anybody even suspected him.

"I wasn't expecting anyone." She shut her sketch pad and placed it on the slatted seat of her chair then got a good grip on the ladderback. She wanted her hands already on the nearest weapon if she had to defend herself. "Angel is fishing. He'll be back any minute. He called moments ago to tell me."

He wouldn't be home before dark, but she didn't want this man to know it. Let him think a tough old man who had battled the swamp for nearly eighty years would soon appear, possibly toting a gun. She'd seen a number of weapons at Pete's Place, and her grandfather's double-barreled shotgun rested in a gunrack in the den. Like the gun Victoria Logan called Old Betsy, they were more than an accessory. They were an essential part of life in the bayou.

Honey Island Swamp was hemmed in on three sides by the Pearl River (Big Pearl), the West Pearl River (Little Pearl), and Lake Borgne. Large portions of it were hidden under the canopies of giant trees with trunks contorted in menacing shapes. Clearly, a dangerous place to live.

"Actually, it's you I came to see. I'm Angel's nearest neighbor, Paul Chenevert."

"Oh." Relief flooded her. "The gallery owner."

"I hope you don't mind my dropping by. Evangeline called to say you were here, and I seized the chance to go over the details of your show."

"Of course." Still, she felt a little weak-kneed that she'd let her guard down, and more than a little relieved that he was harmless. "I've made sunshine tea. Why don't you come inside, and I'll pour us a glass over ice. Unless you prefer it hot."

"Iced tea is fine."

They went into the kitchen where a glass pitcher filled with tea that had steeped in the sun waited for her on the deep sill of a bay window. She poured tea while Paul talked about her art show. "I have clients who will be thrilled by your watercolors. They have a classic feel while remaining fresh and contemporary." He outlined his plans for displaying her work and asked her for input about lighting and groupings.

"I shipped them with a list of how they should be grouped. Evangeline will have that." She asked him about his clients, and he gave her brief vignettes that brought them to life.

It didn't surprise her that a fellow artist should be so observant. What she didn't expect was how much at ease she felt with him. The conversation flowed as if she'd known him forever.

She had not only found a kindred artistic soul in the swamp; it seemed she had also found a much-needed friend and neighbor.

A memory blindsided her—Paul's hands, capable of creating beauty from a block of wood. What else could those sensitive hands do?

Annie blushed just thinking about it, as her heart beat a little faster.

## TWENTY-TWO

Paul meant to stay at Angel's twenty minutes, tops, and then hurry back to his workshop where he could block out his past by becoming a slave to his art. But that was before he met Annie, and fell under her spell.

He didn't know any other way to describe how impossible it was not to become lost in the depth of her incredible eyes. How he could sit on his neighbor's front porch, unaware of time because of the lilting rise and fall of her voice. How her mere presence soothed him.

Even more astonishing was the powerful connection he felt to her spirit, as if they had been split apart and had finally made their way back to each other. As he listened to her talk about how she had found her grandfather and the man who claimed to be her twin, he felt such ease with her that he suddenly realized how he had missed simply sitting and talking with someone who intuitively trusted him. Annie seemed to read his mind.

"I didn't mean to burden you with my problems," she said. "It's just that you are so understanding. Ever since I talked to Lucien, I've felt a sort of desperation. I'm torn between wanting his story to be true, and not." She took the scrunchie out of her hair, and when she shook her head, the sun shot sparks through her mass of mahogany curls.

How could such a simple action mesmerize him? Set him on fire with the urge to sculpt her face, surrounded by that tangle of living, breathing hair?

"You don't strike me as desperate." He was touched by her sincerity and the big heart it would take to not simply reject Lucien's claim outright—particularly since she had to know how she and her family would be ripped from everything they had believed to be true about their mother and themselves. "Not even close. Maybe I can help. I've lived here many years. What do you want to know?"

"What sort of man is Jacques Morel?"

"Depending on who you ask, he's the most admired—or the most hated—man in the Creole enclave of Honey Island Swamp. Whatever they think of him, no one is neutral."

"Why the extremes?" she asked.

"Like several others here, he still makes his living fishing and hunting, running his traps for the hides of the river otter and mink he catches. He's an expert at what he does, and he's generous to share his bounty with anyone having a hard time. Some even say he robs the rich to give to the poor."

"A modern-day Robin Hood?"

"He's called that by many. Others say he's the devil in disguise. Are you familiar with the Creole legend of the Rougarou?"

"I've researched Creole history because of my roots," she said. She struck him as a woman with the intellectual curiosity to do exactly that. "The Rougarou is a man cursed to transform into half man, half wolf. He uses his glowing eyes to stalk and kill prey at night, and he casts a curse on anyone who sees him."

"Many bayou residents think Jacques is the Rougarou. The few times I've encountered him, he encourages the talk."

"What's your personal opinion of him?"

He hadn't formed personal opinions about anybody in the swamp except his closest neighbor, Angel, and Pete Thibodeaux, who was the source of the staples he kept at his bayou house and the gas he used for his boat. Lucien Morel fell into the category of the familiar only because of his involvement with Evangeline. Paul had found out everything he could about the man only because he felt obligated to protect his employees to the best of his ability.

His own conscience called him a liar. Since the untimely and tragic deaths of his wife and daughter, he had felt obligated to protect every female who crossed his path, whether he knew them or not. He'd gotten into trouble more than once for intervening when he saw a man threatening a woman. It turned out, almost nobody wanted strangers in the middle of their business, even if they were airing it in public.

Maybe it was time to start being sociable enough to form opinions and real relationships. To lay his ghosts to rest. It was certainly time to be truthful to the only woman he'd found even remotely interesting since his wife Stella died.

"I'm something of a recluse," he told her. "But Angel is one of the most solid and decent men I know. He doesn't like Jacques Morel, and I believe he must have a very good reason."

Annie picked up the pitcher to refill their glasses. "I can get more ice if you like."

"No." He picked up his tea and felt the condensation on the outside of his glass. "This is great."

Here he was, talking in superlatives. He'd think she might have slipped a magic potion into his tea if he didn't know that she was a sophisticated artist who had traveled so far from her Creole roots there was no hint of them in her speech or actions.

As if she could divine his thoughts, Annie smiled at him. "I wasn't being entirely truthful with you when I said Angel would return soon."

"I know." He glanced at the sun, already low on the western

horizon. How did time slip away so fast? "That was a smart move. You should be very careful. Everybody in the bayou is locking doors and packing heat."

"That's what Grandfather said. I had planned to go back to New Orleans tomorrow with my friend, Toni, but I can't leave without trying to find out the truth. Is Lucien trustworthy? Does he have a criminal record? What kind of man is he?"

He felt her need for answers as if the questions were his own. Though she was an independent woman of formidable talent, he wanted to help her.

*Get real. You want to rescue her.*

The truth settled in his bones like the leaves in Annie's sunshine tea. He was still playing knight in shining armor.

*Get a grip, Chenevert.*

His pep talk fell on deaf ears.

"Lucien is a fisherman and a hunter, usually laid-back, but he can be triggered. He's been in a few public brawls, but he has no criminal record that I know of."

He'd seen the video footage that placed Lucien at Pete's Place with both victims, but it proved nothing except opportunity. That had turned out to be a lucky break for all the suspects, including Paul.

"Lucien is private, an enigma," he added. "But he strikes me as a man who is decent, and from what I've seen, he doesn't share his father's worst traits."

"Can I believe what he tells me?"

"I wish I could help you there, but I don't know."

She nodded and sipped her tea, a woman at peace with herself, a refreshing woman who saw no need for pretense. "Do you know if the Swamp Witch died in a hurricane?"

"Her body was never found, but her house is still standing. I've never heard anyone talk about seeing her since she was swept away in the hurricane, though some say they've seen her ghost haunting the house."

"Is it possible to go there?"

"The house is still there, but I don't recommend it. She lived in one of the dangerous areas of the bayou." He contemplated the level of tea in his glass. It was almost to the bottom. Time to go. Past time, considering how radically his ideas about self-imposed isolation had changed.

He took his last swig of tea and set his glass on the table between them. "I have clients from all walks of life scattered all over New Orleans and the adjoining states. I'll start asking a few questions. Delphine Thierry was well known over a wide area. A celebrity of sorts. If she's still alive, someone, somewhere will know."

"That's great, thank you."

"I'm just down the path if you need me. It's been a pleasure meeting you."

That was the understatement of the year. The least he could do was thank Evangeline for the tip that led him to spend the best afternoon he could remember in many years.

On the walk home, he was revved up, hyperaware, hypervigilant. Each leaf presented itself separately. The tree branches arching overhead created a canopy that gave the illusion of being in a place apart from the outside world, a place where anything at all could happen at the moment you least expected it.

# TWENTY-THREE

## THE SHADOW

The Shadow crept out the door like a phantom, blending with the night as he moved through the thicket at the edge of the parking lot.

His boat was hidden so well, no one would ever see it was there. It was hard to keep from roaring his triumph as he climbed in and glided silently through the water, indistinguishable from the other boats seen on the slowly meandering water any time of day or night. The gear aboard pegged him as a fisherman out at night to check his trout lines, someone ordinary, an insider who belonged.

He'd never been ordinary. And he had never belonged to the land and the water, *any* land and water. They belonged to him. They were there to serve his purpose, whatever he decided it would be, just as the woman he'd left behind was waiting to do his bidding, whether she knew it yet or not. She hadn't even questioned him about why he was leaving her alone while he went out at night to check on fishing lines. She viewed him as some kind of hero.

His chest expanded with pride. He was strong, invincible, ten feet tall. Nothing could touch him.

Darkness and fog surrounded him, and a night that was silent except for the chorus of frogs and the occasional thunderous bass of an alligator. It was the kind of night that called up the past, that opened up the cavernous hole inside him and allowed the old hurts and injustices to escape. The abandonment and humiliation. The years of living a life that was never meant to be his.

*She* was the cause.

Everything he had suffered was because of her. The pain he still nursed like a stubborn toothache was all her fault. The morose feeling that often sent him to find relief in a whiskey bottle threatened to overtake him.

He shoved his pain into the black box of his soul. It was time to make her pay.

He trolled through the backwaters of the bayou, his night vision goggles perfect for spying. They highlighted a pair of gleaming eyes watching from a tangled thicket, a lone fisherman pulling in his trout lines, a dinky boat with a stooped old man and a nubile young woman.

When he came to the isolated cottage where the little blue boat was missing, he hid his boat among the scrub brush where no one would see it, not even if they were looking. Then he sat there watching, invisible as a shadow.

She was in the garden, gathering her things, the faint light of a dying sun lighting the red in her hair. When she walked into the house, a carefree woman of privilege, he felt the monster rise in him, fierce and wild. It grew bigger and bigger until it was so fierce, he could have jerked an oak tree out of the ground by its roots and hurled it at her back.

Hanging onto the gift he'd brought in a burlap bag, he climbed out of his boat and slunk through the bushes until he was in her backyard. A single light bulb in the kitchen window lit the flames in the hair of perhaps the most beautiful woman in the world—and the most selfish. She'd taken everything he had.

He intended to destroy her—and that nosey little friend she'd brought here with her.

TWENTY-FOUR

Long after Paul had disappeared into the shadows of evening, Annie's memories of him played through her mind—the way his blue eyes lit up when he smiled, his quiet appreciation of the simple things, a rocking chair on the porch, a glass of sun tea. And, *oh,* the ease she'd felt with him, the instant pull of attraction, as if they'd been created at the same time then sprinkled with star dust so the glow would always lead them back to each other.

She knew she was letting her fanciful nature color her perception, but she didn't care. It had been a long time since she'd felt even a twinge of attraction. Over the past few years, she had let her art take over her life.

Annie turned her mind to their conversation. It was clear to her that the truth didn't lie with Lucien and Jacques Morel. With so many conflicting opinions about them, she had no way of knowing whether they were spinning lies to protect themselves or for some sort of gain. Instinct alone wouldn't tell her that, and neither would her dreams.

She gathered her sketchpad and the chair from the garden and went into the house. Emptiness pulsed around her, and a strong premonition of danger. She backtracked to lock the front door, and then she walked through the house making sure all the windows and doors were secure.

The grandfather clock sounded mournful as it chimed the half hour. Five thirty. Almost dinnertime. Angel and Toni would be back soon.

If nothing had happened to them. If the killer didn't change his MO and go after a vibrant woman in a small motorboat with a helpless old man, easy pickings in one of the many secluded sections of the swamp.

*Stop it.*

She rinsed the tea glasses, then sat down at the kitchen table with her cell phone. There were no messages from her sisters or her agent, no missed calls she needed to return. Annie went to her Facebook page to make a quick post, and there, waiting for her, was another message from John Davidson.

I know where you are. I'm coming for you.

Fear threatened to paralyze her, the feeling of being trapped in the house. Alone.

A sudden mist swirled around the room, and whispers of danger echoed through the fog. Was the danger to Toni and Angel? They should have been home long before dark.

Annie shook off her waking dream, pushed past her fear, and got up to search out the kitchen window. Was that movement in the trees? A shadow near her grandfather's gazebo? She stood there, peering into the backyard, until her eyes adjusted to the dark. *Nothing.* She was letting the silence and loneliness in her grandfather's house get under her skin.

"You should know I don't scare easily." She shook her fist at the window, then marched to the cookie jar to nab one of the butter cookies Toni had brought from New Orleans. Then she sat at the kitchen table, telling herself Angel knew the swamp like the back of his hand. Surely, he and Toni had just decided to do some night fishing.

Annie pulled out her cell phone to search for Rosalie Edmonds, the woman named in the online newspaper article. There were two in Slidell. The first number, Rosalie June, turned out to be a young mother with screaming children in the background—and the daughter of the same Rosalie Edmonds whose house had caught fire when Delphine Thierry was there doing readings for the guests.

Annie called the number the daughter gave her, and introduced herself with a sketchy account of why she was calling.

"My grandmother, Nina Broussard, was a friend of Delphine's, and I'm trying to find out what happened to her."

"Honey," Rosalie's voice quavered with age, "I'm so old I can't even tell you what happened to me." She followed that with a burst of self-deprecating laughter. "But I remember Delphine like it was yesterday. If it hadn't been for Jacques Morel, she'd have died in the blaze that broke out in my house the night she was here. Most folks called him a hero, but I've always believed he was the one who set the fire."

Annie didn't have a chance to ask why. She didn't have time to do more than draw a deep breath before Rosalie was prattling on about the multitude of loyal followers Delphine had because of the accuracy of her predictions and the great results from the charms and potions she sold.

"Why, Delphine was friends with four governors' wives, two U.S. senators, two actresses, four singers, a movie star, and a Mafia kingpin. And that's just the ones I know about. Jacques Morel thought he was a big shot over there in Honey Island Swamp, and that the Swamp Witch should be at his beck and call. His exclusive fortune teller."

Suddenly, the avenue to finding out what really happened to Delphine was wide open. While Annie waited for a pause, Rosalie plunged right ahead, an engine under full steam.

"You'd be surprised at how people will toe the line if they think you wouldn't blink twice about killing them. Even a formidable old woman like Delphine. I'll tell you one thing. I wouldn't want to tangle with that man."

"Neither would I." Annie leaped into the pause while Rosalie panted from her long monologue. "Do you mind giving me the names of those people who knew Delphine?"

"I can not only give you their names, but I can tell you most of their phone numbers and what color dye they use on their hair."

As Rosalie reeled off the list, Annie wrote it in the sketchpad that was still on the kitchen table. By the time she ended the call, the grandfather clock was striking six. Toni and her grandfather were still nowhere to be seen.

She called Toni's cell but it went directly to voice mail. Alarm skittered through her. Lack of phone service in the swamp was the obvious answer, but Annie wasn't so cavalier about danger that she would rule out a man called the Shadow, leaving bodies of young, nubile victims to turn the water crimson with their blood.

A screech echoed through the kitchen. A woman screaming? Annie dived away from the windows and into a large pantry. She closed the door behind her so the light from the overhead kitchen fixture couldn't reach her. Standing in the darkness with her heart pounding too hard, she strained to hear. There was not a sound. What was happening out there? Had her stalker already crept into the kitchen?

She eased the pantry door open a crack so she could hear and see what was coming. A scratching sound at the back door sent chills through her. Animal? Or human? The predator raked his claws on the door again, dragging them with agonizing slowness down the length of the wooden door.

Annie muffled a scream. Out of the darkness, an eerie scream echoed the one she was holding back. Her stalker's threats roared through her mind. *Only you can make it stop.* Was the killer butchering another young woman right under her nose?

Paralyzed, she could do nothing but wait and listen. The scream sounded again. It was only a screech owl. She'd have recognized it the first time if she hadn't been worried about being alone with a murderer on the loose. A terrible certainty filled Annie. Someone was watching—and the owl had sounded an alarm.

She reached into her pocket for her cell to call Paul Chenevert, but the glow from the screen winked at her from the kitchen table. She could crawl across the floor and reach up to get it, but what if her watcher was close? What if he spotted her and burst through the back door while she was out in the open, without a weapon?

It wouldn't take much effort to break in. Angel's cottage had no security system. It didn't even have adequate locks. Any kid with a hairpin and knack for breaking and entering could be inside before Annie could ever get her phone off the table. Certainly, a man with brute strength could kick through the door and drag her into the bayou before she could scream.

"I won't let you win..."

She got a gallon glass jar of dill pickles off the shelves and hefted it over her head. Then she tensed her muscles for action and waited.

If the killer was out there, he wouldn't take her without a fight.

## TWENTY-FIVE

Toni's fishing pole lay forgotten in the bottom of the boat, her apprehension growing stronger by the minute as she searched the dark water surrounding her and Angel. Not a soul in sight. Not a single landmark she recognized.

They were lost in the swamp, and that's all there was to it.

She curbed her tongue, and watched as Angel made a frame with his thumbs and forefingers then held them up to the sky. What on earth did he hope to see? It was black as the ace of spades out on the water, and patches of fog drifted around their boat like spooks from a horror movie.

"What are you doing?"

"Navigating by the stars," Annie's grandfather told her calmly.

Toni felt sorry for him. The only stars up there were half-hidden by clouds, and looked so puny you couldn't find a nickel on the ground by their light, let alone navigate your way out of a swampy maze.

She held her phone up, turning this way and that, trying to find a signal. *Nothing.* She was doomed to spend the night out here with the alligators and a serial killer. She didn't know which was worse. She rued the day she ever thought it would be fun to go fishing in the bayou.

The hairs on the back of her neck stood up. Someone was watching. She swiveled around and saw a pair of gleaming eyes. They were not on the water, where something awful could be watching, like a large alligator pretending to be a log. They were bigger, meaner-looking, closer. And at eye level. Like somebody out there in the murky night who knew how to move a boat through the water without making a sound.

"Mr. Broussard," she whispered. "Let's go. Somebody's watching..."

Without a word, he looked in every direction. "Bobcat," he finally said. "On the bank in the bushes."

But it was not. Toni was no scaredy cat alarmist. She knew the difference between a watcher who was merely curious, and one who wanted to slit her throat. Her watcher was definitely of the killer variety.

Still, it was Angel's boat, and she didn't have her hand on the tiller. She wrapped her arms around herself and glanced in the direction of the eyes.

They were gone. Was that better or worse? What if the killer had on a wetsuit and was now swimming toward her with the intention of pulling her overboard when Angel wasn't looking? Even if he looked, he wouldn't be quick enough to save her.

Finally, thankfully, the outboard motor sputtered back to life. Angel's small boat moved through the night where every tree and stump and bush looked exactly the same. Dark and scary. Where was her Sicilian courage when she needed it?

She held up her phone again, desperately hoping. Suddenly, a bar. "I got it," she shouted, and Angel startled so hard he almost toppled from the boat.

"What?" he said. "What's wrong?"

"Stop the boat. I've got a signal."

"Who sent it?"

Toni rolled her eyes. Her mother would be spewing Italian words you didn't want your children to hear, and Mimi would be saying her rosary.

"Mr. Broussard, it's a cell phone signal. I can call for help."

"We don't need help. I can navigate every inch of this swamp in the pitch-black dark."

Obviously not.

"I know you can, but I'm not used to long hours in a boat the way you are. I'm tired and hungry." And terrified. How could she forget that? "I hope you don't mind if I call your neighbor for help."

Fortunately, she'd put Paul Chenevert in her contacts at the same time Annie did, because you never knew when a contact would come in handy. Like when somebody was stalking you in a swamp.

Also, it advanced her argument with Angel that, only this afternoon, he had extolled the virtues of the man who *had enough sense to mind his own business.* His words for the owner of the gallery.

He gazed at the pitiful display of stars again as if they held answers, then he sighed and sank onto his seat. "There's no need to bother him."

Toni reached deep and found her inner lawyer, that side her mother said would argue with a brick outdoor toilet.

"We need to get home. Annie's alone, and there's a madman on the loose. Hunting women. As a matter of fact, I think he's here on the water right now, looking to snatch both of us and drag us off into the swamp."

He wouldn't leave witnesses, either. The idea sent a chill through her.

"Nobody's out there," Angel said.

"Maybe not, but what if I'm right and you're *wrong?*"

TWENTY-SIX

Nobody rang Paul's phone late on a Saturday night unless it was an emergency. Instinctively, he grabbed it.

"Paul!" It was Annie's friend Toni. "Angel and I are lost in his boat!"

"We're not *lost*!" Angel shouted in the background. "Tell him the call is all *your* idea."

"Hang on, Toni. I'll come and get you. I need you and Angel to tell me everything you know about your location."

He listened then pocketed his phone. Finding them would be a daunting task.

Ordinarily, Paul would have been happy to race off into the night to rescue someone—just about anybody would do. But Toni's call sent his mind in a different direction. *Annie Logan. Stranded at home alone.*

He made a quick call to check on her, and discovered she had crouched down and crept from the pantry to the kitchen table to get to her phone, all while clutching a jar of pickles.

"Somebody's outside," she whispered. "If he comes in here, he's going to end up with a knot on his head and pickle juice all over his shirt."

"I'll be right over, then I'm headed out to find Toni and Angel." He would take Annie with him. Leaving her alone and scared was unthinkable.

*Another rescue, Chenevert?* He was learning to hate that little voice in his head.

"Hurry to them. Toni will be scared to death. And don't worry about me. I'm already back in the pantry. Nobody is going to get through this door. I can do major damage with the pickle jar, and if that doesn't work, I can give them a slug with the canned peaches..." There was a pause. "Oh, wait. What was I thinking? I can just call 911 now that I have my phone."

"This is not negotiable. I'm on the way."

He ran to his boat. He hadn't moved this fast since he followed the ambulance that carried his wife and child from the wreck to the ER. The past rose up to haunt him, but he rejected it with fierceness and determination. There would be different results tonight.

His boat raced over the water, leaving a wake that sent aquatic creatures scurrying in every direction. Angel's dock came quickly into view. He anchored and hit the boards running.

Armed with a powerful flashlight, a holstered gun, and a dangerous mood, he scouted the woods around the Angel's cottage, working his way inward until he came to the back door. The gory find on the back step spun him back to the carnage on the bridge. Annie was in danger, and he felt almost as helpless as he had been all those years ago.

He pooled his light around the severed head of a black cat, the edges of the cut too sharp and clean to have been the work of another animal. He panned the light around, searching for a note. There was nothing, only the macabre reminder that evil had been right outside while Annie was alone. He pounded on the back door.

"Annie! It's Paul! Let me in!"

She met him with the pickle jar still in her hands. If he had expected trembling and tears, he was mistaken. She was remarkably cool, even fierce and a bit dangerous looking. His first instinct was to hug her with relief. His second was to keep his cool.

"You had a watcher, and he left a calling card." He slid through the door and described the cat's head on her doorstep while she grabbed a garbage bag and paper towels. "Wait here, Annie. I'll take care of it."

He bagged it and left it in Angel's garage so wild animals wouldn't get to it. Tomorrow he would come back and take the cat's head to the sheriff. With a killer on the loose, nothing should be dismissed as a prank.

"It's all clear out there." He went inside to wash his hands. "Grab a jacket and come with me."

"Where to?"

"My boat. We're going to rescue Toni and Angel."

"Is this negotiable?"

"No. I can't see in all directions at once. You're going to help me find them."

Smart woman that she was, she grabbed the jacket closest to her, Angel's old windbreaker, hanging on a hook beside the back door.

Under other circumstances, Annie would have been thrilled to be in a boat in the dark, viewing everything the swamp had to offer through night vision goggles. But her stalker's bloody calling card and fear for two people she loved had her peering through the fog, straining to see the first glimpse of Angel's little boat.

By mutual consent there was little conversation. Both she and Paul strained to hear every sound that might lead them toward their lost friends—or away from any danger lurking in the foggy night. Periodically, she lifted her cell phone for signals, hoping to make contact with Toni.

They hadn't been able to get in touch with her since they left the boat dock. The directions Toni had given Paul earlier were vague, at best, and her grandfather's were not much better.

"If I hadn't spoken to Angel on Toni's cell," Paul said, "I would never believe he's lost. He's lived here all his life."

"I wonder if he's had a stroke? Even worse, what if something awful has happened? Grandfather's boat is *ancient*. What if it sprang a leak and sank? Or what if Toni stood up and capsized it?"

"Don't borrow trouble, Annie."

"I can't help it. Somebody's out here preying on women in the swamp, and Toni's vulnerable and unsuspecting."

"We'll find them."

They both fell silent, scanning the darkness for any sign of the lost. Suddenly, out of nowhere. There it was. A boat-shaped blob.

"Paul, I see something!"

"Where?"

"Around that bend on the right. I see something jutting out!"

He turned the boat, and it skimmed across the water. As the object got closer, her spirits sank. It certainly wasn't a boat.

"It's a half-submerged tree," he said.

"I'm sorry."

"No need. Anybody could have made that mistake."

The chill of the night combined with her own terror had Annie wrapping her arms around herself. Hope was hard to hang onto in the darkness of a place that harbored a killer.

"What now?" she asked. If Paul hadn't been with her, she'd have had a little cry.

"We keep searching in all Angel's favorite fishing places until we get lucky—or you get a signal."

Annie glanced up at the sky. The moon was tucked out of sight behind clouds, and even the stars could barely be seen through the fog and the cloud cover. She pulled her phone from the pocket of her over-sized windbreaker and checked for a signal.

At last, there it was, two bars, a blessed connection to Toni and Angel. She made the call.

It took another thirty minutes to find them. Angel blamed their situation on forgetting to take his afternoon medications. Still, he didn't relinquish control without a lot of gentle persuasion from her and a bit of stern logic from Toni and Paul.

"But who will drive my boat?" Angel sounded shaky and uncertain. "Paul can't drive two at once."

"I will." Toni spoke with some asperity. Obviously, her fear had not snuffed out her ability to power back from adversity. "Annie's going to ride shotgun so I won't lose sight of Paul."

"You don't know a thing about driving boats." Angel was not one to give in without an argument.

Neither was Toni. "Yes, I do. I've driven more ski boats for my brothers than I can count."

As she moved toward the rudder and took charge of the tiller that would guide them home, she reminded Annie of her grandmother, Victoria Logan. Always self-assured and comforting, a bit bossy, and more than a little cantankerous.

But *nothing* could relieve Annie's anxiety. Everything that had happened to her since she came here pointed to one true thing. Someone out there *hated* her.

Would he strike at her again with something more gruesome than a severed cat's head.

Would someone else die?

# TWENTY-SEVEN
## THE SHADOW

The butchered cat on Angel's doorstep last night had been a masterful touch. Another gory warning to *her* that this game was far from over. A smile curved his lips. Seeing all that blood gush out when he sliced off the head had satisfied him as nothing else could.

The kill always thrilled him. He didn't even stop to wonder why. He *was* what he was. A creature of Nature. Kill or be killed. It was the only way to survive in the swamp. He was a killing machine. And no one ever noticed.

Pete's Place was teeming with people, as usual. He strolled through the crowd, munching on a ham and biscuit, pausing to talk to fishermen and inquire of neighbors about their children and grandchildren. Gossip was the key to information he couldn't glean by hiding and watching his target.

Everybody in the swamp was stirred up about the murders and eager to talk, especially about the two outsiders staying with Angel. The Shadow's excitement grew as he listened.

He knew the perfect way to make Annie Logan regret the day she set foot in Honey Island Swamp.

TWENTY-EIGHT

After a harrowing night lost in the bayou and a late lie-in to recover, Toni was glad to be leaving Honey Island Swamp. Paul Chenevert had graciously offered to take her back to Pete's Place in his boat. Angel was obviously in no shape to do it, and considering the cloud of suspicion hovering over Lucien's head since the video footage of Pete's Place aired, she wasn't about to ask him.

Still, Toni had all day. She wanted to spend more time with Annie and make sure the sweet old man was okay. Also, she wanted to squeeze in some time to work on her case before she left. Who knew what fresh problems tomorrow would bring?

She threw on jeans and a gray sweatshirt, some comfortable driving shoes, and then she barreled down the stairs toward the sound of voices. Annie and Angel were in the kitchen. Looking normal. As if the nightmare rescue in the bayou had never happened.

"How are you feeling this morning, Mr. Broussard?" Toni poured herself a cup of coffee and slid into a chair at the table.

It was loaded with platters of bacon, scrambled eggs, and biscuits. Annie had been cooking again, an apron covering her turquoise blouse, her long hair drawn back in a ponytail. Maybe Toni would let her do more in the kitchen when they got back to New Orleans.

"Don't you go treating me like an old man," he grumbled, frowning. "Annie's been acting like I'm half dead."

"Grandfather, I'm just being sensible." Annie upended her coffee cup as if she needed to fortify herself with caffeine. A real possibility, considering the level of stubbornness she was dealing with. "I'm taking him to his doctor tomorrow," she told Toni.

"I'm not going, *ma chérie*."

"Yes, you are. I want to drive that vintage Thunderbird convertible I saw in your garage this morning, and I need you to show me the roads out of here."

He nabbed a biscuit and slathered it with butter. "You're just like Delilah. Always sneaking around, stirring up trouble."

Annie pounced. "What kind of trouble?"

"With Delphine and her love potions, and that skunk Pete."

"Thibodeaux?"

"I'm done talking," he told Annie, then shoved his chair aside and stomped out the back door, taking his biscuit with him.

Annie drained her cup and went to the coffee pot to pour herself another. "I haven't seen this level of belligerence before. I can't bear to find him and then lose him so quickly."

"It sounds like a transient stroke," Toni told her. "Mimi had one a few years ago, and she was mean as a rattlesnake for a while. But she recovered fast... and fully."

"That settles it." Still holding her cup and sipping her fresh coffee, Annie started clearing the table, one-handed. "I'm definitely taking him to the doctor, even if I have to get Paul over here to help me get him into the car." She aimed her coffee cup in the direction of the phone hanging on the kitchen wall. "I'm getting that reconnected, too. He said he didn't need it after Nina died, but he most certainly does."

Toni erupted into a belly laugh. "I believe he's met his match."

"You bet your boots he has."

While they cleaned up in the kitchen, they peered out the window to see Angel in the backyard walking around his gazebo with a hoe, chopping at random weeds and muttering to himself.

"Will you be all right here with just Angel?"

"Certainly, I will."

Toni left the window and stacked the clean dishes into the cabinet. "I don't like the idea of leaving you here you with a stalker. Thank goodness Paul got rid of that cat's head."

"This situation is scary, but it doesn't intimidate me. I was raised by a grandmother so cantankerous even the mountain lions were scared of her. I have every bit of her grit, and more, besides."

The sun was setting when Annie went upstairs to help Toni pack. As Toni tossed the last of her belongings into her backpack, Annie handed her a list of Delphine's followers to tuck into the side pocket with her laptop. It was half the names Rosalie had provided.

"Delphine is the key to the mystery with Lucien," Annie said as she picked up her own list from the bedside table and scanned it. "I think I'll start with one of the local entertainers who was her client. Show businesspeople are most likely to be willing to talk."

"It's not the mystery of your twin I'm worried about. Someone was watching me on the boat last night, and they're spying on you, too."

"I won't run because of a stalker."

"Annie, you listen to me. I've seen all kinds of bizarre things in my work. We don't know who this John Davidson is or where he's from. For all we know, he followed you from Italy and could be in the swamp right now, killing girls."

"You could be right, but I'm not the kind of woman who allows fear to dictate my life."

"I *know*." Toni made a little sigh of exasperation as she zipped up the outside pocket of her backpack. "Still, I wish you were coming back to New Orleans with me. You can dig around in the past from the safety of my apartment."

"I can't leave until I know for sure that Grandfather is okay."

"Bring him, too. We have great doctors in New Orleans."

"He's stubborn and too frail for me to engage in that battle with him right now."

Toni grabbed her jacket. "Okay. I give up. I'll come back and get you whenever you're ready. It's a short round trip. I could make it any day after work."

Annie leaned in to hug her. "You're a good friend."

"What I am is stirred-up and ticked-off. Maybe a little scared, too." From a distance, she heard the sound of Paul's boat approaching Angel's dock. "Gotta go!"

"I'll walk you down."

Annie released her hair from the ponytail, and they headed to the dock. Paul's eyes lit up when he saw Annie. Her smile and their soft greetings of *hello* were fraught with meaning.

*Well, good for them!*

Toni was grinning when Annie hugged her and whispered, "Stay safe."

"You, too."

She didn't even know how that was possible with the Shadow still on the loose. After Toni got into the boat, she turned for one last look at her friend and her heart constricted.

What if she never saw Annie alive again?

## TWENTY-NINE

Pete's Place teemed with people, including a loud group of tourists getting off a Honey Island Swamp tour boat. If the crowd was any indication of the traffic going home, Toni dreaded the drive.

"Holiday crowd," Paul explained. He anchored his boat. "I'll help you carry your things to your car."

"There's no need." She'd left the cooler at Angel's to pick up on her return trip. "I'm going to make a quick detour into Pete's for some snacks, and then I'll hit the road."

Lucien's boat pulled into the dock a few feet away, and she watched as he disembarked with Evangeline. They were a beautiful couple in matching red shirts, their heads together, their dark hair shining.

Toni called, "Hey, Evangeline!" but she and Lucien just kept walking. The moment was strangely charged in a way she couldn't describe.

"Maybe she didn't hear." Paul grabbed a cloth shopping tote. "I'll escort you into Pete's. I have to pick up a few staples."

The inside was as crowded as the outside. Toni recognized the mousy redhead in the spice aisle. But her attention was immediately drawn to the tall man near the coolers, black curly hair sprinkled with gray, broad shoulders, deeply tanned skin. He held a six-pack of beer in his hand, and he still looked very much as he had when he rescued Delphine Thierry from a burning house in Slidell.

"Is that Jacques Morel?" she asked Paul.

"Yes. I'd steer clear of him if I were you. He's known for being unsociable to strangers. Have a safe trip home."

Paul headed toward the deli meats, and she veered toward the junk food. Call it habit. Call it stress eating while driving. She didn't care. She wasn't out to win beauty contests. She just wanted to remain reasonably presentable and healthy. She would eat fresh fruit next week.

As she headed toward the long line at the cash register with her candy and chips, she noticed Lucien and Evangeline in the corner across from her. Evangeline was holding a small paper sack with the end of some shrink-wrapped beef jerky sticking out the top. They appeared to be arguing. Lucien's face was red, and she looked close to tears.

Toni moved up with the line, and their voices drifted toward her, as clear as if she were in front of her TV watching the news.

"Please, Lucien. I don't want to drive home with you mad at me." Evangeline caught his arm and hung on. "Let's not part this way."

"You should never have called to send Paul Chenevert to Annie. I told you we needed to give her some space, and we don't know what he's capable of. He's been questioned in the murders."

Evangeline put her hand over her trembling lips. "Paul is one of the most decent, respectful men I know. He would *never* kill someone. He's just reclusive, that's all."

"A man lets you see only what he wants you to see." Lucien spoke through gritted teeth, and his eyes reflected his turmoil, those astonishing eyes Toni had never seen on anybody except Annie.

Then he went as quiet as the center of a tornado gathering force to destroy a small town while silent tears streaked down Evangeline's face. His transformation was surprising, and a bit scary.

Toni started to rush over and offer some kind of comfort, but suddenly Lucien spotted her and pulled his girlfriend behind a display of parched peanuts. As much as Toni hated the idea of leaving Evangeline to deal with the problem alone, her fight with Lucien was none of Toni's business. She'd drop by the gallery early next week and make sure Evangeline was all right.

She paid for her purchases and headed to her car. The minute she was behind the wheel, she ripped into a candy bar, chocolate filled with coconut and almonds. There was nothing like a greasy, sugary treat to take the edge off anxiety.

She bit into the candy, then started her engine and idled in the parking lot, waiting to catch a glimpse of Evangeline coming out of the store. Something felt... off.

Toni was no Annie Logan. She had no gift of dreams or ability to divine past events from merely being in a certain place, but she was Sicilian, by golly, and they held some of the most deeply felt emotions in the world. Nobody could out-cry them at funerals. Nobody could yell louder in an argument. Nobody could laugh more at a funny joke. And nobody, anywhere on this earth, could throw an iron skillet at a cheating spouse with such rage and accuracy as a Delgado woman.

Toni just hoped she never had to throw an iron skillet. She laughed at herself. Why would she? She didn't even have a husband. She wouldn't have a job, either, if she didn't get a move on and get back home so she could finish the brief that was due in her boss's office on Monday morning.

She was about to back out of the parking lot when Evangeline raced out the door and onto the path that led to the back of Pete's Place. Lucien was right behind her.

Alarm skittered through Toni. She got out of the car and walked across the large parking lot, already shadowed with evening. She squinted through the gathering darkness, trying to see. She saw a shadow near the toilet that might be a person, but could just as easily be a bush. Finally, she spotted two people standing beside a blue Valiant, parked at the back of the lot near the single toilet. Since they were the only couple she saw and she hadn't seen a car leave, she assumed it was Lucien and Evangeline. He towered over her, waving his arms about.

Should Toni intervene? Race back into the store and get Paul? She turned toward the dock and saw that his boat had already gone. After a moment's indecision, Toni got into her car and backed out of the lot. She'd spent enough time with Lucien to believe he wasn't a killer.

No sooner had Toni turned onto the road going home than a horrible idea took hold.

What if she was wrong?


Ten miles down the highway that would take her from Honey Island Swamp to New Orleans, Toni was still arguing with herself over the decision she'd made when full darkness dropped suddenly, like a black curtain. It was another starless night. Clouds everywhere obscured the moon. The first fat droplets of rain hit her windshield.

Out of the blue, she heard a bump, and her car leaped forward. What on earth? The second bump was louder, and her car skidded. The car behind was ramming her bumper.

She gripped the wheel and stomped on her gas pedal. Her car shot forward, but the dark car behind her zoomed around and rammed against her door. It was a black Lincoln. Older model. Toni floorboarded the gas pedal, but the car stayed with her, metal scraping against metal as the other driver tried to force her off the road.

Rage filled her. "You've messed with the wrong woman!"

She stomped on her brakes. After the other car slid past her, she floorboarded the gas pedal again and rammed his back bumper as fast and as hard as she could. Surprised, he over-corrected his skid, and his big car began to weave and wobble.

For a moment, she thought he would overturn, but then he shot down an offramp and disappeared into the darkness.

She pulled onto the shoulder and dialed 911. She didn't start shaking until she'd made the report and was sitting in the dark. Alone.

THIRTY

## HONEY ISLAND SWAMP

Lying in her single bed with a quilt handmade by her Grandmother Broussard tucked around her, and the grandfather clock on the floor below marking off the hours, Annie was caught unaware by her dream. The piercing scream shuddered through her, and she cringed from the contorted face, the upraised hand.

*"No! Please!"*

Was it her dream-self begging? Or was it the woman clinging to the spindly branches of a bush, the lower part of her body already submerged in the water?

Slowly, surely, like cotton candy spun at a carnival, the dream merged with reality. She twitched with pain and a searing sense of betrayal, her legs moving underneath the covers and her fingers clutching the edge of the quilt as if it might protect her from the gleaming blade of a hunting knife.

Blood pouring into her eyes obscured the face of her attacker. Still, she knew him. That face. That familiar face.

*"Please... Not you."*

*"You have to pay."* The male voice, indistinct, muffled by rage and regret.

The scream pierced the night once more, scaring night birds from their perches and sending the wetland creatures who were nocturnal hunters scurrying back to cover. The knife blade flashed, caught by a sliver of moonlight. Again. And again.

Still, the woman whimpered.

The dark shadow stood over her, heaving, drenched with sweat that even the chilly night air couldn't banish.

Where was the moon? Where was that giant yellow spotlight that would show exactly who he was, this monster who owned the night?

Finally, he walked away, and the woman lay still, her right hand still clinging to the bush, her body turning blue in the cold water, her face turned up to the sky. A single star popped out, its feeble light revealing her face.

It was her face.

Annie woke up gasping for air. Frantic, she felt her face and neck, expecting to find slashed skin, wounds dripping with blood. Nothing. There was nothing.

Still caught up in the terror of her dream/vision, she snapped on the bedside lamp. Light flooded the room, illuminating the old-fashioned armoire carved by her grandfather's hands, the ornate cedar chest he'd made to hold Nina's quilts, the rocking chair with the hand-carved roses on the armrests. It moved gently, as if Nina were still there, rocking her only child Delilah.

Always Delilah. At the heart of the mystery, at the center of the days and weeks and years that had led Annie to this moment—standing alone in her mother's childhood home, fearing for her very life.

Annie slept fitfully the rest of the night, as she always did after she saw things no one else could. She woke to find a chilling post waiting on her social media.

Before this is over, you will wish you were dead.

Horror filled her. Her stalker was the killer, she had no doubt. The dream and the post so close together were too much to be mere coincidence. Had he killed again? Would there be another young woman found dead in Honey Island Swamp?

Indecision threatened to paralyze her. "Prioritize." Saying this aloud helped pull her together. She put on black slacks and a matching cashmere sweater and went downstairs.

There was no rich aroma of coffee coming from the kitchen, so she tiptoed to her grandfather's room on the first floor and peeked through the half-open door. He was sleeping on his back, his mouth wide open, his snores loud enough to raise the roof. Maybe he'd feel better after a good rest and be more amenable to seeing his doctor.

In the kitchen, she put on the coffee and turned on the TV. If everything ran true to form, she'd dream-watched another murder in Honey Island Swamp, and it would be on the news this morning.

There was Linda Holloway, sitting on a sofa in the television studio, dressed to the nines and telling her television audience about Annie's upcoming art show at Green Oak Gallery. She announced that plans for the Mardi Gras ball in February were already underway then moved on to hard news.

"In other news, the St. Tammany Parish Sheriff's Department has questioned several more suspects in the Honey Island Swamp murders, but so far, they have made no arrests. The perpetrator has an uncanny ability to remain hidden. Scared residents out in the bayou are locking their doors against a killer they call the Shadow. Anyone with clues that might help solve this case, please call the number on your screen."

No mention of another girl taken. Relief flooded through Annie.

Her cell phone pinged with a text from Toni. Followed by three heart emojis.

*I'm home. Safe. Somebody tried to run me off the road last night. I doubt you'll see it on TV or hear it on the radio, but don't be alarmed if you do. I took defensive action, and the idiot is lucky he escaped from me.*

Fear rolled through Annie, and images bombarded her. Fog and darkness, eyes watching, everywhere, burning with malevolence, metal grinding against metal, a petite woman, lying in a broken heap on an isolated stretch of road, a twisted monster who wouldn't give up. *Ever.*

Chilling current events were coming together to form a deadly center, the formidable eye of a category five hurricane that was moving ever closer. When it hit, she knew it would destroy them all.

Toni was in danger. They both were. Annie had to get out of the bayou and back to the relative safety of New Orleans. She'd have easier access to the law, plus living and moving among crowds of people would provide some protection. It would be harder for the killer to remain undetected if he were surrounded by witnesses. Nothing was worth putting Toni's life at risk—hers, too—not even learning the truth about her mother's past.

But there was Angel. She couldn't simply leave him behind. He didn't even want to go and see his doctor. Getting him to leave the swamp would be a task on the order of herding Hannibal's elephants across the Alps.

Annie reined in her panic and sent a text to Toni. Without emojis. She didn't use them on principle.

*I'm glad you're okay. Be careful. We're both targets. I think my stalker is the killer. I'm coming back with Angel as soon as I can convince him to leave. Hire a bodyguard for yourself. I'll pay.*

Toni's reply zipped right back.

*That's a big negative! The killer is a coward, or he wouldn't be hiding in the dark to do his dirty deeds. If he keeps messing with me, I'm calling my Sicilian grandmother to come down here and work him over with her cast iron skillet.*

A mad emoji followed. Then one of the devil holding a pitchfork.

Annie didn't try to figure out how it was possible to be frightened and find comic relief at the same time. She was just grateful.

Suddenly, a cloud appeared beyond the kitchen window and the sky darkened, Nature was warning Annie that evil waited just beyond the horizon.

## THIRTY-ONE

Annie spent the rest of the morning cajoling Angel into seeing his doctor. Finally, she slid behind the wheel of his antique Thunderbird as he climbed into the passenger seat. It was in pristine condition. She could hardly wait to drive it.

"This is a great car, Grandfather."

"*Humph.*" He was still in a bad mood.

"How far is it to Pearl River?"

"Too far, if you ask me. We've no business going."

So much for trying to cheer him up. She consulted the GPS on her cell phone then backed out of the garage. The road took her through a deeply wooded area she hoped led away from the swamp. The trees with their massive trunks and umbrella-like canopies whispered ancient secrets. The otherworldly feel was so great, Annie felt as if she was driving backward in time.

"Grandfather, is this the right way?"

"You're the one that wanted to go." He sank into a stubborn silence, but she could be just as obstinate. She let him stew. Finally, he said, "I don't know why we're going to the doctor. I'm healthy as horse."

It was on the tip of her tongue to argue, but a big black car came barreling out of a side road and began to tailgate her. She stomped the gas to get away, but the other car increased speed, moving so close she expected any minute to hear the crunch of metal against metal. A quick glance in the rearview mirror showed the driver wearing a baseball cap.

Adrenaline shot through her. "Grandfather, can you see the driver of that car?"

"What car?"

"The one behind us." She fought to avoid a collision and hold the car in the road. Was it her stalker? Did he intend to kill them both?

Angel swiveled around with the painstaking slowness of thick syrup being forced from a bottle. "Nobody's back there."

She glanced in the rearview mirror. The car had vanished, an easy feat on a twisting country road with so many branch-offs. Annie could get lost and never find her way home. If she lost signal on her cell phone, she might not, anyhow.

She was relieved when they reached the city limits of the small, nearby town. Like so many old river towns in south Louisiana, Pearl River was dripping with atmosphere and history. Driving along streets lined with the rich, waxy green of magnolia trees and live oaks draped with curtains of Spanish moss felt like being transported back to the pre-Civil War days of the Deep South. Though any Southerner worth his salt would be quick to tell you there was nothing civil about the war. They called it the War Between the States. Or the War of Northern Aggression. Period. End of argument.

Dr. Glen Sheffield's office was in the heart of the business district, and his diagnosis was far better than Annie had imagined. "He's very fit for his age. I'm reducing the dosage of his blood pressure medicine. Too much Beta blocker has made him dizzy and confused."

He handed two prescriptions to Annie. "I'm adding a mild anti-depressant to help with his agitation, which is not uncommon for his age. He should take a nap every afternoon."

"I doubt he will."

"He might for you. Bring him back in a few days and let me see how he's doing. Meanwhile, call if you need anything."

Before they left Pearl River, they picked up Angel's medicine then stopped at a small market for some much-needed groceries. The minute Annie stepped inside, the back of her neck began to prickle.

She tightened her grip on the grocery cart and glanced around the small store. *There.* A tall man, swarthy, dark haired, oozing charm as mesmerizing as a deadly viper. The baseball cap was missing. Was he even the type to wear one?

He was with the plain-looking redhead Annie had seen at Pete's Place the day she and Toni arrived. The woman saw her and made a beeline with the man in tow.

Annie felt her grandfather stiffen beside her. "Jacques Morel," he muttered.

Blindsided, Annie studied Jacques for any resemblance to her or Lucien. The lush dark hair could have been Lucien's and even hers, minus the red, but wasn't that common among the Creole? His dark eyes were nothing like hers. He used them like lasers, studying her intently as he strode closer. Annie felt as if she were staring into a black, soulless void, but she refused to cringe.

"Annie Logan. I'm Jacques Morel." Without even acknowledging her grandfather, he bent over her hand. For a horrible moment, she thought he was going to kiss it. When he released her, she stood her ground, refusing to show any reaction at all to this man who claimed to be her father. "At last, we meet. It's not often we have a celebrity in the bayou."

"It's so exciting!" The small redhead almost twittered. "I'm the librarian here, Helen Whitaker. We met once before at Pete's Place. I hope you'll do us the honor of a visit. We have a little group that meets monthly for musicales and art lectures and such. They would love to hear you speak."

Before she could think of a polite way to decline, Angel said, "She won't have a minute to spare. She's taking care of me, and I'm a handful." He grabbed the shopping cart and shoved off.

Annie refused a hasty retreat. "Perhaps another time, Miss Whitaker."

Jacques Morel stood beside the librarian, immovable as a mountain, cold as a glacier. He was sizing her up with laser-like focus.

She returned his stare. "Lucien told me about you," she said. "His description didn't do you justice. Goodbye, Mr. Morel."

Jacques could take that as an insult, a challenge, a compliment—whatever he wanted. After today, he would know Annie Logan would stand her ground with anybody.

She could feel his gaze following her as she strolled off, not a care in the world. It didn't take her long to catch up with Angel in the meat department.

"*Baa.*" He grabbed a package of steak and flung it into the cart as if it might bite back. "I spit on him!"

"I do, too."

Angel beamed. "You do?"

"Yes. Now, let's finish up and go home."

Jacques was not in the store when they left, and neither was Helen Whitaker. Annie searched the parking lot, but there was no large black car, either. She wished she'd looked earlier.

Was her visceral dislike of Jacques Morel connected to her fear of the stalker? Or to his outrageous claims that had caused her to question who she was?

## THIRTY-TWO

Surprisingly, after they got back to the cottage, Angel went to his room to nap. Annie could only hope he was taking his doctor's advice, but it was more likely that he still hadn't recovered from his long night lost in the swamp.

Annie grabbed the list of names Rosalie had given her and swooped into the kitchen to make herself a cup of tea. "I'm *not* that man's daughter."

But that still didn't mean she wasn't Lucien's sister. The length of Delilah's stay the year Annie was born made it possible she was pregnant before she left home. With twins. With her hand still on the cream pitcher in the refrigerator, Annie paused, searching inside herself for answers. The bayou tugged at her, but her reaction could be that of a grandchild to her grandfather's home or simply that of an artist drawn to a treasure trove of inspiration.

*Lucien.* His name whispered through her, and she saw his eyes. *Her* eyes. Annie's heart hurt at the thought.

She poured cream into her tea and dumped in more sugar than usual, then plopped her cup on the kitchen table so hard, tea sloshed over. Her Logan stubborn streak took over. "If

Jacques Morel thinks I'm going to buy his lies, he's sadly mistaken."

She took her cell from her pocket and called the first name on her list, Honey LaBelle, a local actress. She had a New Orleans number, and her voice had the raspy quality of someone who was either a heavy smoker or had breathed more than her share of cigarette smoke in her business. Maybe both. Her name, plus the burlesque music playing in the background, suggested she might be a performer in one of the many strip clubs along Bourbon Street.

"If you're calling with a job offer, I'll talk," she said. "If not, get lost."

Annie had a hunch and took a chance. "I'm Delilah Broussard's daughter."

The woman's chuckle was deep and rich with humor. "Well, honey, why didn't you say so in the first place? We were show biz pals. I loved that woman to pieces. Great blues singer. Cried my eyes out when she was killed. Couldn't wear mascara for three days. What's on your mind?"

"I'm trying to track down Mom's friend, Delphine Thierry."

"Now, there's a blast from the past. Just a sec. Gotta light a cig." There was a long pause. The volume of the music inched down a notch, and there was the sound of a long inhale and exhale; Honey LaBelle, dragging on her cigarette. "Everybody knows Delphine's dead. The funny thing is, I can still get that little love potion she mixed up for me over at the voodoo shop on Decatur. Exact same thing I used to drive all the way out to the swamp for. Now, you tell me if the Swamp Witch is dead or not."

Honey LaBelle's monologue only deepened the mystery. She was so forthright it was likely she knew no more about Delphine than she was telling.

"My mom died when I was very young," Annie told her. "I never knew much about her relationship with Delphine, except that she considered the Swamp Witch an aunt. I'd appreciate anything else you can tell me about them."

"The two were tight, that was for sure, but, honey, Delilah was the only woman I ever met who could keep her mouth shut about her own business. She was good to me, bailed me out of jail a time or two, but she never confided in me."

"Did she ever visit you after she married and left show business?"

"Why, honey, yes. You couldn't keep a singer like her off Beale Street. She'd come driving up in her daddy's Thunderbird, out of the blue, and doors would swing open. Everybody wanted to hear her sing. We never could understand why she quit."

Annie's pulse kicked up. "She loved my dad very much." *Did she?* Annie stamped that painful little voice out. "Did you see her back then, about thirty years ago? She would have been pregnant."

"I remember it like it was yesterday. It was dead of winter. Delilah got sick as a dog, and Delphine came roaring out of that swamp like her coattail was on fire, straight to me. My sister Tootie used to be a nurse. Delilah was big as a barrel. They stayed here three days till Delilah got back on her feet."

Hope bloomed through Annie, not the fragile feeling of poetry and song but the sturdy, indestructible assurance that refuses to die, no matter who tries to stamp it out. "Was my mother carrying twins?"

"Nobody ever said, and I'm not the domestic type. To me, knocked up is just knocked up, that's all."

"Would Tootie know?"

"She's been dead fifteen years. God rest her soul."

"I'm sorry to hear that." *Still...* Somebody, somewhere had to know. "Do you know anyone in show business or otherwise who might have been really close to my mom or to Delphine?"

"There was this guy in New Orleans that the Swamp Witch thought hung the moon. Some sort of big shot."

"What was his name?"

"Beats me, kid. I gotta go. My meal ticket's coming over, and I've got to psych myself into acting like I'm his girlfriend."

"If you remember the name of Delphine's close friend, will you let me know?" Annie reeled off her number.

"Sure thing, kid. Good luck."

Annie wrote a note beside Honey LaBelle's name to contact her again, and then stepped into the hallway to listen for her grandfather. The clock in the den chimed the half hour, five-thirty. He'd been asleep far longer than she expected.

Suddenly, she heard his shower running. Relieved, she went back into the kitchen to finish her tea. But the steam coming from her cup billowed upward like fog on the bayou. The Shadow moved through the mist, restless, sinister, his intent as clear as if he'd handed her a note.

*I'm coming for you.*

Lucien's houseboat felt like a cage, even with his friend Boone there, sharing a beer with him. He paced, his emotions burning him up inside. Self-doubt bombarded him so fast and furiously he thought he might explode.

"Sit down, man," Boone said. "You're making me dizzy."

"It's the beer making you dizzy. You've had too much."

"Can't ever have too much. What got you all stirred up? The cops hauling you in for questioning, or Annie Logan?"

"Annie. I'm not worried about the cops. They have nothing on me except one of Pete Thibodeaux's tapes. Half the population of the swamp is on it." With Evangeline gone, it was a relief to have his old friend and confidant here. "Why hasn't my sister called? You think I scared her away."

"I'd be scared if I found out my daddy was Jacques Morel. I'd just as soon be told my daddy was an alligator."

"Yeah, but you're a wimp. Annie's *not*." Lucien sank onto the sagging sofa beside his friend. "What if Delphine lied about who my mother was and how she gave me away?"

"I wouldn't put it past her. Nor your daddy, either. Shoot,

man, you need to put all this out of your mind and just go back to being happy."

Maybe Boone was right. His quest had become an obsession that was almost madness. But how could he let Annie go knowing she was his twin? How could he be *happy* in the place where he *saw* the other half of himself in the mist, in his dreams? How could he be whole without her?

Lucien picked up his barbells and lifted weights for a while. When that didn't ease his tension, he jerked up his pistol.

"Come on, Boone. Let's find that big cottonmouth that's been trying to get in here." The viper had been plaguing him lately, slithering through the water with a predatory eye turned in the direction of Lucien's houseboat. He had no intention of becoming the victim of its lethal fangs.

Though evening was falling, and he hadn't thought to bring a flashlight, he and Boone stood watch at the railing. From a distance came the sound of an outboard motor, the constant lullaby of anyone living on the water.

Suddenly, he caught a glimpse of black gliding through the water. He fired, and splinters shot into the air. He'd hit a large stick, floating in the algae.

"You missed," Boone said.

"I can see that."

It was all Evangeline's fault. Their quarrel circled through his mind, the things he should have said but hadn't, the things he'd said and done that he would regret. But not yet. Not yet.

He took aim and shot at a long, narrow shadow. His bullet hit the water without resistance.

"Missed again." Boone was half drunk, but he was right.

There was no snake, no big stick. Lucien was imagining things. Was he going crazy?

The sound of the outboard motor came closer, and a cry echoed across the water. "Ahoy, Lucien!"

When he was a child, the familiar greeting always filled

him with joy and anticipation. Today, dread settled on his chest like a millstone. This was no jubilant cry of a father returning to his beloved son, triumphant over a huge catch of fish or an unusually large haul of pelts. *No.* This was the command of a man with sand in his craw, a man who was ready to put teeth and claws into the threats he'd made many years ago.

Lucien squinted through the falling light to watch the boat come in, but he didn't return the greeting. He remained unsmiling, and so did Jacques. His dad's pistol was in a shoulder holster, but Lucien held his in his hand, his finger already on the trigger.

Horror filled him. Killing his father was unthinkable, even if Jacques gave him cause to do so. He put his weapon in the cabinet on the deck where he kept life preservers. After what had happened with Evangeline, he no longer trusted himself.

Jacques dropped anchor and clambered aboard, his chocolate-colored eyes almost black with suppressed rage.

"Boone." He nodded in the direction of Lucien's friend then turned to his son. The two of them faced off like two raging panthers, nothing moving except the ripple of their identical black curls in the wind and the tic of a muscle in Jacques' square jaw.

Lucien took the offensive. "You've heard she's here," he said.

"Everybody in the bayou has heard. *'Delilah's daughter'* is all I hear."

"I didn't seek her out. She came to America looking for me." If a partial truth would serve to defuse the situation, Lucien was willing to try. If not, so be it. He was three inches taller than Jacques and thirty-six years younger.

"Send her back," his father said.

"I have no control over her! She's a grown woman. After her art show, she'll go back to the other side of the world, and we'll never hear from her again." Anger ripped through him. Would he go back to his old life? Was he willing to let that happen?

"She has already poisoned your mind. Promise me you'll have nothing more to do with her."

As if on cue, the cottonmouth moccasin Lucien had been looking for reared its ugly head out of the water. He didn't even wish for a gun. He was too mesmerized by the sudden epiphany that the viper's diamond-shaped head was his father's chin, in reverse.

"I can't make that promise, and I won't." Lucien stretched to his full height. If he'd meant to intimidate, it didn't work. Jacques put his hand on the butt of his gun.

"Annie Logan is evil, an outsider. She'll soon be a pariah in the bayou, and you'll go down with her."

Jacques was exaggerating as a ploy to keep him in line. Why had he never seen that before?

"She's an artist with fans around the world," Lucien told him. "A celebrity. They have Teflon hides. Gossip won't break Annie."

"You *fool*." Jacques kicked the side of a cooler, and it slid across the deck. Only the railing kept it from toppling into the water. "She's vindictive and selfish, like Delilah. She takes what she wants and walks away from the ruins. She'll destroy us both." He stared with those piercing eyes that had sent more than one opponent running for cover. "Back off. And wash your hands of her."

Lucien didn't bother saying *I can't* or *I won't*. He made himself larger with a wide-legged stance, and stared back at Jacques. The air became thick with tension, while mists rose from the bayou and twined around them like snakes. He was prepared to stand there all night if he had to. He had more stamina and more than enough righteous anger to last until morning. Even beyond.

"Boone." Jacques whirled toward him. "See if you can talk

some sense into my son." Jacques stalked off and swung down the ladder to his own boat. As it shot through the water and the sound of the motor faded, the only indication he had been there was the wake his boat left behind.

"Maybe he's right?" Boone said.

"He's *wrong*." Lucien took his gun out of the cabinet and peered into the darkness for the viper.

He was itching to pull the trigger, and just about any target would do.

# THIRTY-FOUR

## ANGEL'S BAYOU HOUSE

Annie stepped out of the kitchen to listen for her grandfather. His shower was no longer running. She debated whether she should go to his bedroom and ask if he needed any help, then discarded the idea as overprotective and anxious, two qualities certain to raise his temper.

She went back to the teapot to pour herself another cup. Angel was tired after his visit to the doctor, and slow to dress, that was all.

Her phone pinged with an incoming text from Toni.

*Have you heard from Evangeline? I went by the gallery today, but she never showed up for work. She's not answering her calls, and Lacy said her car's not home, either. I'm worried. She and Lucien were arguing at Pete's Place yesterday.*

Annie felt as if the walls were closing in on her. Images from last night's dream flickered through her mind like a movie reel going bad. Blood, flashing from red to black, a foot fading in and out of the water, the face, Annie's face... but not quite.

She sent a quick text back to Toni.

*I haven't seen her. I'll check with Lucien and Paul.*

Her phone call to Paul went unanswered. She sent him a text.

*I'm looking for Evangeline. Do you know where she is?*

Next, she called Lucien. He answered on the first ring. "Annie, I've been hoping to hear from you. I'd like to see you again."

His voice set off a little shiver of hope, though today it held none of the musical cadences she remembered. In fact, he sounded upset. Maybe Evangeline had come back, and they were trying to patch things up?

"I'd like that, too, Lucien, but I need more time."

"I wish things were different... but I understand."

"Thanks." Annie tried to gauge if he really did, but she couldn't tell from his voice, and her ability to see things others couldn't had suddenly gone on vacation. "I'm not calling about us," she added. "Toni said Evangeline didn't show up at work today. Is she there with you?"

"No." His answer was abrupt, harsh.

Annie found it more than odd that he didn't react to Evangeline's unexpected absence from the gallery. "Have you seen or talked to her?"

He went quiet for so long, she thought he might have ended the connection. In the stillness, she sensed mist rising around him, evil lurking in the dark. Prickles formed along the back of her neck. It was impossible to tell whether the evil was threatening Lucien from the outside or the inside.

"We had a big fight before she left yesterday," he said finally. "I doubt I'll be hearing from her for a while. If ever."

The cool detachment of his reply chilled her. She ended the call as fast as she could without being rude or showing her feelings. She felt as if a fog were closing in around her. A waking vision hovered just on the edge of her conscious mind, but the details were lost in her overwhelming dark premonitions. Was Lucien the Shadow?

The tea in her cup grew cold. The sun disappeared, suddenly, as if it had been shot out of the sky. *An omen?*

Annie found the number for the St. Tammany Parish Sheriff's Department and called to report Evangeline missing. The deputy who took the call was particularly interested that Toni had seen her at Pete's Place arguing with Lucien. "I'm worried sick about her," Annie told him.

"Don't you worry, Miss Logan. Considering that she's a prime target for our killer, we'll make finding her a priority."

Annie hoped her call would make a difference for Evangeline. She thought about brewing another cup or tea or reheating the one she had when a loud crash catapulted her from her chair. Shards of glass flew all over the kitchen, and a rock rolled across the floor. She raced to the broken window and peered out, but all she could see was darkness. Not even a shadow moved among the thick groves of trees and bushes that flourished in the wetland.

Her instinct to rush out and catch the culprit was tempered by the knowledge that he was likely the murderer dubbed the Shadow, a fleeting illusion seen briefly, then gone in a *pouf*.

There was a handwritten note attached to the rock. She made sure the back door was securely locked then picked her way carefully through the glass shards and bent to retrieve the note. On second thought, she backtracked to the sink and slipped her hands into a pair of rubber gloves.

*You are going to pay for what you've done. Before all this is over, you're going to wish you'd never been born. Turn on your TV.*

She slid the note into a plastic bag with shaking hands, and turned on the TV. SPECIAL REPORT WITH LINDA HOLLOWAY flashed across the screen. The reporter sat in one of two plush chairs, her skinny legs crossed at the ankles, the skirt of her red dress flowing around her. Her makeup was heavier than usual, and a self-important smile tugged at her lips.

"This is *Special Report*, and I'm Linda Holloway. In a shocking turn of events, we've learned that the murder of two girls in Honey Island Swamp might be connected to a world-famous artist, whose home is in Italy."

Annie's face leaped onto the screen. Multiplied. A movie reel of photos scrolled by showing her at galleries in Rome, Milan, and Florence, sitting on a stone wall sketching, arriving at her flat in Assisi. All publicity shots the media had used through the years.

But the most chilling was a photo of her arriving at Pete's Place. Who had taken it? Why? There had been no press coverage since her arrival. She would have known. They would have wanted interviews.

Linda Holloway said, "Her name is Annie Logan. Based on a credible source, we started digging. And the facts we uncovered paint a disturbing picture. The artist bears a striking resemblance to the victims. Coincidence?" Her voice dropped to a conspiratorial tone. "Or something more?"

Linda sat in her blood-colored dress while head shots of Annie and the two victims bloomed to life. It took almost no imagination to believe the three young women might have been sisters.

Annie was stunned. How dare the reporter dredge up her family history, point a finger of guilt at her in the name of TV ratings!

"In a significant development," the reporter added, "we have learned that Annie Logan not only has a grandfather living in Honey Island Swamp, but she, herself, is here. And her connection to the victims goes far deeper than similarity in looks and age."

Another photo filled the screen; Delilah as teenager, arm in arm with a woman the TV reporter identified as Julie Bergeron. Annie stared at the photo of her mother, disbelief and anger twisting her into a knot. She was going to ask Toni if this program constituted slander.

Linda Holloway was shameless. "In a stunning twist, we learned that Annie Logan's mother, Delilah Broussard, and the second victim's aunt, Julie Bergeron, were childhood friends. Julie is here on set with us." The middle-aged woman had tamed her curly hair into a sleek French twist. The casual clothes she'd worn on camera when her niece was killed had been replaced by a navy skirt and blazer. "Julie, what can you tell us about your friendship with Delilah Broussard?"

"We were great friends, always doing everything together, even double dating."

Snapshots that showed two teenage couples flashed onto the screen. Delilah's face shone with the innocence of youth, but the awful reporter was trying to turn her mother's past into a prelude to murder. Annie wanted to cry.

Linda droned on, self-important and almost gleeful. "This is the foursome as teenagers, Julie on the right with Pete Thibodeaux, and Delilah on the left with Jacques Morel." Linda turned to the woman beside her. "Julie, can you tell us what happened the day this photo was made?"

"Delilah decided she wanted Pete, and she accused me of taking him from her in the first place."

"A common teenage rivalry," Linda said, nodding. "But in this case, it became more. Julie, can you tell us why?"

"Delilah was vindictive. She said she would never forgive me for stealing Pete, and someday I would pay." Julie choked up. "Now Delilah's daughter is here, and my niece is dead."

They had implicated her in *murder*! Annie's turmoil built to such volcanic proportions, she thought she might explode. It seemed impossible that someone could destroy you with such ease and without regard to facts. Annie could prove she had nothing to do with the murders. This was sensational journalism at its worst.

A shot of the first victim in front of an easel popped onto the screen. Linda said, "It appears no coincidence that Janine Porter was an art student at Tulane. According to witnesses, the first victim of the Shadow met Annie Logan last spring when she gave a lecture there." She paused, dramatically. "Let me be clear that there is *no* evidence to link Annie Logan to the Honey Island Swamp murders, but the coincidences just keep piling up. Is she, in fact, carrying out a decades' old vendetta for her mother?"

*"Unbelievable!"* Annie wondered that her roar didn't shatter the lightbulbs.

A shot of her climbing into Lucien's boat appeared on the full screen. It lingered there long enough to let the seeds of doubt take root. Then a close-up of Linda's face filled the screen. She was wearing blood-red lipstick to match her dress.

"Nobody knows whether the Shadow is male or female." Her serious and self-righteous expression hinted that *she* knew. "What we *do* know is that the bayou is running red with the blood of victims. The cops have made no arrests, and as long as the Shadow remains at large, nobody here is safe. This has been *Special Report* with Linda Holloway."

Annie snapped off the TV. She felt as if someone had pulled a thread and unraveled her. The entire program had been designed to embarrass her, put her under the glare of negative publicity, and destroy her reputation. Many would believe the worst of her until they knew the facts, and then some would continue to associate her with the murders, even after all the facts proved her innocence.

Now, the media firestorm would begin.

# THIRTY-FIVE

## THE SHADOW

That fool reporter had taken his bait. She even spread his lies on TV wearing a dress as red as the blood of those Annie Logan lookalikes he'd butchered.

He couldn't have planned it better himself. His neighbors all over the bayou would tremble. They *believed* in omens and spells and legends of terrifying creatures that would tear your heart out and eat it while you lay dying.

That's exactly what the Shadow *wanted* them to believe. The more confusion, the less likely the eye of the law would land on him.

His laughter echoed through the swamp, chilling, diabolical.

He poured himself another beer and watched Linda Holloway wrap up *Special Report* with the pride of a man who always won, no matter what he had to do.

No matter who he had had to kill.

# THIRTY-SIX

Putting the awful TV special from her mind, Annie found some Italian opera on her music app and busied herself making a chicken and rice casserole for dinner. She let an aria from *La Boheme* wash away her turmoil, and the smell of onions and mushrooms sautéing in butter wipe out the lies and innuendos.

She even sang along to the aria, stretching herself to match the lyric soprano. She loved music, and had once considered it as a career.

She was putting her casserole in the oven when her cell signaled a call. It was her formidable grandmother's ringtone. Relief and dismay vied for Annie's emotions. It was a tossup which one would win.

"Gran?"

"I don't know why you went to that swamp, and I don't want to know." Victoria Logan's voice popped with spunk and determination. "Just hold onto your hat. I'm on the way. Nobody treats my granddaughter this way and gets by with it! I'll take Patrick's shillelagh to that Holloway woman."

The awful TV special came roaring back. Obviously, clips

from the sensational garbage had been picked up and aired nationally.

"Everything that so-called journalist said is easy to debunk. Don't you worry about me, Gran. I can take care of myself."

"You bet your boots you can. No granddaughter of mine would do otherwise. I'm headed out there to take care of the skunks who did this to you. I'll see you in three days. I'm driving a big truck and carrying a big stick."

"Gran?" The line was dead. Victoria had already broken the phone connection. She was probably halfway to her pickup truck by now. There was no use trying to call and talk her out of coming. She wouldn't answer her phone. Once she set her mind to something, there was no changing it.

Her cell rang again. This time, it was Rachel.

"Annie, what on earth is going on down there?"

She stalled for time. "Can you stop Gran from coming?"

"Has anybody *ever* stopped Victoria? She's loading that monster truck of hers so fast my head is swimming. I told her to wait until I can get a substitute to teach my class so I can come with her, but she won't." Rachel took her commitment to her elementary school students seriously.

Annie could hear Gran's voice in the background, "I don't need anybody to babysit me. I'm older than dirt." That was followed by the sound of her boots as she tromped across the wooden floors at the ranch. Rachel called after, "Gran!" but Victoria shouted back, "I'm not waiting, so you might as well not waste your breath."

The exchange, so typical of their childhood on the ranch, made Annie smile.

"Annie." It was Rachel again, clearly rattled. "You never did tell me why you're in the middle of a murder investigation in a Louisiana swamp. Jen's going to be livid."

"Don't worry about the TV show. Linda Holloway's innuendos are easy to disprove. The great news is that I've found our grandfather. I've also found a man who claims to be my twin. He says my father is Jacques Morel."

Rachel's silence was deafening. "Oh, Annie... this is... *unbelievable.*"

"Angel Broussard is definitely our grandfather. Mom's pictures are all over his house, and her playbills are in her old room. You remember how Mom always smelled like magnolias? I even found one of her old perfume bottles. I don't know if Lucien Morel is my brother, but I intend to find out."

"Not by yourself, you don't. I'll be there as soon as I can get my family and my job squared away. And so will Jen. Hang in there. We're coming."

The great thing about sisters is that they never said, *I told you so.* When one of them was in trouble, the other two mounted up and galloped to the rescue.

After they arrived, Annie would tell them about her stalker. When her sisters went after him, he might think twice about his shenanigans.

Filled with purpose and renewed courage, she tapped in the emergency number that would bring cops to Angel's door to collect evidence of vandalism and personal threats.

The coward who threw the rock and threw Annie under the bus with a reporter whose lust for headlines outweighed her decency and common sense had better start running. He had sorely underestimated his opponent... and the Logan sisters.

A feeble-looking and slightly befuddled Angel came into the kitchen while Annie was checking the casserole. She settled him into a chair with a cup of hot tea. The only good thing she could say about her day, so far, was that Angel didn't notice the broken window.

"Grandfather, I'm going for a walk. Our dinner is in the

oven and will be ready in an hour. Will you be okay by yourself?"

"I've been taking care of myself for longer than you've been alive. Have your walk and let me drink my tea in peace." He bent over his tea, dismissing her.

Hoping his fractious temper was a good sign, she slipped the bagged rock into her pocket then hurried outside to call Paul. Turning to him was becoming a habit, and surprisingly, one she didn't mind.

Relief rushed through her when she heard his voice. "Annie, I saw *Special Report*. I'm coming over."

"There's more to it than that." She told him about the rock through her window, and the note. "The deputies will be here soon, and Angel's in the kitchen. I'd rather he not be a part of this. I'm going to wait outside, and I need you to keep him occupied."


Annie's request set off a battle between Paul's voice of reason and his conscience. He'd rather be anywhere except in the vicinity of the cops. In cases involving the law, justice was not always done, and the truth was not always found. He had no desire to come under their radar again. Still, this was Annie. In distress.

"I'll be right there." He imagined a heavy suit of knight's armor closing around him. His habit of rushing to the rescue was going to be his undoing.

Maybe he needed therapy. The deaths of his wife and child had been accidental, a rainy night, a slick road, and an oncoming car that veered into Paul's lane. He had swerved to avoid a collision, but his brakes didn't hold. His car skidded and hit the bridge. Maybe a professional could talk him out of his guilt, and then he could get back to normal and let others take care of themselves.

*Not happening tonight. Not with Annie.*

There was something special about her that wouldn't bear too much scrutiny. He was not ready to risk upending life as he knew it.

"Paul, I hate to be an imposition. I don't usually go running to other people for help, but considering the circumstances, I have to do what I can to protect my grandfather."

"You're never an imposition, Annie. Whoever threw that rock could still be out there. I'll cut across the path and wait for the deputies by the dock while you and Angel remain safe inside."

"Thanks, but no."

"Is this negotiable?"

"No."

His medieval knight side wanted to protest, but why waste time? "I'll be there in five minutes."

He found his flashlight and ran the trail to his neighbor's house, training his beam into the semi-gloom of the bushes and trees for any sign of Annie's trespasser. He was alone in the woods.

Annie let him in, wearing Angel's too-big windbreaker and holding a flashlight. If he weren't an artist who sees every detail, he might have believed she was merely a lovely young woman, happy to greet her grandfather's next-door neighbor. Was she a woman who handled stress well, as he had first thought? Or was she just very good at hiding things she didn't want the world to see?

*Like you.*

He brushed the pesky voice of his conscience aside. Easy to do with a beautiful woman standing beside him and a heavenly aroma coming from the oven.

"The casserole's in the oven," she said, "and I've set the timer so you can take it out if I don't get back."

"I learned my way around the kitchen a long time ago. Don't worry. I've got this."

"Great. I made coffee for you." She touched his arm, an easy gesture of friendship, but the shock of awareness that roared through him was anything but platonic. "Thanks, Paul."

When she left, he watched until she was out of sight, then stood in the doorway listening until her footsteps no longer echoed across the wooden floor of the den. Making sure she didn't get waylaid between the kitchen and the front door. Protecting someone who had unknowingly become important to him, perhaps even necessary.

He poured coffee and sat beside Angel. He had a job to do.

"My granddaughter sent you, didn't she?"

The old guy was too cagey to believe a lie. "She did, so let's act like we're having a good time. We don't want to disappoint her."

Angel's laughter was hearty. "Talk of fishing ought to do it. I've got more tall tales than I'll ever live to talk about."

Paul's easy laughter masked his deep concern that Annie was being threatened again. And he didn't know how to stop it.

## THIRTY-SEVEN

Annie walked to the end of Angel's pier and aimed the beam of her flashlight over the water. There was no sign of a boat bearing deputies from the St. Tammany Parish Sheriff's Department. Or maybe they were arriving the back way by car. They didn't say.

She sank onto the end of the pier to wait. The night was quiet around her except for a small tapping sound coming from below. Annie dangled her legs over the pier and aimed the beam of her flashlight toward a large piling that supported the end of the dock. A shoe. She leaned as far as she dared and trained her light closer. It was a woman's shoe, caught in a tangle of algae and bumping against the piling with every movement of the water.

Annie stretched her full length on the pier then reached down to snatch the shoe. It was an espadrille mule wedge, somehow familiar. Alarms bells sounded. She knew that shoe.

But where had it come from? A sweep of her flashlight around the immediate area showed nothing unusual. She studied the movement of the current. Angel's property stretched in both directions from the pier. The current flowed around a deep curve on her right where a well-worn path threaded into a heavily wooded area.

Electrified, Annie took off running, pounding on the wooden pier, propelled by sheer horror. The bayou and the woods around her came alive, beckoning, calling to her, urgent.

*I'm here. I'm here.*

At the end of the pier, she veered onto a path that curved into a deep tangle of trees, bushes and overgrowth. The path had been cleared but appeared to be neglected from disuse. Had Angel built a picnic area he was too old to visit? Had he created a grotto in a little hidden nook, one of those perfect spots where he had once come to meditate? His property was huge. Anything could be at the other end of the trail.

Even a killer...

Annie paused, waiting for the wooded trail to reveal itself, expecting waking dreams, impressions that would identify this secluded spot as good or evil. Nothing came except a whisper.

*Find me.* The phrase was from her dreams, but this voice was female.

She sent her flashlight beam into the treetops then swept it across the forest from eye-level to ground. There was nothing to set off alarms except the plaintive cry of a screech owl she'd heard calling in the night. The wail sounded again, as if Nature's creatures had fled this section of the swamp, leaving behind the owl to mourn.

Annie stood still, listening. Who was the owl mourning?

*Save me.* The call vibrated to her very soul, creating an urgency that sent her racing along the dark path once more, swinging the flashlight in a never-ending arc.

*There.* A hand. Icy blue. The fingers curled around a spindly bush.

Shock and horror brought Annie to a halt. The beam of her flashlight picked up an arm, the bruises and slashes cruel in the harsh light; a shoulder, the clothing ripped away and hanging in tatters. A face.

Annie leaned over to retch. The darkness closed around her—and sudden terror.

*Get it together!*

"Evangeline!" Annie raced to her side. She was so still, so cold. Most of her body was curled on the bank, but one foot was still in the water, floating on the surface, a blackened, swollen limb. Dried blood was everywhere, on her clothes, her hair, spattered on the ground around her. The thicket of bushes had protected it—and her—from the weather.

Annie screamed her name again. Did her chest move? Was she alive?

She caught Evangeline's wrist, and the marks on her arm bent Annie double, heaving. *Claw marks! The Shadow has been here!* She heaved, but nothing came up.

*Get it together!* She checked for a pulse, but she couldn't tell. She didn't know.

"Evangeline, can you hear me?" There was no response. Not even a flutter of her eyelids. "Wake up, wake up!"

*Nothing.* Panic threatened to be Annie's undoing. She was wasting precious time. She set off running toward the cottage, screaming Paul's name at the top of her lungs.

A burly figure blocked her. Large hands closed around her shoulders.

Annie fought against her attacker, landing a perfect kick to his groin. He doubled over, but suddenly another man was there to take his place. Before she could get off a roundhouse kick, he had her in a vice grip, immobilized.

*Breathe. Breathe.*

He was in uniform. Both men were. She'd just disabled a sheriff's deputy.

"I'm Annie Logan, the one who called you. Angel Broussard's granddaughter. I've just found Evangeline Aguillard, and I think she's still alive."


The night came alive with shouts, lights, new arrivals, frantic activity. Deputies fanned out in the woods, searchlights bobbing, a tracking dog loping alongside them through the tangled overgrowth. Paramedics from the Pearl River fire department arrived and raced toward the cove where Evangeline was hidden.

"Got something!" The shout came from the woods. "A blue Valiant."

Evangeline's car, hidden on Angel's property. The news sank into Annie like a stone. Linda Holloway would have a field day with that. To make things worse, she could hear the paramedics working on Evangeline. Disjointed commands. "Blankets!" "CPR!" "Pressure cuff!"

Was she dead or alive? All Annie knew was that they were administering the care she had been unable to provide.

Finally, someone yelled, "She's alive!"

Music to Annie's ears. And yet she'd *seen* Evangeline. To the naked eye, there were no signs of life. Arms closed around her, broke her shivering. "I'm here." Paul. Suddenly beside her in the dark. An unexpected rock in the middle of a storm.

"Where's Angel?"

"I waited with him until a female deputy came in to stay with him. She's in the kitchen now, serving up your casserole."

Helicopter blades split the air, the beams from their powerful searchlights aimed at the fragile figure on the gurney, being carried from Angel's hidden cove.

There was a sound like a wounded animal, and Annie realized it was her, grieving.

Paul tightened his hold. "They're going to airlift Evangeline to the trauma unit in New Orleans."

"I need to call Toni." She fumbled as she searched for her cell phone, almost dropped it on the trampled ground.

"Annie, wait." He put his hand over hers. "The hospital won't let anyone but family see her. If she survives, there'll be police guards outside her door."

"She *will* survive." Annie broke loose and raced toward the gurney. Coma victims could still hear.

"Ma'am." A young, earnest detective blocked her. "You need to step back."

Just beyond him was Evangeline's thin, still body, her bloodless face turned slightly in Annie's direction. Through all those layers of darkness, did she sense Annie's presence?

"Evangeline, listen." She made her voice huge, imperative. "Come back to us. Be strong. *Fight!*"

"Ma'am." A burly, gray-haired man with a voice as scratchy as sandpaper came up beside her, followed by Paul. "We'll need you to come down to headquarters to sign an official statement." He turned to Paul. "You, too, Chenevert."

"I can't leave Grandfather here alone. He's not well."

"Deputy Wanda Sparks is already in the house. She'll stay with him until you return."

Annie felt only a small relief. The Shadow had been all over Angel's property, and he was still out there somewhere.

Waiting to strike again.

# THIRTY-EIGHT

Annie rode with Paul to the St. Tammany Parish Sheriff's Department, but they were separated as soon as they arrived.

"Annie?" He glanced over his shoulder. "Will you be okay?"

"Certainly. I have nothing to hide."

Her footsteps echoed on the tile as she followed a uniformed officer down a long, narrow hallway. Suddenly, she caught a glimpse of dark hair, lanky frame, familiar profile. The man was being led into a room two doors down and on her left.

"Lucien?"

He paused a moment, his posture stiff, his dark hair disheveled, and then he disappeared into the room without ever looking back at her. They would have picked him up for questioning the minute Evangeline was found. Annie wished he'd turned to face her. Would she have seen sorrow or guilt?

She waited, hoping to read the room. But nothing came to her except the buzz of the heating unit. Lucien's story remained locked as tightly as the door.

She turned to her escort, a stern-looking man with a military-style haircut. "That was Lucien Morel, wasn't it?"

"I'm not at liberty to say." He showed Annie into a bare

room with a plain wooden table and two chairs, functional lighting, nothing lying around to pick up and use as a weapon, not even a pencil. "Wait here."

She sat in a straight-backed chair and waited. Patience had never been a problem with her, and she wasn't one to panic at the unknown.

They were watching her. She could feel them through the two-way mirror, their preconceived notions and unanswered questions swirling around them like rain clouds. She remained still, her conflicting emotions tamped down, her hands folded in her lap, and her legs crossed at the ankle.

The man who finally came through the door was the gray-haired one who looked like he might be somebody's grandfather. His innate kindness trailed along behind him like a faithful puppy. Regret over the cases he could never solve made his shoulders slope downward, as if he always carried a burden he couldn't throw off.

He introduced himself as Sheriff Harold Debeau, then sank into the chair opposite Annie and placed a file on the table. "Miss Logan, you are not a suspect here, in spite of what Linda Holloway implied. We have verified you were doing an art show in Italy when the first murder occurred, and were in New Orleans with Toni Delgado when the second took place. I don't let television reporters do my work for me."

"Thank you."

"I knew your mother personally. Delilah was never mean or spiteful. She was a talented, gifted woman. There's no vendetta going on here." The sheriff steepled his fingers. "Furthermore, you called in a missing person's report on Evangeline Aguillard, and if I ever saw real grief, it was you after you found her. For the record, though, I'll need details of how you know her and how you found her."

Annie told him everything, from the day she met Evangeline at the art gallery until the horrible moment she found her, comatose. He jotted notes, never interrupting her narrative flow with questions.

After she had finished, she reached into her pocket and handed him the note. "I called you for this, too. It was on the rock that came through Angel's window."

"Bagged, thank you." He scanned the note, frowning, then called for forensics to take it for fingerprint analysis. Afterward, he opened the file on the table. "We have the report of you and Toni Delgado discovering a snake in her car at Pete's Place. Walk me through the threats to you. Start to finish. Don't leave anything out, even if you think it's unimportant."

Annie started with her first threat on social media and her incident in the plaza with the stalker in Italy. With her eye for detail, she painted a vivid and complete picture of her online threats and the array of animals left to intimidate her. She even included her prescient dreams.

"I know all that must sound crazy to you," she told the sheriff. "But based on my dreams and everything that has happened to me during the time frame of the recent murders, I have every reason to believe my stalker might also be the killer you're looking for."

"Miss Logan, I've seen everything in St. Tammany Parish; voodoo, snake charming, claims of zombies. Nothing shocks me." His answer revealed nothing of his investigation or his thoughts about the killer. He tapped the file on the table. "Tips are still coming in about the snake in your friend's car, but nothing we can verify yet. We're going to need to take a look at the threats on your social media. Forensics will take you back to the computer room."

"Certainly."

He stood up. "Stay safe. Barring leaks, we're going to keep word that Evangeline is alive off the news. I don't want the killer thinking she might have talked. Otherwise, he'll come after both of you."

## THIRTY-NINE

By the time she and Paul got back to Angel's, the stars had vanished and storm clouds had gathered in their place. He parked his car beside the St. Tammany Parish patrol car and came around to open Annie's door. A revelation for her—and a pleasure. Manners that harkened to a simpler, gentler time.

They stood for a moment, letting the evening air wash away the stress of one of the worst days Annie could remember since her sisters were in jeopardy.

"Feels good to just breathe," Paul said.

"Yes, finally." The wind picked up, setting the chimes hanging on Angel's gazebo in motion. Annie turned toward the silvery sound, and her eye caught movement. An object of some kind, no clappers. It definitely wasn't the windchimes. "Paul, there's something hanging on the gazebo."

He grabbed her hand, and they crossed the backyard cautiously, looking and listening for an intruder. As they got closer, Annie said, "It looks like a doll."

Paul trained the penlight hanging on his keychain on the object. "It's a voodoo doll."

Primitive-looking, green button eyes, dark yarn hair woven

with red, a pin stuck through the body where the heart should be. There was a note attached to the leg. Three chilling words.

*You are next.*

Fear whispered through Annie. "It's meant for me."

"I know. Don't touch it."

Paul led her toward the back door. Deputy Wanda Sparks waited for them in the kitchen, alone. The television was on. Linda Holloway was already at the St. Tammany Parish Sheriff's Department office, giving her own breathless commentary about his brief press conference.

"The body of Evangeline Aguillard was found on Angel Broussard's property earlier this evening by none other than his granddaughter, the famous artist, Annie Logan."

Annie had no intention of listening to any more of that woman's lies. She grabbed the remote and turned off the TV. At least the Holloway woman hadn't mentioned that Evangeline was still alive.

"How's my grandfather?" she asked the deputy.

"He's fine, Miss Logan. He's a tough old gentleman who has probably seen worse than what happened here this evening. He had supper and went to bed about nine." The deputy began to gather her belongings.

"There's a voodoo doll with a note threatening Annie hanging on the gazebo." Paul poured two cups of coffee, and handed one to Annie. "You'll want to take it into evidence."

"How is that possible?" Wanda was already taking an evidence bag from her gear. "I was here all evening."

"My stalker is so silent and elusive, he's like a shadow," Annie told her. "Did you hear anything?"

"You couldn't hear yourself think over all that commotion on the property. But after everybody left and things quieted down, I didn't hear a thing except a screech owl. What did the note say?"

"*You're next,*" Paul said. "I'm going to stay here with Annie and Angel tonight." He turned to Annie. "Not negotiable."

Lightning flashed and thunder cracked. She had a moment of comic relief in thinking it could be Nature, agreeing with Paul.

"I'd better hurry before this storm hits." Wanda headed toward the door. Annie thanked her then settled at the kitchen table with her coffee cup.

Paul joined her. "I'm going back to New Orleans tomorrow," he said. "Lacy can't run the gallery by herself, and I need to be there for Evangeline and her mother."

"Where does her mother live?"

"Baton Rouge, but she's been in Paris for six weeks with her new husband. Her fourth." His implication was clearly that Evangeline's mother was far too busy to even notice her daughter missing. Sudden rain slashed the window. Its ferocity matched the growing feeling of impending disaster. "I want you and Angel to come with me. My New Orleans home is in the Marigny, not too far from his. You're not safe here, Annie."

"I know. Neither is Angel, as long as I'm here. And I certainly don't want Toni to have to come back to the bayou to get me. I'll drive Grandfather's car, and we'll follow you."

"Annie, I'm beginning to think the Broussard stubbornness is all a myth."

Paul flashed her a heart-stopping smile, and the night ahead loomed in Annie's mind—him on the sofa, her upstairs, the storm outside raging, and the force of their mutual attraction making sleep impossible.

Annie knew she had found more than danger in the swamp.

# FORTY

## NEW ORLEANS

Toni usually loved brainstorming a case with the smart attorneys at the DA's office, but Annie's news from the swamp last night had her tied in knots. She couldn't wait to head to the hospital.

"If there are no new thoughts, that wraps it up." The DA, a tall, solidly built family man who commanded respect, closed his file and strode back to his office.

Toni hurried down the hall to her own, a cubicle compared to his. Still, she didn't mind. She loved her job. She'd work on a park bench out of a shoe box, if necessary.

She was typing up notes when the text she'd been waiting for came in from Annie.

*I've driven both my grandparents crazy. Victoria is barreling toward New Orleans in that truck of hers, and Angel has aged so much he's moving at snail speed. We won't be in New Orleans until late this evening, probably around seven. Have you heard anything about Evangeline's condition?*

Toni shot back her reply.

*No. Everybody is under orders not to talk. It's the only way to keep her safe. But don't worry. I have a plan. By the time you get here, I'll be at the Marigny with news.*

Toni parked her bike in the rack at the hospital, swapped her sneakers for high heels then finger-brushed her short bob, slashed on red lipstick, and pranced to the reception desk in the massive lobby. No matter how fancy it was, it still smelled like sickness and grief.

Thankfully the lobby was empty except for the receptionist at the desk. The middle-aged woman in a tight bun that matched the severity of her dress looked up from her paperwork. "May I help you?"

Toni plopped her purse onto the top of the reception desk. She had ditched her usual backpack for a Kate Spade bag, designed to impress. She pulled out a business card from the DA's office and flashed it just long enough for the woman to see ATTORNEY AT LAW written large across the top. Flustered people never remembered important details. Especially a difficult name like Antonia Gloria Delgado.

"I'm here on official business."

The woman opened her mouth to respond, but Toni hurried in the direction of the elevators, giving the impression that she was too busy with pressing legal matters to wait. Unless the receptionist was unusually observant, that's what she would remember. In Toni's experience, most witnesses missed the small details.

She got off on the ICU floor and glanced down the hall. An officer from the New Orleans PD sat outside one of the doors, easily visible from the nurses' station. Considering the circumstances, the hospital would want to ensure as many eyes were on the room as possible.

The officer was solidly built and young. *Good.* He would be easier to deal with than a more seasoned cop, and she wasn't above a little flirtation if it helped her get to Evangeline. If she played her cards right, he might not call to ask his superiors if he could let her in.

She showed her business card, hoping a glance would suffice, but he reached for it. Undeterred, Toni nodded toward the room.

"I'm from the DA's office, but I'm an old friend, too." She was careful to protect Evangeline's identity, and she didn't have to fake the tears that leaked down her cheeks. "I understand she's comatose, but it's imperative to know every detail in order to build an air-tight legal case."

He glanced from the card to her, his eyes lighting up with appreciation and more than a little interest. "I'm supposed to call this in."

"But do you have to? The DA's office will get quick approval, and I'm in something of a hurry."

"You know, you're right." He handed the card back. "Five minutes only. I'll be standing at the door watching you."

"Perfect!" She flashed him a smile then went inside. Who knew when she might need his assistance again?

The sight of Evangline almost wrecked Toni. She was unrecognizable. Bandages covered her head and large portions of her body, IVs dangled from both arms, and an oxygen tube snaked out of her nose. The skin that was visible was purple with bruises. The shape of her legs under the covers showed that she had lost considerable weight between the time she vanished and the time she was found. But it was Evangeline's feet that shocked Toni most. The outline of one foot was clearly visible under the covers. The other foot was missing, the leg shortened and thick where the stump had been bandaged.

Monitors beside the hospital bed showed the vital signs of a healthy young woman making a steady recovery from the brink of death. A relief and a blessing.

Toni had dealt with many victims over the course of her career, but none that tore at her heart the way Evangeline did. She moved closer so she could be heard inside the room but not outside.

"Evangeline, you are going to get well, and I'm going to fight for you... and win. Stay strong. The person who did this to you will be punished. I'll *personally* see to it, I promise."

At the sound of Toni's voice, Evangeline's eyes moved from side to side beneath her closed lids. She was searching, listening. The intensity of Toni's relief and gratitude loosened her tears. She got a tissue from the box beside the bed and dabbed her eyes.

The young cop blocking the door was also listening. Though he had his hand on his holster, he couldn't maintain his stern façade. *Good.* In case he remembered her name from the business card, Toni didn't want any blowback to the DA's office. She needed his discretion.

Toni touched Evangeline's cheek. "Everybody's pulling for you. Be strong. You're a survivor." She turned toward the cop, who was visibly blinking. "What you've seen today is protected under attorney/client privilege. Plus, she's in your care under a strict gag order. I trust you will say nothing."

"You can count on it, ma'am."

# FORTY-ONE

## THE MARIGNY

It was late evening when Annie parked Angel's Thunderbird in his garage at the cottage in the Marigny. Already the day felt as long to her as if it were midnight. It had taken Angel most of the day to pack two small bags and get ready to leave the home he loved in Honey Island Swamp.

In addition, Annie's calls to check on her grandmother's progress toward New Orleans had gone unanswered. Was that Victoria being stubborn, or Victoria in trouble?

Paul pulled in behind them and grabbed their bags from the trunk.

Annie's heart broke a little as they all walked up the porch steps to her grandfather's cottage. Angel was more stooped than when she first met him, his movements slower, his face stamped with fear that hadn't been there before.

He fumbled with the key, but Annie didn't risk making him feel feeble by offering to help. Neither did Paul. She shot him a look of gratitude.

The inside of Angel's cottage held fewer mementos of his life with Annie's grandmother and mother than his estate in the bayou. Still, it had the charm of a home where the two occupants once enjoyed simple pleasures and each other. Two wooden rocking chairs on the front porch, an identical pair beside the fireplace in the front room with matching crocheted blankets thrown over the back, twin beds with carved headboards side by side in the bedroom downstairs, two pairs of reading glasses resting on a bedside table beside a paperback novel harkening back to another era—a western by Louis L'Amour.

Paul stood in the doorway with the bags. "Where do you want these?"

Angel nodded toward the closet. "Put mine there. Guest room's upstairs, follow me."

It took them twice as long to navigate the stairs behind him, and Annie was pleased to see how respectful Paul was toward Angel. If there was one lesson that she had learned from being brought up by her grandmother, it was respect for those who have lived many years, and appreciation of their experience and wisdom.

Sunlight poured through the dormer windows, a welcome respite from the thunderstorms and the horrible events of the previous evening. The room was frillier than the one downstairs, obviously Delilah's. A perfume bottle and a framed photo of her sat on an antique dressing table with a triple mirror.

Regret pierced Annie. How she and her sisters would have enjoyed playing in this room, running down the stairs to sit in the lap of their grandfather, racing outside to play underneath the magnolia tree where Angel would have hung a rope swing.

Paul touched her arm. "Annie, we're heading downstairs to make coffee."

"I'll join you in a minute. I need to call Gran first." Though Victoria was notorious for not taking calls when she didn't want her granddaughters to know what she was doing, Annie kept getting flashes of storm clouds gathering over her grandmother.

Was bad weather heading her way, or disaster? Thankfully, she answered on the third ring.

"Gran, where are you?"

"Eating supper."

"That doesn't tell me a thing. I want to know if you're safe and when you expect to get here?"

"Of course, I'm safe. You're talking to me, aren't you?" Her grandmother's stubborn logic caused Annie to sigh. "I heard that," Victoria added with more than a little asperity. "I'll get there when I get there."

"Are you having any trouble with your health or the traffic? Are you stopping to get plenty of rest? I'm worried about you, Gran. I'm okay down here, and I have lots of support. Why don't you think about going back to the ranch and rooting for me from afar?"

"Rooting from afar, my foot! I've got my boots on, and I'll use them for a good kicking when I find that Holloway woman."

Victoria at her most stubborn was both maddening and lovable. Annie wondered if she'd be that feisty at her grandmother's age. "Where are you? Specifically."

"Eating at a tacky booth in a dinky restaurant."

Now what? Was she lost somewhere between Colorado and Louisiana? "Gran." There were a dozen things Annie wanted to say, but they would only rile Victoria further and produce no results. "I love you, wherever you are. Please take care."

"I love you too, baby. I'll be there when I get there." Victoria paused, and Annie could hear silver clinking against the side of her plate. "I ran into a speck of trouble."

"What kind of trouble?"

"The kind where you're backing up at Wal Mart, and somebody's truck bumper just jumps out at you. The owner is an old man so mean he ought to be shot."

"Good grief, Gran! Where are you? Somebody needs to come."

Victoria chuckled. "Hank flew in. By the time he gets through straightening out that old man, he'll be shriveled up like a snail somebody doused with salt."

"Who's looking after Rachel's children?"

"They're having the time of their lives. Hank's brothers and their families came to the ranch for Thanksgiving and some of them are still there." Gran made kissing noises then hung up without even saying goodbye.

Annie stared at her cell phone as if it might be the culprit. The only good thing that came of the call was the knowledge that her new brother-in-law would not hesitate to use his private plane when the family needed him. *Good for Rachel!*

The doorbell pinged. *Toni.* Annie raced downstairs to open the door.

Toni grabbed her in a bear hug. "I'm so glad to see you alive I don't know what to do." She stepped back to wipe her eyes. "Crying was not part of my plan."

"You saw Evangeline?"

"Yes. That's why I'm so thrilled to see you healthy and in one piece."

"Toni, you're scaring me. How is she?"

"Still in a coma, but she's going to live."

"That's worth a celebration." Paul came up behind them and slid an arm around Annie. It felt so natural she leaned into the embrace. "Dinner at my house tonight. We'll figure out how we can help Evangeline get through this." He glanced at Toni. "You can bring a guest if you like."


Paul's home in the Marigny blended French and Spanish architecture and nestled among live oaks trees as if it might have rooted there. As Annie and Angel stepped through the wrought iron gates, its nineteenth-century heritage whispered of gaslights and horse-drawn carriages, gloves and beaded gowns, long-lost elegance and faded gentility.

Much to Annie's surprise, Angel had donned a tuxedo from another era for the occasion. "In my day, we always dressed for dinner," he'd said. With his wide satin lapels and red satin cummerbund, he looked as if he might be heading to a Mardi Gras ball in the seventies. His attire, alongside his improved attitude, made him look fifteen years younger.

"Grandfather, you're going to be the best-looking man here."

"I plan to. I'm with the prettiest girl here." Annie was in her white cape and blue Italian silks, the long scarf and palazzo pants flowing around her as she walked. Her single adornment was a diamond clip in her hair. He pointed to a star-studded sky. "Nina, look at me now. I'm in high cotton!"

The respite was a welcome release for Annie. She counted her blessings. She'd had no more threats since she left the bayou, and Evangeline was still alive.

"Angel... Annie." Paul opened the door and took both her hands. His smile was possibly the most endearing one she'd ever seen. "Welcome to my Marigny home."

They were the first to arrive, so he gave them the tour. The inside of his house had the same easy elegance as the outside—banks of windows everywhere that would let in the light every artist needs to function; French doors opening from room to room and onto wrought iron balconies that ran the length of the house upstairs; a courtyard out back with a curving path that led to a secret garden, Annie's childhood dream come true. Moonlight plus lights strung among the tree branches illumi-nated a water fountain and benches tucked among lush green-ery, winter-blooming camellias, and late-blooming roses. A perk of living in the Deep South. There was even a tree swing under-neath a massive live oak, swaying in the breeze that had sprung up with the chill night air coming off the river.

"I used to dream I'd one day have a garden like this," Annie said.

"Sometimes dreams come true, Annie." The look Paul gave her said a thousand things if you were looking for them. She found herself looking. A revelation to her, a sharp turn in the direction she had mapped out for herself.

They went back inside, and Toni, in a simple black cashmere dress, arrived with the kayaker in tow. Annie recognized him as the man who had discovered the second victim in the swamp. A chilling premonition swept through her, as if a dark cloud had suddenly dropped over the group standing in the sparkling light of a chandelier. The horror wasn't done with them yet.

She glanced around the room expecting to see a dark man peering at her through one of the windows, or a rock to come crashing through. Anything at all could happen. The other shoe was getting ready to drop. The gift passed from Delilah told her so. And it was never wrong.

Paul, quick to pick up on her moods, leaned close. "Are you okay?"

"Yes." She smiled to show she meant it. She wasn't about to let the Shadow, or whatever that evil monster wanted to call himself, ruin her evening.

Toni introduced her friend, and Paul greeted him with enthusiasm. "Brick, I've heard your jazz band play on Frenchman's Street. It's great."

"We try." Brick Beaufort was modest, and obviously very talented. Paul was not the kind of man who passed compliments lightly. Annie loved seeing Toni so happy and at ease with a very attractive man who obviously was smitten with her. He even had a cute pet name for her. *Jersey*.

"If you don't already have a manager," Paul said, "I'll be glad to introduce you to a client of mine." With the ease of a man who had once moved in many social circles, Paul led them to the dining room and slid back into the role of a charming host who knew how to make an evening memorable. Annie saw his past billow behind him like smoke then disperse in a puff that left nothing behind except fresh air. She breathed easier with him.

But the sudden dimming of the chandelier and swaying of the curtains whispered of unspeakable things to come.

The Shadow was not done with Annie yet.

FORTY-TWO

When Annie and Angel got home from dinner, he lit the gas logs in his fireplace and settled into a rocking chair. "I always watch the ten o'clock news." With one flick of the remote, he turned the TV on.

Today's news was sure to spoil any mood. Annie hated to let go of the beauty and peace of the evening, but she sank into the rocking chair beside him, anyway.

Linda Holloway bloomed large on the screen. Bright lights picked up a long pier, a curving path, and a raised Louisiana cottage in the background. Angel's house.

Annie's heart sank. The other shoe had dropped.

"I'm Linda Holloway. Tonight, I bring you exclusive, breaking news on the third victim of the Honey Island Swamp murders, Evangeline Aguillard. Reliable sources say she survived the attack by the killer..." A dramatic pause was followed by a faked look of wonder, mixed with worry. "That's right. I said *survived*."

The camera panned outward to reveal a full view of Angel's house and grounds. "Evangeline's location and her condition are undisclosed, *but* what we do know is that she was found at this very location." Photographs of Angel and Annie appeared on the screen. "I'm standing in front the home where Angel Broussard, a retired furniture maker, lives with his famous granddaughter, the watercolorist, Annie Logan. Both are unavailable for comment."

"I'll give her a comment," Angel roared. His face was twisted, livid. "The next time she sets foot on my property without my permission, she'll be looking at the end of a double-barreled shotgun."

"Don't upset yourself." Annie felt the hot breath of the monster Linda Holloway had unleashed. "If you want me to, I'll get Toni to file trespassing charges against her. I'll file defamation charges, too, for pointing a finger at me as a suspect in the murder of those poor girls." Annie hated controversy, and she despised the idea of having to waste time in court when life offered so much joy. But it was time somebody called a halt to Linda Holloway's loose grasp on moral responsibility and her lack of journalistic integrity to report the facts. Even worse, the lies she spread for a very wide audience had turned a killer's sights back to Evangeline, and probably Annie.

"Throw the book at her!" Angel shoved up from his chair so hard it continued rocking. "I'm going to bed. See how she likes *that*."

The news had shrunken him back to a feeble old man. He tottered off, and Annie snapped off the television.

Her cell phone rang. *Jen.* Relief washed through Annie. She couldn't think of anyone she'd rather talk to.

"Annie, I'll be in New Orleans in the morning. Pick me up at the airport at ten. We'll wait for Rachel. She'll be coming in on the red-eye."

"You saw the news?"

"Who didn't? Since that TV witch got you involved, the

swamp murders are now international news with you as the centerpiece. Linda Holloway had better be shaking in her boots. She *does not* want to tangle with your sisters."

# FORTY-THREE

## NEW ORLEANS AIRPORT

Relief poured through Annie when the monitors at the airport announced the arrival of Jen's flight. Shortly, her sister strode through baggage claim, vivid as a light bulb, her natural color high, her signature red sweater coat flying out behind her. "Annie!" Her gold bangles slid along her arm as she swooped in and drew her into a bear hug. "I don't know whether to spank you or kiss you. I might just do both."

"You'll do no such thing." Annie was smiling and crying at the same time. *Nothing* topped the reassurance of having her beloved sisters in her corner.

Jen dragged her back toward the carousel and nabbed her oversized tote. "I'm starving. Let's get something to eat while we wait for Rachel. I want to hear everything about our Broussard kin. Did Angel come with you?"

"No. He's a little bit frail, and I thought it best for him to wait at home. But he knows you're coming."

"And?"

"He's very happy, Jen. You and Rachel are going to love him. The feeling will be mutual." As Annie led them down the street to a small bakery and coffee shop, she studied her sister.

Jen was good at masking her feelings. Always had been. "How do you feel about having a grandfather you never knew?"

"Same as you. Curious, excited, and more than mystified that Mom kept him from us."

"He explained why." Annie told her about Angel and Delilah's disagreement over her marrying Patrick. "He has regretted that."

"Likely he has, but I'll withhold judgement until I see for myself. I'm pretty upset at you, though. Why on earth would you keep Angel and Lucien from us?" Jen ordered coffee and muffins for both of them, and they settled into a table beside the window. The shop was full of travelers with their bags beside their chairs, but the sound of airplanes drowned out their conversations.

Annie toyed with her muffin. "I had hoped to learn the truth before I told you. Maybe we should wait for Rachel so I won't have to go over it twice."

"If I wait another minute, I won't be responsible for what I'll do."

Annie related everything Lucien had told her, as well as what she had learned from Angel, Paul, and even Pete Thibodeaux. Jen took the news with the same neutral expression she had practiced over the years, listening to her patients spill secrets so horrible it would make your hair stand on end.

"That's all I know, so far." Annie cradled her coffee cup as if holding it could anchor her to the version of her life she had always known. "I've really struggled with the idea Mom left a child behind, but the most awful thing has been thinking Jacques Morel might be my father."

Jen waved her arms in dismissal, setting her bracelets atinkle. "You are *Logan*, through and through. DNA tests will prove with ninety-nine percent accuracy that Jacques Morel is *not* your father. DNA testing for siblings is far less conclusive. It will take us a while, but I promise you, we *will* find out what happened in that swamp before you were born. Nobody gets to claim kin with a Logan unless it's true." Jen glanced at her watch. "We'd better get back. Rachel's plane should be landing now."

Back at the airport, they watched as Rachel made a beeline toward them, her hand-tooled cowboy boots clicking smartly on the tile, her buttery colored leather jacket with a hint of fringe announcing her Western roots. She glowed with the happiness of a recent bride and the contentment that had always made her the most easy-going of the sisters. Looking at her, you would never guess she was as fierce as her sisters if you threatened her or those she loved.

The three of them climbed into Angel's convertible with their bags, all talking at once, trying to bridge the gap of years since they had been together. Annie and Rachel both broke the news to Jen that Gran was barreling toward New Orleans in her new red pickup truck.

"Why am I not surprised?" Jen, who rode in the passenger seat, had flung a red scarf over her hair, but it still blew out behind her like a dark flag. As did Rachel's.

"She's had a fender-bender somewhere, but she wouldn't say." Annie glanced in her rearview mirror at Rachel. "Have you heard from Hank?"

"Yes, I called him when I changed planes. They're in Memphis. Everything's okay, nobody's hurt. Gran should be here late tomorrow afternoon. He wanted to fly her down and hire a driver to deliver her truck to Colorado, but she wouldn't hear of it."

"Naturally not," Jen said. "She's tough as nails... and we're all just like her." She leaned over to squeeze Annie's arm. "That includes you."

The shroud of uncertainty that had hung over Annie for so long lifted in the presence of her sisters and dispersed on the crisp winter air as she navigated back toward the Marigny where their grandfather waited.

Angel was sitting on the front porch, his hands shading his eyes, watching. He'd combed and slicked down his silver mane, put on a tie with his white shirt, and polished his shoes to a high shine.

Rachel beamed when she spotted him. "He dressed up for us. Isn't that adorable?"

"Handsome, maybe. Definitely tough." Jen studied Angel while Annie parked the car, and then she turned to Rachel. "But I don't think adorable runs in this family unless it's you."

Angel came down the steps to meet them. "My granddaughters. At last." He opened his arms wide, and Rachel walked right into his embrace. Jen took a wait-and-see stance nearby, a half-smile on her face. "If only Nina could see me now." Angel patted Rachel's face then slid a sly glance Jen's way. "Your momma practiced that look on me. It won't work."

Jen burst into laughter and linked her arm through his. "Intimidation never worked on her, either. I think we must be related."

"Looks like it, Jenny girl."

Jen rolled her eyes, but Annie could tell she liked Angel, and she was more than willing to let him use the nickname she'd never tolerated from anybody else.

As Annie followed her sisters up the steps, she felt a chill along the back of her neck and a tug on her sweater as if unseen fingers had grabbed ahold to pull her backward. She turned and saw Angel's ancient neighbor across the street, sitting on her front porch, her hair tucked into a yellow scarf. She was not alone. Beside her sat a younger woman, a mousy redhead who looked like the librarian from Peal River. The redhead smiled and waved when she saw Annie, as friendly as you please.

What was she doing in the Marigny? Annie lifted her hand to wave then drew it back as if she had been shocked. Evil floated in the air, electrical currents of it flowing down the street as if the entire Creole neighborhood was under siege.

Jen and Rachel both stiffened, then turned to stare across the street. Their faces were suddenly shadowed by their awareness of danger.

"Grandfather." Annie caught up with him at the front door. "Do you know the two women across the street?"

"That's my neighbor, Molly Guidry and her niece, Helen Whitaker. You remember her from the grocery store in Pearl River. They're thick as thieves. Gossipy old biddies, but harmless. They've been sitting together on that porch for years."

Harmless wasn't the word Annie would use to describe them. A fog came out of nowhere and tangled her in its murky depths. Just beyond her reach, the two women rocked, years of envy floating in the air above their heads, their blood flowing hot with accumulated resentment that had finally reached a boiling point. Nothing would stand in their way of finally getting what was owed to them.

Angel's footsteps echoed through the fog, and it slowly lifted. But Annie was still heavy with the weight of her waking dream.

*The gift never lies.*

Danger was all around them.

## FORTY-FOUR

Annie was touched that Angel considered meeting his other granddaughters an occasion for celebration. He had spread his table with a checked cloth and used Nina's fine china to serve up chicory coffee and a cream cake he'd ordered from the bakery. Her sisters noticed, too, and Rachel got teary-eyed.

Though Annie and Jen had eaten muffins at the coffee shop, they piled around the table and dug into the cake. Angel and Rachel had their heads together, looking at pictures of her two children, her new husband, and even her dog Sam. She opened her tote and pulled out photos she had framed.

"These are for you, Grandfather, and an open invitation to the ranch anytime you want to come. We'll send you a ticket. Or Hank can fly out here and get you."

"You are so much like my sweet Nina, I can't even believe it. It's like she's come back to me." He shot another sly glance down the table at Jen. "And you, Jenny girl, are just like me. As solid as a rock, and as stubborn, too."

"That fits."

His face softened. "I know it does, *ma chérie.*"

As if their conversation had conjured it, a rock smashed

through the dining room window, sending glass flying in every direction. A shard caught in Annie's hair, and she glanced anxiously to see if Angel or her sisters had been hurt.

"I'm fine!" Angel roared. "Go get him!"

Jen was already sprinting toward the door with Rachel right behind her. Annie caught up, and the three of them raced after a figure running down the street. Annie caught a glimpse of the two women still on the front porch across from Angel's cottage, Molly Guidry still sitting and Helen Whitaker standing at the railing, watching the figure racing toward an alley. Helen's mouth was moving, but Annie couldn't hear what she said.

"He's trying to get away!" Jen yelled. "Split up! I'll go after him."

Annie and Rachel peeled off in opposite directions, and Jen ramped up her speed to chase the fleeing figure through the alley. He wore a baseball cap and a loose denim jacket. Though he was slight and not very tall, he was fast. Obviously very physically fit. If Jen didn't catch him, hopefully Annie and Rachel would have him blocked on both ends of the street, so he'd have no means of escape.

Annie's height gave her the advantage over Rachel. She rounded the corner first and saw the culprit burst out of the alley and glance her way. He was just a kid! Still, only the guilty ran. He pivoted to run in the other direction, but Rachel burst around the corner, and he paused, undecided.

Jen pounced, grabbing the back of his collar, and spinning him around. "Got you."

He was even younger than Annie had thought, a little boy, no more than ten years old, black frizzy hair curling underneath his baseball cap, defiant dark eyes, and bony fists hanging by his side. He glared at them, one by one, trying to act defensive and brave, but his bottom lip trembled.

"Who sent you to throw that rock?" Jen asked.

"I ain't telling you nothing!"

"I don't think you want me to call the police." Jen said it like she meant it.

Annie didn't know if she had the heart to question him. She wanted to give him cookies and milk. His jacket hung on his scrawny frame as if he had missed more than a few meals.

"I still ain't talking! I ain't scared of no police!"

Jen wavered. Her twins had just turned thirteen. She had a mother's heart and a philanthropist's urge to make the world a better place for little kids like him.

Rachel—the quintessential comforter who not only filled the role for her own two children but for the stream of eight-year-olds who passed through her third-grade class—knelt beside the little boy.

"I bet somebody paid you to toss that rock," she said. The little boy stuck out his chin at Rachel and clamped his mouth into a tight line. "I bet the person who sent you didn't even tell you his name, is that right?" The little boy hesitated, then nodded. *Yes.* "That's what bad people do, but that doesn't mean you're bad."

"You not gonna turn me over to the cops?"

"No," Rachel told him calmly. "You tell us everything you know about this person, and we'll let you go."

"You won't come lookin' for me?"

"We won't."

"Cross your heart and hope to die?" He turned his big-eyed gaze on Rachel, who melted.

"Hey, kid." Annie wasn't about to put Rachel in the position of answering the little boy. Her sister hadn't said *hope to die* since her first husband died fighting for his country. "I cross my heart and hope to die," Annie said. "And they do, too."

"I dunno." He glared at all of them. "There's three of you."

"We all promise, kid." Jen glared right back at him. "Now, start talking."

"You ain't as nice as she is." He pointed to Rachel.

"That's right, kid." Jen was losing patience. "Spill it before I change my mind."

Rachel shot Jen a look that she ignored, but the little boy was already talking. "It was a big man, 'bout the size of a grizzly bear, I s'pect. He was scary as all git-out. *Hey, boy, wanna make a buck?* He pulled this big ol' dollar bill outta his pocket and laid it on me. All I done was throw the rock he give me. I ain't no criminal."

"Besides being big, what did he look like?" Jen asked. "What color hair did he have? Did he have a beard? What was he wearing?"

"He wore a baseball cap, same as me. No beard. Kinda funny-soundin' when he talked. I dunno nothing else."

Annie thought of the red-haired woman on the porch. "Was anyone else with him? A woman, maybe?"

"No. Ain't nobody there but hisself."

"You're sure about that?" Annie said. "You didn't see any other people nearby, maybe a woman with red hair."

"I dunno." The little boy looked down at the ground and rubbed the toe of his sneaker on the pavement. "Maybe. They's lots a folks in N'Awlins."

Rachel was still kneeling by the child. "Where did you see the man who gave you money?" Her face and voice were so gentle, the little boy smiled at her. It transformed him from defiant criminal-in-the-making to innocent kid wishing he was on a baseball field or on a sliding board in the park. Anywhere but standing at the edge of an alley with three sisters determined to discover the truth.

"'Round yonder at the park close to where that ol' man with the white hair lives. I was playing ball with my buddy Jonesy when he come along and offered me a dollar. Can I go now?"

"You have to promise something first." Rachel adjusted the little boy's baseball cap and cupped his cheeks. "Promise me you won't throw any more rocks—not at the white-haired old man's house or anybody's house. Okay?"

"'Kay."

"And promise you won't let anybody talk you into doing things that are wrong. I want you to grow up to be a great man."

"Cross my heart and hope to die." He studied Rachel a while, then leaned in to give her a hug and whisper in her ear. "Maybe I'll be Pres'dent one day. You can come see me in that great big ol' White House."

"I will." Rachel reached into her pocket and handed him a lollipop. He grabbed it then raced off down the street, while Jen observed with a bemused expression. "You know I always keep them in my pocket," Rachel told her with a smile.

"Big softie." Jen turned to watch the little boy disappearing down the street. "I don't think he was telling the truth."

"I don't think so, either," Annie added. "Did you see his face when I asked about a red-haired woman?"

"He could have been lying," Rachel agreed. "But he could have just been scared. My third-graders sometimes look guilty when they're scared. What I want to know is why would anybody throw a rock at Angel's house? He's such a sweet old man."

"Because they're after me," Annie said, and her sister studied her, dumbfounded.

Jen was the first to recover. "Are you saying the swamp killer is after you?"

"I don't know. Maybe." Annie gave a rundown on the text messages and notes, the dead animals and the voodoo doll planted by her stalker while Jen's face became more and more thunderous. "The description the little boy gave fits the man I believe has been stalking me. And he could possibly be the killer."

"Angel's alone!" Jen broke free and raced off toward the cottage with Annie and Rachel keeping pace beside her.

## FORTY-FIVE

As they approached their grandfather's cottage, Annie stopped, panting.

"Wait. The killer is only targeting young women. We don't want to upset Angel by racing in there with our fear hanging out."

Even as she spoke, a waking nightmare hit her. Danger wafted from the cottage like steam from a teakettle.

"You're right, Annie, but look at *that*." Jen pointed to a flock of black birds gathering in the magnolia tree in the front yard. "We're in the presence of evil."

"Black crows!" Rachel gasped. "And I smell magnolias everywhere!" There was not a magnolia flower in sight. Even in the Deep South, they didn't bloom later than September.

The sisters joined hands against the warnings from their mother's gift. Jen finally broke the spell. "Listen, we are *not* going to let the Shadow, or whatever he wants to call himself, win. I don't intend to lose my grandfather the day I found him."

Annie watched her older sister erase her frown and push open the door with a smile on her face. It died the minute they walked into the front room.

There sat Molly Guidry and Helen Whitaker, rocking away in the chairs in front of the fire. Angel was nowhere in sight. Fog swirled around Annie, damp and pervasive, carrying the stench you would only find in hospitals... or the morgue.

Annie fought her way back from her waking vision, her heart hammering in her chest, and her mouth dry. "Where's Grandfather?"

"Don't you worry, dear." Helen leaped out of her chair—spry for a woman her age—and patted Annie's arm. Her touch burned like fire. "We saw the commotion over here, and came to sit with him."

"He was very agitated." Molly's smile was ghoulish. "We gave him some tea and put him to bed." She pushed out of her chair while Rachel raced off in the direction of Angel's bedroom. "You should be glad we're here. Bad things can happen when you're not looking."

Molly trotted toward the door, followed by Helen. Jen pushed between them and caught both of them by the arms. Her smile was possibly as scary as Molly's.

"We wouldn't think of letting you go back by yourselves, would we, Annie? Not after everything you've done for us today."

"Absolutely not." Annie grabbed a firm hold on Helen Whitaker's other arm. No way could she get loose from the two of them. "We'll see you safely into your home. You never know what's waiting for you. As you said, bad things can happen when you're not looking."

She and Jen almost frog-marched the nosey little old ladies back across the street.

When they came to the front steps, Helen balked. "Thank you for the escort." She didn't look thankful at all. To Annie, she looked a little bit scared. Or was it guilty? "We can take it from here."

"We wouldn't think of it." Jen used her most authoritative

voice, one designed to keep her uncooperative patients in line. "We're coming in with you, aren't we, Annie?"

"Absolutely." She tightened her hold on Helen. "We wouldn't think of letting you face an empty house with a killer on the loose."

Molly was suddenly too confused or possibly too scared to say a thing. She began muttering that she forgot her key, and they might have to call somebody to get them in. Maybe even the police. Annie plucked a hairpin from her thick mane and slid it into the lock.

"Where'd you learn that?" Jen said.

"Toni. She knows all kinds of interesting things."

Jen refrained from comment. Though she had moved on from the episode last spring, she would keep her distance from anybody who threatened her or her family. That's just the way she was. Annie made a mental note to keep the two of them apart as much as she could. It would be uncomfortable for both Toni and Jen.

Annie jiggled the hairpin until she felt the lock give. She pushed open the door then froze. The sight that greeted her was almost as terrifying as finding Evangeline in the swamp.

"Voodoo dolls!" Jen swept past her and began snapping pictures with her cell phone.

Helen and Molly raced around the room, snatching up dolls, but not before Annie spotted one with red yarn woven through her long dark hair and a pin sticking out of the red heart stitched over her chest. The green button eyes stared back at her.

"What are you two doing, practicing voodoo?" Annie blocked the door so neither of the women could bolt. Not that they could ever outrun her. A vision of the voodoo doll twisting in the storm at Angel's swamp house roared through her, and she felt the winds of evil.

"These are our crafts." Helen tossed all the dolls into a large sewing basket and slammed the lid shut. "Molly's a vital part of the ladies' circle at my library. I come here once a month to take her back to Pearl River. We take great pride in studying the crafts of all different cultures."

"That's right. I know about the spirits." Molly adjusted her yellow scarf, which had gone askew in the march across the street. "You need to go home now so I can rest. I don't know how much longer I can protect your grandfather. There's some strong black magic at work around here."

"That's right," Helen added. "You girls be careful now."

Annie and Jen linked arms and walked out as one. They didn't speak until they were halfway across the street.

"Jen, did you see the voodoo doll meant for me?"

"Saw it and got a photo, too. If those two are involved in the threats against you, they won't get away with it."

Rachel met them at the door. "Come and see what's under Angel's bed."

"Is he okay?" Annie asked.

"Yes. I checked his pulse, and his color is natural. I don't think they drugged him, if that's what you're thinking." Rachel slipped on rubber gloves she'd brought from the kitchen, then knelt to retrieve a small, smelly bag from under the bed. "I wanted you to see it before I bag it."

"It's a *gris gris* bag," Jen said. "Early cultures used them for protection, but through the years they became used for black magic. Bag and get it out of the house."

"Where?" Rachel held the bag at arm's length.

"Angel's car." Annie fished the keys out of her pocket. "We'll lock it in the trunk."

"You need to see this first." Rachel reached onto the bedside table with her free hand for a note sealed in a plastic bag. "This was wrapped around the rock that came through the window."

*Haven't you had enough yet? GO HOME... or this time Evangeline dies.*

"Are you serious?" Horrified, Jen grabbed the bag. "Annie, what on earth is going on here?"

"My stalker is still tracking me," Annie said. *But how?* It would have been easy in the swamp to sit on the water in a boat and watch her comings and goings. But here? Annie closed her eyes and Angel's old Thunderbird swirled through the mists, taking the curves to Pearl River, the black car following; navigating the way back to the Marigny, the rocks still crashing the windows no matter where she went. Suddenly, she knew. "There must be a tracking device on Angel's car!"

She raced out the door with her sisters behind her, and they scoured the antique Thunderbird. Jen found the device tucked behind the back bumper.

Annie placed a call to Sheriff Harold Debeau to report her whereabouts and recent events in the Marigny. "Be careful," he told her. "We have reason to believe the killer will try to silence Evangeline after somebody leaked that she was alive to that reporter. It looks like you're in jeopardy, too. The connections between your stalker and the Honey Island Swamp murders are lining up."

"Do you have any idea who is leaving all these notes and dead animals to scare me?"

"So far, we've only found partial prints. Whoever is behind this is smart. I'm going to have police protection put on you."

Within minutes, he'd sent the FBI and the New Orleans PD to the Marigny. Rachel went back inside to stay with Angel in case he woke up, while Jen and Annie gave their reports and handed over the evidence, including the photos of voodoo dolls Jen sent to them from her phone.

In the cottage across the street, the curtains lifted and two faces pressed to the windows, watching.

FORTY-SIX

It was late afternoon when Paul drove past the Broussard cottage on his way to the airport. He was relieved to see four silhouettes through Angel's open curtains and his ancient car sitting in the driveway. That meant Annie had picked up her sisters and arrived home safely.

His relief was almost palpable. Whether that was fear of the threat to her from the Shadow or his own dread that he could lose the people he cared about in a heartbeat, he didn't know.

He parked his car in the airport's lot and went inside to meet Evangeline's mother. Because of the leak, Evangeline had been moved to a secret and heavily guarded location within the huge hospital complex. No one would have access to her except the doctors, specially appointed nurses, and her mother, Estelle Aguillard Riley Walker Demoville.

She was waiting for him in the baggage claim section, a petite woman whose most attractive qualities were her charm and the warmth in her big brown eyes.

Paul knew it was all fake. Through the years he'd watched as this cold, selfish woman kept Evangeline at arm's length while she pursued her own pleasure. He'd often seen his treasured employee at her desk crying after a telephone conversation with Estelle. That's why he had asked Toni to meet him at the hospital after he picked Estelle up at the airport. He didn't want to spend any more time alone with her than he had to.

Estelle's visit to the hospital was a carefully coordinated, clandestine operation. He and Estelle went through a back entrance, out of sight of the news vans parked near the front, and two plainclothes policemen in business attire were waiting.

Toni was already inside. The two of them were led to a private waiting area, and Estelle was whisked off in another direction. Finally, Paul could breathe again.

"Coffee?" Toni said, and he nodded. She poured two Styrofoam cups from the carafe on the table in the corner and handed him one. "She strikes me as a cold fish. Will she even tell us Evangeline's condition when she comes back?"

"I think so, yes." He took a long swig of his coffee and waited for the warmth to spread through him. The police cars and FBI van he'd seen at Angel's cottage had ratcheted up his worry. "Have you talked to Annie today?"

"Yes, right before I left to come here." She gave him a rundown of the two sisters' arrival and the events that had brought the law to Angel's door. "They're putting police surveillance on Angel's cottage."

The news should have relieved Paul's mind, but it didn't. The puzzle of murder and intrigue was scattered in so many directions, he didn't see how it was possible to put all the pieces together. And he found that he cared more deeply than he'd ever imagined.

"I would sleep in the cottage on the sofa until this is resolved, but I want Annie to have the time she needs with her sisters." Paul met Toni's scrutiny head on. There was no use pretending with her. He gave her a little nod. *Yes.* "Annie's that important to me, and I know how close she is with her sisters. The problem of Lucien's parentage involves them, too."

"I know. I feel the same way. I'm trying to help Annie find Delphine, but it's as if she vanished off the face of the earth."

"Annie might have to give up the search..."

"She won't," Toni said. "It's not in her DNA to quit."

Estelle came back into the room, leaning heavily on one of the plainclothes men, her eyes red-rimmed. Toni jumped up. "What happened? Is she okay?"

"They cut off her foot!" Estelle wailed. "She can never wear high heels again!"

Paul couldn't believe his ears, and Toni looked as if she wanted to smack the woman.

"Estelle," he said, "how is she, otherwise?"

"She can't talk." Estelle brought her handkerchief to her face and sobbed.

"You have to control yourself," Paul told her. Since the leak, news vans were parked outside the front of every hospital in New Orleans, and he didn't know how many of them were enterprising enough to sneak around to the back. He walked over and patted her on the shoulder. "An emotional display will tip off reporters. We can't jeopardize Evangeline like that."

"All right." Estelle held both hands in front of her face as if she were warding off pesky insects. Miraculously, her tears quickly vanished. "I can be brave." This woman made everything about herself.

He put his hand on Toni's arm to hold her in check. "Estelle." Toni all but barked the woman's name. "What did the doctor's say about Evangeline? Word for word."

"They don't know when she will come out of her coma. But she's improving every day and should eventually recover completely. She will be fitted with a prosthetic..." Her lips trembled. "...f-f-foot." Estelle shot a challenging glance at Toni as if to say, *Satisfied?*

Paul couldn't wait to get this woman back to her hotel. She would be heavily guarded in case the killer tried to get to Evangeline through her. After today, he could consider his job with Estelle done. He had more important things than babysitting her.

Keeping Evangeline and Annie safe from the Shadow topped his list.

Toni shucked the business suit she'd worn to the hospital and dressed in jeans, a hoodie, and sneakers. Then she headed toward the elevators up the hall from her apartment and rode three floors down without thinking twice. Let Paul be noble. There was no way Toni was going to deliver the latest news about Evangeline over her cell phone.

She unlocked her bicycle and headed toward Angel's cottage. So... she would now encounter Jen Logan Turner, the woman whose husband she had tried to steal last spring. It seemed so far in the distant past that the memory of it was little more than a small blot in Toni's mind. She knew with a dead certainty that she was no longer the deluded woman who had temporarily ditched her upbringing, her principles, and her common sense to go after Benjamin Turner.

Better to face Jen head on, than shove it under the rug. It would lie there like a dead rat where it would eventually stink up everything between Toni and the Logan family, including her friendship with Annie. She refused to risk that, even if she had to face her own culpability again, as well as Jen's wrath.

The night had turned colder, and a stiff breeze whipped the

tops of trees as Toni pedaled through the Marigny. She was thankful her hood was up, and that she probably looked like a boy. For the first time that evening, it occurred to her that the killer was somewhere out there, and that she was one of his targets. In hindsight, she should have driven her car. Or asked Brick to take her.

Thinking of him, she smiled. While she'd been paying attention to other things, he had quietly slid into her life and became the other half of a twosome. She was already planning a big Christmas dinner with Brick at her table. She thought Mimi would approve. She might even get her grandmother to fly down from New Jersey.

Toni breathed a sigh of relief when Angel's cottage came into view. She parked her bicycle and rang the doorbell. It wasn't Annie who came to the door, but Jen. For a heartbeat, she stared at Toni as if the walking dead had landed on the front porch. Toni pulled back her hood and let Jen have her moment. It wasn't up to her to set the mood of this meeting. She was the wrongdoer. Not Jen.

Voices drifted through the doorway, Annie's musical one blending with another female voice so like hers it could only be the other sister, Rachel. Still, Jen studied Toni, her face a mask that gave away nothing.

Finally, Jen said, "You have courage. I'll give you that." Toni nodded in agreement, giving the other woman complete control. "I appreciated your letter," Jen added, "and I know you've been a good friend to Annie. I've put the past behind me."

"I have, too."

"Good." Jen's color was high, and she wore a half smile when she opened the door wide. "Come in." She led Toni into the front room where Annie and Rachel waited. All the sisters looked startlingly alike except for the eyes and hair. "Look who's here."

Annie jumped out of her chair to embrace Toni and whisper in her ear. "Are you okay?"

"You bet." Toni didn't realize she'd had a two-ton elephant of guilt sitting on her chest until Jen had removed it with a simple act of forgiveness. Toni took a seat and drank tea with the Logan sisters as if she were one of them. She told them the good news about Evangeline, and they brought her up to speed about the strange events going on next door. "That Pearl River librarian keeps popping up in the strangest places," Toni said. "Everything in my work at the DA's office tells me that's no coincidence."

"I agree," Annie said. "All the law enforcement agencies involved are aware of it, and I'm sure they're checking that lead." Her cell phone rang, and she excused herself to walk into the kitchen and answer it.

Rachel took up the slack in the conversation by asking Toni how she liked living in New Orleans and explaining how she'd always wanted to come and try the beignets and café au lait her mother used to talk about.

"We can make that happen tomorrow, right after work," Toni said. "I'll meet all of you there. Annie knows the place."

"What place?" Annie was back, her cell phone still in her hand, her face a study in barely suppressed excitement.

"Café du Monde," Toni told her. Then she saw the look on Annie's face. "Wait, what's up?"

"That was Honey LaBelle. She wants to meet me tomorrow at her apartment. I think she has a good lead on Delphine."

FORTY-EIGHT

As talk of Delphine swirled around her, Annie's eagerness slowly gave way to a creeping sense of trepidation. She kept battling against a dark vision that wanted to consume her—fog, a dilapidated shack, a stunning sense of loss.

When Toni announced it was time to leave, Annie insisted on driving her home. "You shouldn't be out there alone in the dark," she told her.

"I don't want you out at night, either. I'll call Brick to pick me up."

Even that news, as well as Toni's excitement when Brick arrived to take her and her bicycle home, couldn't entirely lift the fog from Annie. After she and her sisters cleaned up the tea things and headed off to bed, she opened her laptop to check her social media. And there it was, the source of her fear.

Three pretty girls, thinking they have won. Along came the Shadow, and then there were none.

Annie grabbed her laptop and went across the hall to the

bedroom her sisters shared. Their voices drifted to her, and she tapped on the door. "It's me."

"Annie?" Jen swung the door open. "You look like you've just seen a ghost."

"Worse." She perched on the bed where Rachel was sitting and opened her laptop to show the post. "My stalker is the killer, and now he's after all of you, too. It's all my fault."

"You are *not* going there." Jen sat down on the other side of Annie, and both sisters put their arms around her.

"Absolutely not," Rachel added. "We knew we were walking into danger, and we would do it again for you."

"From now on, we stick together," Jen said. "Whoever this evil coward is, he does *not* want to tangle with us."

FORTY-NINE

THE FRENCH QUARTER

The next morning, Annie and her sisters headed to the French Quarter after breakfast with their grandfather to find Honey LaBelle.

Her apartment was above a strip club on Bourbon Street. Annie found a parking spot for the car, and shortly she stood with her sisters on the sidewalk, at war with her own feelings. Above them was a swinging sign with TOOTSIE'S JOINT painted in large letters.

They had left Angel alone in his cottage with strict instructions not to open the door to strangers and especially not the two batty women across the street. "Alert the police outside the cottage at any sign of trouble," Rachel had told him, and Jen had added, "Do you have a weapon?"

"Jenny girl, I was born knowing how to take care of myself. Go and find out who is the father of Delilah's babies. If it's that skunk, Jacques Morel, I plan to give him a tongue-lashing he won't ever forget."

As Annie stood beneath Honey LaBelle's apartment, her heart rejected any father except Patrick Logan.

"Ready?" she said to her sisters, and they both gave her the thumbs-up sign.

Jen added, "No matter what the LaBelle woman tells us, we can handle it. We're all warrior women. Remember that, Annie."

They went through a side door to the strip joint and up the narrow staircase, single file. Honey's apartment wasn't hard to find. It was the third door on the left that featured a hand-painted sign decorated with red hearts and silver tinsel. Her name was written large in ornate script with pink paint.

"If the inside is like the outside, I'll need these." Jen whipped on her sunglasses, while Annie and Rachel covered their mouths to suppress giggles. It was almost like being a child again, with their older sister finding ways to make them laugh after they had lost both parents.

"Take them off before we go inside," Rachel said. "You won't want to hurt her feelings."

"Honey seems like the kind of woman who will appreciate the glamor," Annie said. "It would be even better if the frames had rhinestones." She punched the buzzer, and Honey, herself, appeared at the door, awash in feathers and rhinestones, dazzling in a swooping neon pink caftan. Her brassy blond curls were arranged in a beehive, and teetered on her head like a bird-cage. Annie introduced herself and her sisters.

"Come in!" Honey swept an arm loaded with rhinestone bangles toward a room with so much fringe on the lampshades and curtains that Annie picked her way toward a plush blue velvet sofa, careful not to get tangled up and fall. "I've made my special brand of tea. Sweetened with honey, of course." With a broad grin that transformed her face from ordinary to warm and pleasing, Honey LaBelle grabbed a tarnished silver pot and began to pour her tea into four delicate silver-rimmed cups. "It's not often I get to entertain real ladies."

Annie had a sudden vision of a lonely woman putting her

body on public display, the crowd around her hooting and hollering, while she longed for a real connection with women who led ordinary lives. She smiled at Honey warmly. "My sisters and I love tea. It's a ritual in the family."

"We certainly do," Jen said, her high-wattage personality on full display. "And we are so grateful you let us all come here today. Obviously, Annie's paternity affects all of us."

"Naturally." Honey LaBelle settled back against her velvet wing chair, sipping her tea, in no hurry to move the meeting along. "I don't know how much help I can be, but I'm just thrilled to meet all Delilah's daughters. Y'all look a lot like your mama. But I guess you already know that."

Annie exchanged glances with her sisters. Not a single one would rush this woman so they could leave and track down whatever lead she could provide. Annie loved that about her family. Their compassion. Their patience. The way they made genuine connections to the people who came into their lives, no matter what the circumstances.

"That's wonderful to hear, Miss LaBelle." Rachel was always the one with the most manners. "We're eager to find out what happened to our mother that year she came to the bayou and returned with baby Annie. We are most appreciative of anything you can tell us that might be helpful."

There it was. Rachel's gentle nudge. Annie didn't know if she could have pulled it off, and she suspected that Jen certainly couldn't have.

"If anybody would know, it's Delphine Thierry. She had her finger on the pulse of Honey Island Swamp." Honey took her time setting down her teacup and blotting her hot pink lipstick with an embroidered linen napkin. "They say she's dead. But if anybody would know for sure, it's Vincenzo Poretto."

"Great." Jen whipped a pen and pad from her purse. "Is he still in this area, and do you know where we can find him?"

"I know, all right." Honey LaBelle made the sign of the cross over her heart. "But, if I was you, I'd be careful about messing with him."

"Why?" As always, Jen was blunt and to the point.

"Rumor has it he used to be part of the Carlos Marcello crime family. They were in racketeering, illegal gambling, and conspiracy. They were even investigated in President Kennedy's assassination."

"This is serious." Rachel set down her own teacup, her face sober.

"You've got that right, kiddo." Honey shot her a sympathetic look. "If I was in your shoes, I'd go on with my life and forget about digging around in Delilah's past. Let the dead stay buried."

"You said *used to be*." Annie was already up to her neck in murder. She wasn't about to stop now. "What's Vincenzo Poretto like today?"

"Word is, the New Orleans Mafia died out, and those that were left went legit. Vinnie owns a large real estate firm and several fine restaurants in New Orleans and the surrounding area. The most popular is Vinnie's, up in the swanky Garden District. If you're dead set on finding him, that's the first place to look. They say he's there every day at lunch with his favorite aunt, like clockwork. But only in wintertime. He and his family travel all summer."

Jen took notes while Honey gave them the address of the restaurant and described the owner. Before they left, Rachel exchanged personal addresses with Honey and promised to send Christmas cards and pictures of her children.

Annie thanked her and hugged her close, but she made no promises. She saw Honey LaBelle surrounded by the dark shroud of death. The cigarettes she smoked had already darkened her lungs with cancer that spread like wildfire. She wouldn't last long beyond Christmas.

# FIFTY

## THE GARDEN DISTRICT

Annie's heart was heavy as she and her sister's left Honey LaBelle's house and piled into Angel's convertible to head toward the Garden District. It was a beautiful day for driving, one of those warm, sunshiny days that can fool you into thinking the icy fingers of winter wouldn't dare lay a hand on the city.

"Has anybody heard from Gran today?" Annie followed her phone's GPS directions down an avenue shaded by live oaks and magnolia trees, filled with mansions set in lush gardens awash with greenery and bloom.

"I sent her a text but heard nothing," Rachel said. "Hank said she was fine when he left this morning, and excited about seeing us this evening. She'll be okay." She twisted to look at her surroundings. "This is gorgeous. No wonder Mom kept coming back."

"Now we know why she never brought us," Jen said. "She was hiding too many secrets."

The residential neighborhood gave way to a commercial section filled with old buildings and charm. A sign bearing the name VINNIE'S came into view. It hung over a door painted with black lacquer and flanked by gaslights. The building was red brick, aged by time and seasoned by history, sitting discreetly in the middle of a block of equally tasteful shops and eateries.

Parking was on a small, paved lot in the back. Annie found a slot for the convertible, and they sat there a moment, second-guessing their decision.

"Maybe we should have called first," Rachel said. "Honey LaBelle could be wrong about Vincenzo Poretto's habits."

"My hunch is that she's right," Jen told her. "If we had called, I don't think he would have talked to all three of us." She pointed to a tree in the corner of the lot where blackbirds had begun to gather. "You see that? Danger is here and more is heading our way. That means we're on the right track."

The sight of the birds made Annie shiver. Jen getting signs from Nature doubled the impact of Annie's warnings. Something momentous and horrible waited for them. Was it inside the restaurant or lurking somewhere they couldn't see?

"I'll take the lead," Annie said. "If Vincenzo knows anything about Delphine, he'll know she predicted my return."

They all agreed, and headed inside. Impressions bombarded Annie. Old wood paneling and white linen tablecloths. Candles in crystal holders, a single red rose on each table, a violinist in the corner playing Bach. Wealthy female patrons in pearls and diamonds scattered among tables widely spaced for privacy. A couple of tables filled with businessmen in suits. The air was heavy with secrets... and something else that sent icy chills along the back of her neck.

Annie's attention was drawn to a table for two in the back, near the swinging doors to the kitchen. A small, elegant woman sat with both hands on her teacup, her gaze fixed on Annie, her black eyes piercing. She had burgundy colored hair, cropped short and stylishly mussed, diamond studs in her ears, and a silver ring with a large ruby on one hand. She wore a smart robin's egg blue designer suit with a ruffled white blouse, and her tiny feet were encased in blue velvet Mary Janes.

*I see you.*

The woman's thought seared through Annie with the force of a branding iron. A waitress in a black and white uniform said, "Follow me," but Annie had a hard time looking away from the woman in the corner. "Is this table all right?" the waitress asked.

It was out of sight of the strangely compelling women. "We would like that one." Annie pointed to an empty table for four that was closer to the ancient woman then settled into a chair facing her. She and her sisters decided to order the rich dishes typical of New Orleans and were soon in diner's paradise with stuffed eggplant with river shrimp, strawberry glazed pork loin, and Cajun ratatouille.

"I have a feeling." Annie leaned close to murmur to her sisters. "Pay close attention to the woman in the blue suit."

"We have to be careful," Jen whispered. "Look at the shadows on the window..." Blackbirds were gathering, their wings outspread, as if they intended to peck out the glass and come inside.

Patrons drifted to the old woman's table, both male and female, sometimes alone, often in groups of three or four. Snatches of their conversation drifted Annie's way.

"Maria, how nice to see you."

"Maria, I love your new hair color."

"Are you keeping that nephew of yours in line?"

"*Do* come to our Christmas party, Maria. I'm going to insist that Vinnie and Paula bring you."

Rachel leaned in close. "The owner's aunt?"

"I don't think so..."

The woman they called Maria looked so different from Honey LaBelle's description of the owner, she couldn't possibly be a blood relative. Annie swept her gaze over the restaurant, searching for any sign of Vincenzo Poretto. Honey had said he was tall and physically fit, a dark eyed, dark haired man with streaks of gray at his temples that emphasized a large Roman nose. He was nowhere in sight. Were they too early? Too late? Maybe Honey was wrong about him coming every day.

When Annie turned back to the tiny woman called Maria, she only saw an empty table. "Where did she go?"

"I didn't see," Jen said. "A group of people were surrounding her table, and when they left, she was gone."

"Something's off here," Rachel said. "Does anybody else smell magnolias?" Annie and Jen shook their heads. There was not a magnolia blossom in sight in the restaurant, and no one was wearing the popular Deep South scent as a perfume. The heady scent was cloying, and would have been easily detected. "I thought not," Rachel added. "The danger is getting closer. We should be very careful."

"Maybe we should go?" Annie glanced around, searching for the all-too-familiar sight of her nemesis, a swarthy man in a baseball cap. "I don't like putting the two of you at risk."

"We're not quitters." Jen signaled to the waitress. "Let's order dessert and see what happens."

They were well into their bread pudding with Southern pecans when a tall, elegant man appeared at their table, his smile stretched wide beneath a Roman nose, the silver wings in his hair shining in the glow of candlelight. Unmistakably Vincenzo Poretto.

"Welcome, ladies. Are you enjoying your meal?"

"Enormously." Jen gave him an equally broad and bold smile. "It's a culinary experience."

"I'm glad you find it so." He turned to Annie. "If I'm not mistaken, you're the famous artist from my home country, Annie Logan."

"Yes, I'm Annie. I hope you'll attend my showing at Green Oak Gallery."

"I'm a great lover of art, and so is my aunt. Would you mind accompanying me to my office? It would be a great honor if my aunt could meet you and get your autograph. She's your most ardent admirer."

Vincenzo had the kind of voice that could be projected at will. His invitation lost all sinister undertones when other patrons heard it and turned toward Annie's table to smile. He smiled back at them, obviously a successful man who knew exactly how to achieve the desired results. He wanted Annie to feel at ease.

Jen noticed, too, and nodded at Annie. Her way of saying, nothing was going to happen in broad daylight in the office of an upscale restaurant filled with patrons and two sisters ready to leap into battle.

"Certainly," Annie said. Still, the air felt electric, and she caught a chilling glimpse of green water and an isolated shack.

Her vision vanished as she followed Vincenzo Poretto into a large office with narrow windows set high on the wall so no one could see inside. The furniture was leather, large and masculine, dwarfing the tiny woman who sat in a wing chair in a grouping of chairs and a sofa opposite a six-foot desk. She had shed her jacket, and the stark white of her blouse contrasted sharply with a face as wizened and dark as a chestnut. Her feet rested on a footstool and a large sheaf of letters lay in her lap, tied with a faded yellow ribbon.

She studied Annie in silence. Finally, she said, "I've waited years for you to come back."

# FIFTY-ONE



As Annie sank into a chair opposite the old woman, there was no doubt in her mind that she was face to face with Delphine Thierry. Still, she waited. Why would a woman who had had gone to great lengths to stay dead suddenly reveal herself to Annie? Why would a man, reputed to have once been part of the New Orleans Mafia, permit her to know the identity of the woman he had obviously protected for years?

"Miss Logan, you are wise to remain silent." Vincenzo Poretto sat on the leather sofa, spreading his arms along the back, a confident man at ease with himself. "Your expression tells me you know who this is. Yes?" Annie nodded. "Smart girl. Aunt Maria said you would be." The emphasis he put on *Aunt Maria* was a clear warning to Annie not to speak the name Delphine Thierry.

"What are the rules here?" Annie could be just as bold as Vincenzo.

"This room is soundproof. Nothing spoken here can be heard. If one word of this conversation is ever repeated, except to Rachel Logan Maxey Carson of Manitou Springs and Jennifer Logan Turner of Gulf Breeze, all of three of you and your entire family—including the children, Jen's and Rachel's spouses, and your grandmother, Victoria Logan—will disappear. Angel Broussard, and your friend, Toni Delgado, will also vanish." His thorough knowledge of her family and friends was sobering. He steepled his fingers and moderated the threat with a genuine smile. "I say this without malice. Though I am now a mere businessman, I guarantee you that I can still do exactly what I say."

"I understand. You're as fearlessly protective of your aunt as I am of my own family."

"Precisely. Aunt Maria's life depends on your silence." He nodded his approval. "The only reason you are here is that she says you will never reveal her identity beyond your sisters. Her predictions are never wrong. I've built an empire because of them. Without her, I would be behind bars. She protected me, and I protect her." He studied Annie for a long while. "My word is my bond."

"So is mine. I won't tell a soul, except my two sisters, what is said here today. And you can count on their discretion."

"Good. I'll leave the rest to you and Aunt Maria." He leaned back, seemingly at ease. But he had the look of a tiger, capable of eviscerating his foe with one swipe of his claws, watching to see if the need arose.

The question Annie had been waiting to ask the Swamp Witch burst from her. "Is Lucien Morel my twin brother?"

"Yes." The truth took Annie's breath away. "I brought both of you into the world. You first, squalling like a banshee, and then Lucien, quiet as a little mouse." The old woman's face gave away nothing, but sorrow and regret rose from her in waves that swirled between them like smoke. "We could play question and answer all day, but let me tell you a true story."

"I want to know everything." Annie settled back to listen, the truth of her brother already taking root in her heart, the question of her father burning through her like wildfire.

"And so you shall." Delphine Thierry shifted her feet on the stool, and hunched her shoulders as if she were lifting off a burden that had bent her almost to the ground. "I loved Delilah like my own child, but I loved Jacques Morel, too. He was a needy child with an abusive drunk for a father and a weakling for a mother. I tried to fill the gap for him, but he was impatient, impulsive, and obsessive. There was something dark in him, too. I always saw it but overlooked it out of love. His biggest obsession was your mother. He spent his whole life trying to attract her favor, even after she married Patrick Logan."

It wasn't lost on Annie that Delphine spoke of her love for Jacques in the past tense. What had happened to make that change?

"Besides Vincenzo, Jacques was my biggest fan and supporter, always bringing new customers my way, spreading the word about me until I became the famous Swamp Witch. I owed Jacques. I think he even staged a fire in Slidell to make me more famous." She smiled at her benefactor. "I owe Vincenzo my very life."

Vincenzo acknowledged her with a gracious nod, and Delphine continued her story. "That summer when your mother came to the swamp, Jacques asked me for a love charm. I knew who it was for. Charms don't take away free will. They're more about the power of suggestion. I thought Delilah would rebuff him again, and he'd get her out of his system. I even sent Pete Thibodeaux to protect her if things got out of hand."

"Where did Jacques and Pete take my mother?"

"There's a clearing in the swamp with a little love shack where the young and the foolish go to practice their own kind of black magic. They build bonfires and drink bad liquor and sometimes even handle snakes. They know nothing of voodoo, but they practice their version of the rituals, anyhow."

This was a recipe for disaster. "Why did my mother go? She

had a family at home, and her gift would have told her trouble was brewing."

"Friendship is one of the strongest connections we have, and she always trusted Pete. That night Delilah rebuffed Jacques, just as I knew she would. Pete got drunk, thinking that was the end of it, and Jacques seized his chance to use a date-rape drug. Then Delilah became pregnant."

A vision stole over Annie—her mother, young, vibrant, beautiful, dancing naked in front of a fire, reeling from the drug, the world swimming in and out of focus, the crowd around her oblivious, the man at her side catching her as she falls. The two on the bed, entangled, hidden behind mosquito netting, Jacques dreaming of a glorious future with the woman of his dreams, Delilah drifting on a fog, transposing red hair and an Irish brogue onto the man with her. And then the awakening. The terror. The gut-wrenching realization. The soul-stealing remorse.

The vision dissolved, leaving behind a taste as bitter as vinegar in Annie's mouth. She wanted to take her mother in her arms and comfort her. The idea of Jacques as a father was repulsive. The idea of being only half-sisters to Jen and Rachel was unthinkable.

The Swamp Witch studied her, her eyes bright. "I see you have your mother's gift."

"Yes. So do my sisters."

"Good. With the gift comes the habit of secrecy." Delphine nodded her approval, then continued with her story. "When Delilah showed up at my house months later, she was distraught. I knew she carried twins, a girl and a boy, but she didn't know whether they had been fathered by Patrick or Jacques. She was beside herself with worry, and I saw the enormous scope of the wrong I had done her."

Remorse had settled heavily on Delphine's face, etching deep lines of sorrow around her lips and across her forehead.

All the sophisticated cosmetics, the trappings of wealth, and the new identity Vincenzo supplied could not erase the past stamped so clearly on the Swamp Witch's face.

"Jacques wasn't long finding Delilah's whereabouts from Pete," Delphine continued. "He came to my shack and begged Delilah to stay with him. Jacques said she could sing again, and he would move to the Marigny with her and work in construction. He promised her a good life. She told Jacques he repulsed her, and she never wanted to see him again as long as she lived. After that she became a hermit. She wouldn't even talk to Angel about what had happened. Besides me, Pete Thibodeaux was the only one she'd let near her."

Hope seized Annie. This was not the story of a woman who willingly left her infant son behind in the swamp with a man she hated.

"Jacques was furious," Delphine said. "He claimed Delilah and Pete were in cahoots to ruin him. Before you and Lucien were born, he came to me privately and asked me to steal his son for him. When I refused, he said if I didn't do what he wanted he would burn my house down with Delilah and the babies in it, and then he would destroy me."

Caught up in the past, the sophisticated woman in front of Annie vanished and in her place was the Swamp Witch, her eyes and face vacant, her lips mumbling spells to hold back the evil. Annie glanced toward Vincenzo, but he put a finger to his lips. Everything in the office took on a greenish hue, and the air shimmered like water.

Finally, Delphine shook her head as if she were throwing off the effects of a drug. The room righted itself, and she continued with her story. "When the babies were born, I told Delilah her son had died, and then I secretly carried him to Jacques. I knew if I didn't do what he wanted, he would kill us all. But I stole her charm bracelet so I could use it to try and right the wrong I had done to Delilah and Lucien."

All the pieces of the story Lucien had told Annie fell into place. Everything now made perfect sense; the lies Jacques told him, Lucien's longing for the sister he had lost.

"Did my mother believe you?" Annie asked.

"Temporarily, she did. She grieved for her baby boy. But in her heart, she believed her son was alive. Her gift of seeing would have told her so. After she got back to Colorado, she started sending letters to me. The first one had a little note to me: *If you know where my son is, give my letters to him.*" Delphine handed the packet of letters to Annie. "Don't open them until you and your sisters are in a secure place. Never tell anyone where they came from, not even Lucien and Angel. Say you found them under the quilts in the lining of the trunk at Angel's. Make up anything. If Jacques finds out I'm alive, he'll kill me."

"Why would he destroy you? You gave him a son."

"When I gave Lucien the charm bracelet, he was too young to read, so I kept the letters. Jacques found out what I had done and put out word all over the swamp he was going to kill me. I staged my death then went to the only man powerful enough to protect me." She glanced toward Vincenzo with the gratitude you'd show if you saw the only lifeboat left on the *Titanic*.

He pushed back from his chair, a sign the interview was over. "My aunt is getting tired."

Suddenly, it seemed to Annie that the woman who had become a legend was an umbrella spreading over her entire life —sheltering her mother, protecting her on the drive to Honey LaBelle when she was sick, helping her through the birth, then making sure Angel saw his newborn granddaughter before Delilah left the swamp. The Swamp Witch had even risked her own life to tell the truth, shielding Annie from the heartbreak of never knowing.

"Thank you for trusting me with the truth and the letters," Annie said. "I won't betray you." The words shimmered in the air between them, a small grace, a gossamer bridge from the past to the future.

The Swamp Witch teared up, and Vincenzo nodded his approval. "If my aunt ever needs to talk to you again, I'll get in touch with you. Understand?"

"Perfectly." Annie handed Vincenzo her business card, then leaned down to hug the Swamp Witch. "You have given me back my brother."

Delphine caught both Annie's hands, her grip strong, the ruby in her ring coming to life, shooting sparks. For a dazzling instant, Annie saw her mother, smiling and happy, Patrick at her side. "Do you forgive me?" Delphine's voice cracked from years of carrying the burden of guilt.

"Yes, I forgive you." Annie kissed her wrinkled cheek then released her. "I would love to see the owner of Vinnie's and his charming aunt at my art show at Green Oak Gallery."

"I think you can count on it." Delphine winked at her. "Delilah would be proud of you."

Vincenzo escorted her back to her sisters' table and loudly thanked Annie for taking so much time with his beloved aunt. Diners at the neighboring tables turned to smile at them, their thoughts so transparent they might as well have popped up in bubbles above their heads. *Such a nice man, that Vincenzo Poretto. A pillar of the community. So devoted to his aunt.*

"We look forward to seeing you at Vinnie's again soon." His manner was suave, his smile perfect and seemingly uncalculated.

"You can count on it." Annie was equally adept at performance. Hadn't she stood in art shows smiling and chatting with patrons through disappointments, large and small, the aftermath of prescient dreams so graphic she could feel the blade of a knife slicing skin, and the fear that her sister Rachel would die before anybody ever found the madman who took her?

Her sisters were equally good actresses. They curbed their

curiosity until they were back in Angel's Thunderbird and on the way to the Marigny.

"What did you learn?" Jen was the first to ask.

Annie glanced around as if spies might be hanging from the Spanish moss and the glossy leaves of magnolia trees, swinging in the wind, itching to broadcast her every word to the world. "You'll find out when we get back to the Marigny."

# FIFTY-TWO

## HONEY ISLAND SWAMP | THE SHADOW

The Shadow had eyes everywhere. And he was gleeful at what he saw. Annie was racing around with her sisters, flaunting Delilah's gift in his face.

*Let her!*

She was already paying for what she had done. *Anxious. Suffering* because of Evangline. And he wasn't through with her yet.

People all over New Orleans were staring at posters of her, discussing her beauty and her talent.

When he decided the game was over, he would rip her face off with his claws.

But before then, he would make her suffer so much she'd wish she had never been born.

And he knew just how he was going to do it.

Lucien was a man shrinking under the weight of guilt. The bayou was on fire with speculation and fear but, for him, the question was not who killed the girls. It was why had he betrayed Evangeline.

He docked his boat and climbed the steps from the pier to Pete's Place, every step a nail driven into his heart, an echo of the fight they had the last time he saw her. And now she was gone. Held in a secret location to keep the killer from finishing the job. Would he ever see her again? Would he have a chance to say *I'm sorry*? Would he ever get to say the words he should have whispered to her in the moonlight on the deck of his houseboat when things were good between them? *I love you.*

He could make excuses for himself, but he wouldn't. He wasn't the only man who ever had a hard life. He had botched his relationship with Evangeline, and with Annie, too. He had even picked a fight with his own father. His need to be seen, to be appreciated, had made him self-centered and moody.

He could blame the culture of his people. He could even blame the swamp itself, the brooding, murky water, and the mists that curtained them all in secrecy; but he was done with blame. He was determined to live in the here and now.

He entered the store, and Pete Thibodeaux patted him on the back, all but shouting his usual effusive greeting. "Lucien! How are you? You're looking good, boy!"

Pete was cordial to everybody, but for the first time Lucien wondered why he was always singled out for this extraordinary exuberance. Was Pete overcompensating for the past?

Lucien recalled a stormy night from his childhood, the nightmare that sent him flying from his bed, screaming in terror. Jacques was sitting in front of the fire, empty liquor bottles scattered around him. *Tell it to Pete Thibodeaux,* he yelled. *He's the reason your mother left us behind. He turned Delilah against us.*

Jacques had yelled at Lucien to get out and leave him alone, and never speak of it again.

Facing Pete now, Lucien had the strong feeling there was some truth in his father's story. He shrugged to throw off Pete's hand, saying, "I can't complain," and the big man's booming laughter made people turn to join in the fun.

"If I was in your shoes and had to put up with old Jacques Morel, I'd complain."

Pete's response brought more laughter from the crowd. All the locals knew Jacques, and they either hated him or loved him. There was no in-between. But they also knew Jacques and Pete were lifelong friends, prone to bicker and jest, all in good fun. Or so they believed.

"What can I do for you?" Pete added. "Buy some product?"

"No furs to trade today. I'm just picking up supplies."

Lucien moved to the back of the store where Pete kept the staples and started filling his cloth bag with flour and cornmeal, sugar and Cajun spices. He was headed toward the cooler when a commotion at the front of the store caught his attention.

He turned to see two FBI special agents and St. Tammany Parish's Sheriff Harold Debeau marching Pete off to his office, followed by a host of other deputies, one of them holding the leash of a police dog. Something big was going on to draw this much police power.

Everybody had stopped to stare. For a moment there was dead silence, and then the murmurs started, like so many bees.

"They have a search warrant."

"Pete did it. I always knew it."

"He couldn't possibly be a killer."

"I heard some woman is in on it."

"Probably Pete's wife. I never did like her."

As if the gossip had conjured her up, Pete's wife Erma slipped into the store through a back door marked PRIVATE and hovered near the meat cooler, her hands pressed so hard against her face that her fingers made deep grooves in her cheeks. Sweat dripped from her like dew, tainting the air with the smell of sorrow.

Driven by a sense of disbelief, Lucien eased past Erma and found a spot near Pete's office. The low rumble of voices filtered through the closed door—and the sounds of a noisy search as drawers were pulled open then slammed shut. When the door finally opened, Pete was in handcuffs, flanked by two FBI special agents and followed by Sheriff Harold Debeau with his deputies and the canine officer.

But it wasn't the sight of handcuffs that held Lucien's attention: it was the plastic evidence bag held by Deputy Wanda Sparks. The bottom dropped out of Lucien's world.

Inside the bag was a hank of dark hair and a cuff bracelet, hand-hammered silver with a raised fleur-de-lis on top. *Evangeline's.* If that weren't enough evidence to convince the skeptical, the dent Evangeline had put in the side of the soft silver when she accidentally banged her arm against the edge of a display shelf at the gallery was filled with a rusty-looking substance that could only be blood.

Lucien balled his hands into fists. He wanted to tear Pete

from limb to limb, not only for Evangeline but for the way he had betrayed Lucien's father. He wanted to truss him up and throw him to the alligators. Even being alligator bait was too good for Pete. Except for him, Lucien would have had a chance to patch things up with Evangeline. Except for him tainting Delilah's mind against Jacques, Lucien would have grown up with two parents... and a twin sister.

Deputy Sparks turned to stare at him, and he realized he had his teeth clenched, his anger on full display. He tried to relax and let her pass on by. His relief was echoed by the crowd watching. "It's over," someone said, and then, "We can all sleep at night again," followed by, "Hanging is too good for him."

Despite his personal grudge against Pete, Lucien wanted no part of the instant judgement involving a murder charge. Pete was innocent until proven guilty. Mistakes had been made before. But also, justice was often done. It was not up to Lucien to decide.

He paid for his purchases and went outside in time to see the fleet of official vehicles and boats vanishing in the distance. He sensed the bayou sighing with him, ridding itself of the shroud of suspicion and fear. He breathed deeply of the fresh air. Today was a new day. Pete's arrest was the ending of a reign of terror, the laying to rest of an old grudge, and the beginning of a new life for Lucien.

He climbed into his boat and secured his bag of supplies. He was turning the key in the ignition when his cell phone range. *Annie.*

"Lucien?" Her voice held a lilt—such a small thing to foster hope. "I found old letters from my mother in the lining of a trunk in her childhood room at Grandfather's house in the Marigny. They're proof that you are my brother."

Sometimes, suddenly, there was mercy. Lucien sank onto the seat of his outboard motorboat. "I'm glad, Annie." He refrained from telling her that he knew it all along.

"I'd like to see you again. And Jen and Rachel want to meet you, too. Can you come to the Marigny?"

"I can, but why don't you bring... our sisters... here so they can see where Delilah grew up?" Lucien savored the feel of the word *sisters* on his tongue. "It's safe to come here now." He told her about Pete Thibodeaux's arrest.

"I'm surprised it's Pete, but relieved to know the killing is over. Hold on a minute." He could hear Annie's brief consultation with her sisters, and then she was back. "We'll be there tomorrow. Gran will be with us, and I think Grandfather will be anxious to get back to the bayou, too."

After he and Annie said goodbye, Lucien sat a while in his boat, his face lifted to the sky while the sunshine poured redemption over him, and the bayou hummed its ancient song.

## FIFTY-FOUR

### THE MARIGNY

Annie pocketed her cell phone, and faced her sisters. They were all in sweats, relaxing after a day spent with Honey LaBelle and the Swamp Witch. The hard part was over. She had already shared Delphine's story with Rachel and Jen, and the burden that came with it.

"That's done. You'll meet our brother tomorrow, after Gran gets here. I'll tell Angel our travel plans as soon as he wakes from his afternoon nap."

Her sisters said nothing, but their faces spoke of the years they had thought of themselves as three and the sudden knowledge that the Logan family had forever changed. Annie reached out and they all joined hands, solidarity in sisterhood, comfort in the familiar, strength through blood kin.

Delilah's letters lay in the middle of her childhood bed, while Annie and her sisters sat cross-legged around them, reluctant to open the door to their mother's past. Simultaneously, they burned with the desire to discover a clue to her dark moods and unexplained disappearances. The yellow pages carried the scent of age and secrets that, once unearthed, could never be hidden again.

"Gran won't want to go." Rachel was buying time. She was the one most hesitant to tear apart their history and try to put the pieces of themselves back together in a way that made sense to them. "She never approved of Mom. She still calls her the Bohemian. She certainly won't want to go poking around the bayou where Mom was born."

"I'll change her mind," Annie said.

The ever-practical Jen guffawed. "Good luck with that. It will be like telling Pikes Peak to move over so you can see the view."

"I can do it. You'll see." Annie pictured the conversation would be much like Jen had described. Still, as the youngest in the family, she had always been given the most leeway by their grandmother.

"Has anybody heard from her?" Rachel pulled out her cell phone to check her text messages. "I've sent her three texts today, and she still hasn't responded to a single one of them."

"Victoria is barreling our way in that monster truck your husband gave her, pedal to the metal, trying to get here before dark," Jen said. "You know this as well as I do, Rachel. Let's get these letters behind us before she arrives." She picked up the packet of letters and untied the frayed ribbon. "Annie, do you want to read?"

Like Rachel, Annie saw her past unraveling with the ribbon. The future appeared to her, vision-like, shrouded in shadows that hid dark figures moving toward her with ill intent. Confused, she shook the image off. The killer was in jail, so why was her vision filled with evil?

Maybe the letters would tell Annie more. "You go ahead, Jen."

Her sister unfolded the first letter, and in a voice eerily similar to Delilah's she began to read.

*Dear Lucien,*

*I named you before you were born, loved you before you came into this world. Stillborn, Delphine told me, and my heart broke in half. I left the swamp mourning you, and I mourn you, still. But my heart says you are there somewhere, alive and longing for a mother's love just as I yearn for you.*

*No matter what anyone tells you, I loved you then, I love you now, and I always will.*

*You mother, forever and always,*

*Delilah*

Annie's relief was so palpable she was unaware of the tears streaking down her face. "I can't wait to show Lucien. This will fill the hole in his heart."

"Don't expect too much, too soon, Annie." Jen's voice of reason and experience was like a bracing wind off the Mississippi River. "Healing takes times." She picked up the second letter and began to read.

*My precious, long-lost boy,*

*Do you look like your twin sister? All curls and giggles and mischievous behavior? Do you have the same smile that can melt away a mother's fatigue and turn aside her anger in a twinkling? Do you have a hint of fiery red in your hair that otherwise could be either Broussard dark or Morel black?*

*Are you and Annie Patrick's children or Jacques'? The timing was so close, the answer could go either way. But I don't dare ask Patrick for a paternity test. He would want to know why, and the reason would break his heart. I don't dare even get his DNA and do a test in secret. Victoria Logan knows everything. And what she doesn't know, somebody will tell her. That's how powerful the Logan family is, both a blessing and curse to me.*

*In my heart, I believe you are Patrick's. In my deepest longing, I cling to the hope that you are his. In spite of my long stay in Honey Island Swamp, he believes Annie is his, and that's good enough for me. He dotes on her, in fact.*

*Still, that awful night only three days after I arrived in the bayou haunts me. My soul is shredded with guilt. I remember, and try to turn events into a nightmare that can't possibly be true. I flee my life here and try to hide my shame behind my father, who knows nothing of it. Every time Annie smiles, I ask myself, What if she is Jacques' child? What if she carries the blackness I always saw in his soul?*

*What if you do? Did he find a way to get you? Oh, I hope not. Better that you had been stillborn than face life with a father like Jacques Morel.*


*With much love,*


*Delilah*


Annie felt herself falling backward into her mother's uncertainty, floating in a dark abyss where the father she cried out to was not the red-haired rancher with a quick smile and a ready hug, but the brooding, black-souled man who slunk through the darkness with a date-rape drug in his pocket. Her sisters, quick to sense her distress, squeezed her hands.

"You are not his," Jen said, and Rachel added, "You are more Logan than any of the three of us. You're the only one with Irish red in your hair."

"I know, but still, I had hoped the letters would prove that."

"Don't worry. There are other ways of finding it, and we will." Jen picked up the last letter. The date would have put Annie and Lucien at four years old.

*Dearest Lucien,*

*Patrick almost caught me writing this, and I can't keep it up. I've already given him more grief to forgive than any other man would bear. And this painful void in my soul has caused me to neglect my beloved daughters. They deserve more.*

*You might never get the letters anyhow. Delphine will not risk Jacques finding out, and I don't want to endanger her. She has been too good to me. After Nina died, she was my mother. Not like a mother, but a true mother in every sense of the word.*

*All the signs tell me you are thriving. I can't see where you are or who you are with, only that you are surrounded by swamp water and that Angel and Delphine will both make sure you grow up, unharmed. I cling to that. I hide all knowledge of you deep in my heart because I know what the future holds. Someday Annie will find you. And she will love you, this fierce daughter of mine. Just as I do.*

*Be strong, my son. Be brave. The life you long for is waiting for you.*

*All my love forever,*

*Delilah*

FIFTY-FIVE

Long after Jen read the last word, Annie and her sisters sat quietly on the bed, their hands joined, listening to the echoes of their mother, searching for memories in their childhood when the love Delilah expressed in her letters came shining through. Her absences and her darkness took on new significance, and one by one, they forgave her. There was no need for talk among them, no idle chatter to explain what each sister knew in her heart.

The sun dropped below the horizon, and shadows of evening crept through the window. Downstairs, they could hear Angel's footsteps as he left his bedroom and went into the kitchen. Soon, the sound of the teapot whistling brought them out of the past and back to the cottage where their maternal grandfather waited downstairs, and their paternal grandmother would come roaring up the street any minute in her red Dodge Ram pickup truck.

Annie's cell phone pinged with an incoming text. She glanced at the screen. "Victoria," she said, and then read the text aloud.

*There has been a delay. More later.*

Jen snorted. "She wouldn't dare send that to me. Text her back, Annie. Tell her to stop her shenanigans and tell us what's really going on."

"She won't respond to that, Jen." That was Rachel for you, always the peacemaker. "Tell her we're worried, Annie. Ask for details."

Annie fired off a text, her way.

*Gran, we've ordered shrimp po' boys for supper. There's nothing like them here in New Orleans. You'll see. How long is the delay?*

She watched her screen for the reply. As the minutes crept by, her sense of foreboding grew. A crow flew onto the windowsill and pecked at the glass, causing a sharp intake of breath from Jen. She hopped off the bed and began to pace.

Rachel rubbed her hand under her nose. Was she smelling magnolias? Or apricots, the scent of killing oleander? Her sudden pallor was the only signal Annie got that Rachel had a sign trouble was brewing.

Finally, the little ping signaled another text from Victoria.

*A few days. I caught a virus and stopped to rest. That's all.*

She turned the screen so her sisters could read.

"Good grief!" Jen threw her hands up in the air, and her gold bracelets slid together with a clink. Growing anxiety magnified the sound. "Find out where she is, Annie. We'll postpone our visit with Lucien. Rachel can stay with Grandfather while you and I go to get Gran. I can drive that ridiculous truck of hers back here."

Annie texted back.

*Where are you?*

They waited for a reply that never came.

"If that's not just like Victoria Logan!" Jen marched to the window and shooed away the blackbird that still perched there. "Get out of here. We want nothing to do with you." She turned to her sisters, hands on her hips. "Let's go downstairs and have dinner with Angel. We've got to let him know he has a grandson."

"It won't be easy," Annie reminded her sisters. "He despises Jacques Morel and has let that feeling carry over to Lucien."

"Delilah's letters will convince him." Jen grabbed the letters, and they all trooped downstairs, their apprehension floating behind them like blue smoke.

A delivery boy was at the door with the shrimp po' boys they'd ordered for dinner, and they decided to eat before they got cold. Annie told her grandfather about Lucien during the meal. As she had predicted, Angel didn't welcome the news that Lucien was her twin.

"Bah! It's just another one of Jacques Morel's tricks. I spit on them all, every Morel by name."

Rachel was the one to placate him. She served tea, then sat beside him while Jen and Annie cleared the table and Angel read the letters. Annie watched Rachel work her magic, leaning her head close, murmuring encouragement to their grandfather, pointing out passages that highlighted Delilah's love for Lucien and the guilt and heartbreak she'd carried for so many years, alone.

By the time Annie and Jen returned to the table with their own tea, Angel had tears in his eyes and was saying, "I always knew Lucien had Broussard blood." Rachel winked at them, and they gave her a thumbs-up.

They carried their teacups into the front room where they sat beside the fire. Angel talked about his remorse and mourned the years he could have spent with the grandson who was under his nose all along while Annie and her sisters offered comfort.

At ten, Angel turned on the news, and there was Linda Holloway, standing in front of Pete's Place, illuminated by portable TV lights, her hair whipping in the wind and her yellow rain parka a sure sign the dark clouds beyond would soon bring rain.

"The FBI and the St. Tammany Sheriff's Department descended on Pete's Place earlier today, in force. Sources say they were following a tip that led to a search of the premises and the arrest of Pete Thibodeaux."

A large photo of Pete filled the screen. He had his head back, laughing, the exact opposite of what you would expect from a murderer.

"Thibodeaux, a local businessman and an icon here in Honey Island Swamp, had long been a person of interest in the murders of Janine Porter and Sylvie Bergeron Hopkins." Photos of the victims flashed on the screen. "Thibodeaux had also been questioned as person of interest in the disappearance of Evangeline Aguillard."

As if Nature were mourning the dead girls, night dropped its black curtain around the cottage, and the wind picked up. Its sharp breath brought in a cold front and a hard rain.

On the television screen, the camera shot widened to show a distraught, overweight woman huddled inside a man's black rain slicker, standing beside Linda Holloway. "I have Thibodeaux's wife Erma here with me. Can you comment on your husband's arrest?" The reporter held the mic toward Erma.

"He didn't do it."

"So, you think the FBI and the St. Tammany Parish Sheriff's Department made a mistake?"

"I don't know what they did. All I know is that Pete's innocent. I would know if my own husband cut those girls up. He didn't do it."

"What leads you to so strongly believe in his innocence?"

"I just told you. Now, I'm done." Erma pulled up the hood of her rain slicker and stormed off.

"Good for her!" Angel pounded the arms of his chair. "That pushy Holloway woman ought to be drummed out of television." He grabbed the remote and the screen went black. "I have a hard time believing it, myself. Pete never struck me as somebody who would do such a thing."

"Grandfather, most people present a façade in public. I see it all the time in my practice." Jen began to gather the empty teacups. "One of the most famous killers was called Baby Face Nelson."

"Jenny girl, you don't spend as much time with your patients as I did with Pete Thibodeaux. He's no Baby Face Nelson."

Annie and Rachel started giggling at the stand-off. Jen turned toward them, grinning. "All right, go ahead and laugh. I know I've met my match."

"Two peas in a pod," Rachel murmured.

Angel was chuckling when he kissed them goodnight. After they finished cleaning up the tea things, Annie and her sisters headed upstairs.

On the landing, Rachel said, "While you were in the kitchen, Grandfather said he's not going to the bayou tomorrow. He needs more time to get used to the idea of a grandson."

"I'm not surprised," Annie told her sisters. "He's every bit as ornery as Gran. He won't change his mind. I'll get Paul to stay with him while we're gone."

"Annie, is Paul somebody we should meet?" Rachel asked.

"Maybe? I don't know yet."

"You don't have to know yet. Let life unfold." Jen caught Annie in a tight embrace, and then she and Rachel said their goodnights and went into their bedroom to call their families.

Annie went into hers to make her calls. Paul readily agreed

to watch after Angel while they were gone. He was gracious and warm in a way that felt personal. Under different circumstances, Annie would have been eager to explore their relationship. As if he could read her thoughts, Paul told her, "Annie, now that the killer has been caught, this will all be over soon. I'd like to take you to dinner when you return from the bayou. Just the two of us."

"I'd like that." It surprised Annie how much she would enjoy a quiet evening alone with him.

Her next call was to Toni. It was easier to tell the truth of Lucien over the phone so she could keep Delphine's secrets without looking her friend in the eye.

"Annie, I think you've known the truth all along. Once the two of you put the past behind, you're going to love having a brother. Most of the time." Toni laughed. "Take it from me."

After the call, Annie checked her social media and was relieved to see no new messages from her stalker. Had it been Pete Thibodeaux all along? Had his own obsession with Delilah driven him to stalk Annie and then murder those girls in the swamp who resembled her?

She had heard of stranger things. As she dressed for bed, she hoped Linda Holloway didn't discover that Pete and Delilah had stayed in touch up until Annie's birth. She could imagine the horrible story the reporter would weave for her television audience with that tidbit.

She padded barefoot to the chair beside the window and opened her sketchbook. Streetlights transformed the trees bending in the wind into a macabre dance of Nature that contained its own eerie beauty. She began to sketch, hoping to hold back the sense of unease that grew larger with each moan of the gathering storm. Lightning split the sky and thunder turned the air into a prolonged drum roll.

By the time Annie put the final touch on her sketch and closed the curtains and climbed into bed, it was the witching hour. The storm lashed the windows in earnest. The hands of Angel's clock shivered her for a moment, and then she pulled up her covers, hoping the killer's capture would be the end of her dream warnings.

She slept peacefully for two hours, and then the scream sliced through her dreams. A banshee yell, more of outrage than fear. Annie jerked in her sleep, fought against the dream pulling her into the bayou, shrouding her in mist and darkness. A boat slipped through the water, gliding among curtains of Spanish moss, deep in the swamp.

Her dream-self wandered in the green haze of water and trees, calling, "Who's there?"

A chorus of frogs answered her, then silence so profound it felt as if the world had ended. Annie's heart picked up speed and sweat beaded her brow. When she kicked at the covers, they had turned to water, swirling around her ankles, sucking at her feet, intent on devouring her.

Delphine floated among the mists, not in her blue designer suit but in a red turban, her hands holding a swaddled child, her ruby sending a light that blinded Annie.

"What's happening?" Annie asked her. "Where am I?"

"Don't you know?" The deep male voice struck terror through her soul.

"Who are you?"

"Don't you know?" His wicked laughter made her think of spiders covering her skin, smothering her face, her eyes, her nose. She struggled to breathe.

*Don't you know? Don't you know?*

The echo was even more frightening than the original answer. It was followed by a scream that woke Annie, and shot her out of bed.

## FIFTY-SIX

When her sisters swarmed into her room the next morning, Annie was still asleep. Sun shot watery light through the window, still streaked with rain, and wind from the cold front set tree branches lashing against the panes.

"Annie, wake up!" Jen's voice filtered to her through layers of lingering anxiety from her dream.

"What?" Annie pushed her thick hair out of her face. "What is it?"

Both Jen and Rachel plopped onto her bed. It was like being teenagers, all over again. "Rachel woke up smelling apricots all over the house, and there are so many crows gathering in the tree outside my window, the sky is almost black with them. Danger is everywhere."

"I know." Annie told them about her dream. "Maybe my stalker is not the killer, and he's still out there somewhere?"

"Maybe," Jen said, "but this feels bigger. We need to be prepared."

Rachel jumped up and started rambling through the closet. When Annie climbed out of bed and reached for her sweats,

Rachel handed her a pair of jeans and a blue sweater. "Wear this. It matches your eyes."

"What's this for? We're just going to the bayou." Annie took the sweater anyhow and pulled it over her head.

"There's a very handsome man by the name of Paul downstairs, and I want my baby sister to look her very best."

Jen rolled her eyes. "My sister, Rachel, the hopeless romantic."

"It never hurts to be prepared. Put these on." Rachel tossed a pair of black boots to Annie, and she vanished into the bathroom to bathe and dress. "Is there a cast iron skillet in this house?" Rachel added.

Annie peered around the doorframe, her toothbrush in her mouth, and nearly choked, laughing. Rachel looked like a cowgirl in her Western boots and buckskin jacket, her hair escaping in ringlets from her bun, her hand on her hips. "Good grief, Rachel, you look like you're reaching for a six-shooter. Why do you want a skillet?"

Rachel huffed when she took her hands off her hips. "With all three of us getting warnings of danger, I'm not going to the swamp without a weapon."

"That's a great idea," Jen said. She was in comfortable navy-blue sweats and sneakers, her only nod to fashion her gold bracelets and a red scarf thrown around her neck. "But we don't want to alarm Angel by taking one of Nina's skillets. We'll stop at a hardware store. We need rope, duct tape, some of those long garbage ties, and some hornet spray." Jen began to tick off items on her fingers. "Maybe a hammer. Oh, and a hatchet, for the swamp, right?"

"I draw the line at a hatchet," Rachel said. "We're not killers like Baby Face Nelson."

The long list of household items Jen chose for weapons and Rachel's argument against the hammer would have been amusing if Annie didn't know that their journey to meet their brother had taken a turn toward evil. As she brushed her hair, she made a fierce face in the mirror.

"Bring it on. The Logan sisters are ready for you." Making the promise aloud boosted Annie's spirits. Then she went downstairs with her sisters to greet Paul and say goodbye to Angel.

Still, the creeping sense of impending disaster remained with her as they loaded their bags into the car—and the certainty that someone was watching. She searched in every direction, looking for a glimpse of her stalker. Instead, she saw movement across the street, a curtain being raised, two faces appearing at the window. The nosey old women who made voodoo dolls.

A premonition whispered through Annie and a vision began to form, gathering shadows, painted with blood. Lucien swirled at its center.

Was her brother in danger, or was he the source?

FIFTY-SEVEN

Armed with their makeshift weapons from the hardware store and content in the knowledge that Angel was in good hands with Paul Chenevert, Annie and her sisters set out to the bayou, Annie at the wheel of the ancient Thunderbird convertible.

Once they left the city behind and entered the outskirts of the bayou, the scenery changed drastically. Last night's storm had left the earth saturated, and fog that had not yet been burned away by the sun swirled around the car.

"Annie, are you sure we're on the right road?" Rachel was anxious, and had been ever since they left the Marigny. She'd tried twice to get in touch with Gran, both times without success. "It feels like we're on the way to Perdition."

"Good grief, Rachel. Please, *chill.*" Jen flung off her red scarf and let the wind turn her mop of dark curls upside down. "We'll hear from Victoria when she wants us to. Not a minute before."

"Something's out there waiting for us," Rachel reminded her.

"Nothing the three of us can't handle." Jen turned from her view at the window. "Right, Annie?"

"You bet your boots."

Jen laughed. "You and Rachel are the ones wearing *boots*. I'm wearing sensible jogging shoes."

"Mine are packed." Annie took the turn that skirted Pete's Place, pointing it out to her sisters, and then headed along the river road. The canopy of massive trees made it feel as if they were in a tunnel. In spite of having no new threats on her social media, she found herself searching the thick woods for a watcher. Nothing but birds stared back at her. Still, she couldn't shake the sense of foreboding, especially when Rachel said, "I smell magnolias all over this car."

As Annie took the last turn onto Angel's property, both her sisters gasped. "It's spectacular," Jen said, and Rachel added, "No wonder Mom kept coming here."

"Wait until you see the inside." Annie parked in the garage, and they hurried through the back door with their overnight bags. Rachel instantly fell in love with the quaint kitchen and the table Angel had made, but it was the wall of photographs in the front room and the sight of Delilah's things in her bedroom upstairs that enthralled them.

"It's like stepping back in time." Jen picked up a photograph of her mother and ran her fingers around the contours of Delilah's face. "I'm sorry I ever told you not to come, Annie."

"That's okay. You knew I wouldn't pay you any attention." Annie lifted the lid of the trunk to display the quilts. "You and Rachel can share Mom's old room, but you'll need these tonight."

"Where will you sleep?" Rachel asked.

"I'll be right down the hall from you."

"But you're the target," Jen said. "You're sleeping in here with Rachel." She set the photo back on the dresser. "I don't want you alone tonight... and don't you argue."

"I won't, but just this one time." Annie grinned to camouflage the uneasiness she'd felt ever since they came back to the bayou.

While Jen left to stow her bag in the guest room down the hall and Rachel shucked her jacket to unpack, Annie sat on the edge of her twin bed and sent a text to Victoria.

*Gran, you need to tell us where you are. We're getting worried. If you're still sick, we can come and get you.*

"Are you checking on Gran?" Rachel sat down beside her then nodded her approval when she read the text. They waited in vain for Gran's reply. The grandfather clock chimed the hour, the sound drifting up the stairs and magnifying their worry. "This is getting ridiculous."

Rachel sent her own text message.

*Gran, if you don't let us know something soon, I'm going to think you're senile and getting too old to drive that truck you're so proud of. TEXT ME! I mean it!*

The sisters watched their screens with their heads together. Time moved so slowly Annie imagined she could hear it mincing across the floor on little mouse feet. She sighed. "Rachel, we can sit here forever, and Gran still might not text us back."

"You're right." Rachel headed toward the door. "When I get old, tell me if I start acting as stubborn as Victoria."

"Same here."

Jen swooped toward them from the other end of the hall, her gold bracelets gleaming, her signature red caftan flowing around her. Neither sister raised an eyebrow. They knew she enjoyed looking like the queen of a small country.

Together, they trooped back downstairs where Jen and Annie made sandwiches from the deli meat and cheese in the refrigerator while Rachel got their Grandmother Broussard's pottery plates from the cabinets.

"These are exquisite." Rachel ran her hands around the intricate design that was distinctly African. "I wish I had known Nina."

Despite the love Delilah had expressed for her children in the letters she left behind, there would always be a little empty space in their hearts that only the grandmother they never knew could have filled. As they stacked sandwiches on their plates, the loss was reflected in their faces.

Jen sat in Angel's chair at the head of the kitchen table. "Annie, before we call Lucien to come over, I want to know as much as you do about him. And don't edit the story."

"When have I ever edited?"

"All the time."

"That's because she was born creative, Jen." Rachel set her plate carefully on the table. "Annie, ignore bossy Dr. Turner over there... but be sure to tell us everything."

By the time they finished talking and Annie called Lucien, it was mid-afternoon. While they waited for him, Annie made café au lait and Rachel made chocolate chip cookies.

Jen leaned against the counter and watched. "I'm the taster. Pass me the spoon, Rachel."

The front doorbell rang, and Annie's sisters froze. "The cookies aren't done, yet." Rachel wiped her hands on Nina's apron, and Jen ran her finger around her mouth. "Do I have cookie dough?"

"Relax, you two. Lucien won't bite." Annie left them scurrying around the kitchen. Doing what, she couldn't imagine. She flung open the door, and her brother stood on the front porch, as nervous as her sisters.

*Yes. This.* Her thoughts were already spooling toward the future—holiday meals together and family celebrations, both large and small.

"Annie!" Relief washed over his face, then he ran his hand through his dark hair. "Do I look all right?" He was dressed simply in jeans, a white shirt, and a black leather jacket.

"Perfect. They're going to love you as much as I do. Before we join Jen and Rachel, tell me whether you want to read Mom's letters with us or read them in private."

A quietness stole over Lucien, the same kind of stillness Annie sought when she wanted to mull any issue of great importance. "I think I'd rather read them by myself."

"You've got it. I'll give them to you before you leave." She led him into the kitchen. "This is Lucien." She gestured toward her sisters. "That's Jen in red, and Rachel in cowboy boots."

They studied him with the kind of awe you'd reserve for weddings and funerals; fearless women, their dusky skin a match to the brother standing before them, their dark eyes drinking in his ocean eyes, chiseled features, lush lips, and the height that mirrored their sister, Annie. The air turned blue with the regret of years lost, and the far-off sound of weeping echoed through the room, Delilah shedding tears of joy as her children found each other.

All of them saw the tinted air, heard their mother crying. Then they saw each other, really *saw*, and they knew. They were Broussards—Creole, and they were Logans, too, their Irish blood fierce.

Rachel blinked back tears, and Jen was the first to recover. She hurried over and caught his face between her palms. "It's astonishing how much you look like Annie."

"Extraordinary. Both of you have ocean eyes, and this amazing, charismatic presence." Rachel smiled at him, a mother to an aching child. "I've made cookies."

"Rachel's an elementary school teacher," Annie told him. "She thinks cookies are the answer to every problem."

"I'll subscribe to that." Lucien's smile turned to a chuckle, and soon all four of them were whooping it up in the kitchen as if the years and their complicated past had never separated them.

Finally, they settled around the table with café au lait and cookies and began to share stories about their childhoods, weaving a net big enough to hold them all together, three sisters and a brother, a family, newly minted.

The sun and the grandfather clock in the den marked the passing of time. Evening dropped a veil of shadows over them, and they shared a makeshift supper of sandwiches and soup Rachel concocted from cans of vegetables she found in the pantry.

They were putting away the dishes when Annie's cell rang. All of them turned toward the sound, knowing as only they could that the caller would be bringing bad news.

## FIFTY-EIGHT

Annie glanced at the screen of her cell phone. "It's my agent. I'm sorry, but I have to take this."

She slipped through the back door and into the backyard, lit only by a sliver of moon and a sprinkling of stars. "Hi, Bea. What's up?"

"I got a call today from Rocco Salvatore. The police caught the man who was stalking you in the Piazza del Commune. It turns out he's a serial stalker with a fixation on pretty young women."

Annie reeled at the news. *Did she have two stalkers, one in Italy and one in Honey Island Swamp?* "Was his name John Davidson?"

"He's Luc Giovanni."

*Where had she heard that name before?* "That name sounds familiar..."

"It should. He does maintenance for the flat you rent."

Though she'd had occasion to use him only once for faulty bathroom plumbing, she had almost recognized him in the plaza. He could have easily used the John Davidson alias to send messages on the Facebook page. But it made no sense that a serial stalker from Italy would fly to the States, wreak havoc with snakes and such, all while posting comments on her social media that would implicate him in the murders in Honey Island Swamp, and then casually fly back to Italy in time to be arrested.

The new twist brought danger that coiled through Annie, as real and terrifying as the rattlesnake at Pete's Place.

"Has Luc Giovanni ever harmed anyone?" she asked.

"No, he just likes to look and get a reaction. Don't worry, Annie. He won't be bothering you again."

"Thanks, Bea."

Annie crossed to the gazebo and sank into a wicker chair so she would have a quiet place to think. If her original stalker was in police custody in Italy, then who had put the rattlesnake in the car and left the dead animals and thrown rocks through the window? Who had planted vicious rumors about her to Linda Holloway? Who had killed the girls?

If the culprit was Pete Thibodeaux, then was the threat over?

Annie had a sudden vision of herself caught in the middle of a spiderweb weaving tighter and tighter around her. The darkness around her seemed oppressive, and the air turned heavy, making it hard to breathe.

On a hunch, she pulled up her social media on her cell phone. And there was another threatening comment from John Davidson.

I see you. You can run from me, but you can't hide. I will destroy everything you love. You will curse the day you were born.

She raced into the kitchen, her hair plumped up by the humidity and her face flaming. Rachel set down her coffee cup and stared, while Jen and Lucien gaped at her as if she were an escapee from a maximum-security prison.

"Pete Thibodeaux is *not* my stalker." Annie showed them the latest comment on her Facebook account, posted long after Pete was behind bars without internet access. "My online stalker has repeatedly referred to the killings in Honey Island Swamp. He and the Shadow are one and the same. Pete *didn't* kill those girls."

"Then who did?" Lucien asked.

He touched the huge knife that had been strapped to his leg in a leather sheath every time Annie saw him. She saw flashes of a remote shack guarded by snakes and alligators, caught glimpses of rope and a primitive wooden chair. She heard echoes of diabolical laughter and felt the web tighten.

Everyone she loved was being threatened, and they were scattered in so many places Annie couldn't possibly know what was happening to all of them. She had a flashback of the creepy old women peering out the curtain when she and her sisters left the Marigny. "I'm going upstairs to get Mom's letters for Lucien, and I'll call Paul to check on Angel."

"Great idea," Jen said. "I'll go with you." She grabbed Annie's arm and led her upstairs to Delilah's old room.

"What's this all about, Jen?"

"Lucien is a very troubled man, Annie." Jen flipped on the light switch then sank onto one of the twin beds. "I've seen enough patients like him through the years to know."

"Is he dangerous? Is Rachel safe with him?"

"No, he's not. And yes, she's safe." Jen ran her hands through her mane of curls, her bangle bracelets flashing in the overhead light. "We all need to slow down with Lucien, that's all I'm saying. Rachel's getting ready to tuck him under her wing like a mother hen, and you're not far behind with the hearts and flowers thing." Annie opened her mouth to protest, but Jen said, "Don't tell me you're not. I can read you like a Harry Potter book."

"I feel a twin's unbreakable bond with him, and he's lovable in ways you haven't seen yet."

"I'm sure of that, Annie. But back me up on this. Let's take it slowly, and I can get him the help he needs."

"Reading Mom's letters will help him... a lot. Maybe he just needs to get out of the swamp."

"You could be right." Jen patted the bed. "Sit down. You don't need to tower over me."

"Was I?" Annie sank to the mattress beside her sister.

"You always do. It's because you're so tall and beautiful you look like you own the world." Jen slung an arm around her and pulled her close. "You're not alone in this, kiddo. I'm not going to let anything happen to you. Or to anybody we love. You know that, don't you?'

"I do." The target on Annie's back felt a little lighter.

"Good. Don't forget it, because all the signs are saying things are going to get worse. Now make that call."

As Annie pulled her phone from her pocket to call Paul, she tried not to think of the carnage left behind by the Shadow and the many ways he could wreak havoc on his chosen targets.

Paul and Annie's grandfather sat in front of the fire in Angel's cottage, the checkerboard on a table between them and the television on, blaring non-stop coverage of Pete Thibodeaux's arrest for the murders in Honey Island Swamp. Linda Holloway was in her element. Paul couldn't help but picture her as a lonely woman whose only pleasure came from broadcasting the misfortunes of others.

"Don't think you're babysitting me," Angel said crossly.

"I don't."

"Good." Angel moved his black checker across the board, taking down the last of Paul's red pieces. "Ha! Got'cha. I win."

"You're too sharp for me." Paul began to lay out the pieces for another game.

"If you want to beat me, you'd better start paying more attention to the game instead of worrying about Annie."

"How did you know?"

"It shows all over you. Are you sweet on her?"

"Looks like it." Not only was Annie burrowed so deeply into his mind that he couldn't stop thinking about her, but she had woven some kind of spell over him. He found himself picturing what it would be like to spend more time in front of the fire with Angel, have a family meal with Annie's two sisters, maybe fly out to the ranch for Spring break, and drive over to Gulf Shores for the Fourth of July. He saw himself in a way that he never imagined would happen again—part of a family.

His cell phone rang, and he smiled. "Annie," he told Angel.

"Well, don't just sit there. Go upstairs so you can say something sweet to her. You won't ever win my granddaughter sitting like a lump on a log."

Paul answered with, "Hello, Annie," then strode off and took the stairs two at a time, propelled by the musical sound of her voice.

"*Paul!*" Was that lilt due to him, or did she talk that way to everybody? "Are you and Angel okay?"

"We're great." He told her about their game of checkers, and the quiet day they'd had together. "Just two old bachelors, hanging out."

Annie's laughter resonated through him with the peacefulness of cathedral bells. "Have Angel's neighbors across the street bothered you?"

He thought the question strange until he remembered the creep factor that arrived with the women when they showed up on Angel's front porch shortly after he arrived.

"They came over soon after you left, bringing cupcakes, and asking where you were going and when you would be back. I told them your agenda was private."

"That's good, Paul, especially in view of recent events." As she told him everything that had happened since they arrived in the swamp, he kept seeing his car crashing into the bridge, hearing the crunch of metal, hearing the screams, seeing the carnage. He felt as helpless as he had the day his wife died.

"Annie, you have to call Sheriff Debeau, and tell him everything you told me. According to Linda Holloway, the search for the killer is over. The sheriff needs to know they might have the wrong man."

"I'll do it as soon as we hang up."

"Is Lucien with you now?"

"Yes. And he's armed with the knife he used to kill the rattlesnake."

"Good. Don't leave the cottage without him."

Her silence spoke volumes.

"Annie, listen to me. Lucien is brooding and reclusive, even hotheaded, but he's a good man. I've known him for years. He'll protect you."

"I believe you, Paul. We'll be very careful. Hug Angel for me."

Just like that, she was gone, and he hadn't said a single thing to let her know how he felt about her. But *you're special to me* seemed inadequate, and *I think of you all the time* sounded needy. Love was not a word he had used lightly, or ever would. His heart might be pulling him in that direction, but common sense said it was the wrong place, and not yet the right time.

Honey Island Swamp came to him, remote and wild, Annie and her sisters on Angel's property, unprotected, with the killer still on the loose.

*What if you never get another chance?*

# SIXTY

## HONEY ISLAND SWAMP

When Annie and Jen came back downstairs to report on Angel, and hand Delilah's letters to Lucien, the conversation turned in a different direction. Lucien stayed with his sisters far into the night, discussing all the angles of the Shadow's murders, and how they could be proactive, but also safe.

"Don't go anywhere without me," Lucien told them. "I know this bayou like the back of my hand, and not many people around here want to tangle with a Morel."

"We're not going anywhere," Annie said, and Rachel added, "Come back in the morning in time for breakfast so we can spend the day with you."

Lucien left the cottage with mixed feelings. His twin, as well as Jen and Rachel, had been gracious to him. Warm, even. But that was in the beginning. From the moment Annie showed them the cruel comments from the man who called himself John Davidson, Lucien had felt a seismic shift in the mood. The three women had been sisters forever, and he was the outsider. He carried a Bowie knife with a twelve-inch blade. His father was still the Boogie Man to Annie, and Lucien, himself, was largely unknown to her.

Reminding himself that becoming part of the Logan family would take time, he made his way along the shell path and down Angel's long pier. Fog swirled around him, and the crescent moon provided barely enough light for him to climb safely into his boat and head toward home. When he was out of sight of the dock, he powered down the motor and let his boat idle. Then he sat on the still water while the night closed around him, and read his mother's letters by flashlight.

Years of longing fell away, and the love she expressed felt like being held in his mother's embrace. Knowing he had not been abandoned lifted the stone that had sat on his heart since he first understood he didn't have a mother.

Other sections of Delilah's letters were deeply disturbing. Something had happened in the swamp that terrified her. And her hatred of Jacques was very clear. The exact opposite of his dad's stories about them being sweethearts.

Annie also had a visceral dislike of Jacques. She was not only an intelligent and talented woman, but she had mystical gifts he'd only seen once before—in Delphine Thierry. What did she see in Lucien's father that he was missing?

The curved slice of moon held no answers, but the nocturnal animals who slid through the darkness of the forbidding forest beyond him whispered a warning. *Find out.* Suddenly decisive, Lucien increased the power and turned his boat in the direction of his childhood home. It was much deeper in the swamp than the small but thriving enclave where he kept his houseboat, a route he would never have attempted in the darkness if he hadn't known it by heart.

As he glided through the meandering channels and murky backwater, he calculated the time it would take to get there and then return to his houseboat for a few hours of sleep before heading to breakfast with his sisters. He could make it.

Soft moonlight light filtered through the thicket of overhanging branches and Spanish moss, gilding his skin and his boat, giving everything around him a silver sheen. Many of the wildlife photographers who flocked to Honey Island Swamp chose the night to make pictures that highlighted the brooding and dangerous nature of the wetlands, and then later called the timing *perfect*.

But there was nothing perfect about the night or Lucien's life. As he tied his boat to the dock and climbed the steep steps to the small shack on stilts, memories of his childhood assaulted him.

"Lucien, if you want any supper, pick up that gun and shoot that squirrel. The swamp is no place for wimps."

The variation of that theme was Jacques yelling, "Kill that wild hog before he kills you," or "Gut that deer, boy. Be a man."

Killing was a way of way of life for his father. Lucien knocked on the door and called out, "Dad. It's me."

There was only silence. No sound of boots pounding across the floor. No yell of "Wait a minute. Let me get my boots on." No spicy scent of squirrel stew in the pot or pungent smell of the cigar Jacques occasionally smoked.

"Open up, Dad. We need to talk." What would he say when Lucien told him about meeting all his sisters? But even more important, how would he respond to the accusations in Delilah's letters?

He waited on the small porch while the swamp breathed around him—the familiar sighing of his childhood, the trees whispering, the swamp creatures calling and chattering to each other in the dark.

He took his key out of his pocket and turned the lock. Jacques' old hunting jacket hung on a hook beside the door, and a twelve-gauge shotgun had been broken down for cleaning, the parts scattered on a burlap bag to keep grease off the floor. But there were no lingering scents of bacon or cigar smoke, no damp towels in the bathroom, no rumpled sheets on the bed.

Where was he? Jacques was messy. He always left a trail.

Lucien's heart picked up speed, and his nerves jangled. *"Dad?"* he called again, knowing there would be no answer. The place looked as if Jacques hadn't been there in days.

What if his father had met with an accident in the swamp? It happened all the time. Predators weren't picky about their victims. A rattlesnake didn't care if you were beloved or hated. Neither did a wild boar. Or an alligator. You were simply the enemy encroaching on his territory.

He started his search in Jacques' bedroom, the most likely place to find clues, not only to his whereabouts but also his past. The bed revealed nothing except that the sheets needed washing. There were no clues among the jumble of matches, receipts, and loose change on the bedside table.

Lucien rambled through the chest, pulling out every drawer and finding only loosely folded jockey shorts and socks, an assortment of tee shirts and blue jeans. The closet doors were ajar. No surprise there. It didn't take him long to go through the pockets of Jacques' clothes. He didn't own many. Never had.

"Never burden yourself down with possessions, son," he always said. "Not in a swamp or anywhere else. If you do, they'll end up owning you."

That might have been the closest thing to wisdom he ever heard from his father. Lucien spotted an oversized tackle box on the floor of the closet, as out of place as his and Boone's favorite exotic dancer would be wearing feathers and revealing costumes at a Sunday morning church service. Honey Labelle. That was her name. He wondered if she was still dancing.

He sat on the floor and opened the rusted tackle box. Jacques' fly-fishing lures littered the top compartment. Lucien pulled that out and lost his breath. Disbelief churned through him, followed by despair.

The silver bangle bracelet with a random pattern of rhinestones belonged to Evangeline. He'd seen the locket with the carved rose design in the photograph of the first victim, Janine

Porter. Did the small plastic bag of fingernails painted bright pink belong to Sylvie Bergeron Hopkins? There had been nothing in the news about her fingernails being gouged out, but that was the kind of detail the cops would keep a secret. Only they and the killer would know.

Lying among the mementos of the dead was the severed paw of a bobcat, the large lynx-like creature that prowled the swamp looking for prey. Its claws were covered with the dried blood of the women the Shadow had butchered,

Lucien was a man turned to stone. He couldn't move, couldn't think. After a while, he realized the dampness on his face was tears. He was mourning for the victims and for the father he had just lost. No man who killed so ruthlessly would ever deserve to be called Dad again.

His mind began to whirl. Lucien had been questioned in both the murders of the girls in the swamp and the disappearance of Evangeline. If he turned over this evidence, no one would believe he hadn't planted it there to implicate Jacques.

He got a damp washcloth from the bathroom and scrubbed the tackle box free of his fingerprints. Then he covered it with a large towel, shoved it back into closet, and threw the towel into the dirty clothes hamper. Too late, he realized he had also scrubbed away Jacques' prints. It couldn't be helped now.

*What next? What next?*

The question was a broken record in his head. His first instinct was to hunt down Jacques. *And then what?*

Suddenly, his twin sister exploded through his brain like a detonated bomb. Annie was in immediate danger.

SIXTY-ONE

The dream tossed Annie about as she lay under her grandmother Broussard's quilt in the twin bed that had once been her mother's.

A shack appeared, vivid, tucked among ancient trees and tangled vines, and filled with paraphernalia only a mystic would have. A crystal ball. A red turban. Tarot cards. Shelves lined with potions and *gris gris* bags. Chants and spells whispered through Annie, cast in a sing-song voice, a lullaby that quickly turned to a nightmare.

Two shadowy figures moved around the shack, while evil swirled around them in a green fog. Tree branches beat against the windows, and a snake, hanging from a limb, bared its fangs through the glass. Danger loomed in every direction.

"*Annie! Annie!*" The voice calling to her in her dreams was female, a bit fragile. "*Find me, Annie.*"

The plea tore out Annie's heart, while a man's diabolical laughter echoed through her dreamworld. She kicked at the covers, fighting the unknown danger.

"*Annie!*" The voice was a roar this time. Male.

"Annie," a softer, female voice called to her, followed by

Rachel shaking her shoulder. "Wake up. Someone's downstairs."

Rachel snapped on the light while Annie leaped out of bed and grabbed her robe. Jen hurried into the room, her hair sticking out every which way like the head feathers of a mad rooster. Her red robe was belted around her, and she clutched a can of hornet spray.

"Lucien's down there." Jen picked up the old-fashioned bedside clock. "It's two a.m." The sisters exchanged worried looks while Rachel scrambled around for her cast iron skillet.

"Something awful is happening," Annie said. She grabbed a pencil, and they all raced downstairs to open the front door, weapons drawn.

Lucien stood on the welcome mat, distraught and bleary-eyed. "Quick." He grabbed Annie's arm. "Back inside."

They hustled into Angel's front room, and Lucien locked the door behind them. "Jacques killed the girls and hid evidence in a tackle box in his closet. Evangeline's bangle bracelet was there, too. Annie's in danger. All of you are."

"I've known of the threat all along," Annie said, and her sisters flanked her, still clinging to their weapons.

"We all have." Jen swept her arm around the room to include Lucien, clearly terrified of his own dad; the grandfather clocking ticking toward the wee hours of the morning; and the three of them, half-dressed and dependent on hardware store items for protection. "This is when the monster jumps out of the closet wielding a machete."

"Gran's not sick like her text said." Rachel put down her heavy skillet and sank into a chair. "She's *missing*. The scents are telling me so."

"I'm calling her right now." Jen punched in Victoria's number, and the ringtone was a ticking time bomb in the utter silence of the room. There is nothing more frightening than a phone call, unanswered by a person you fear is missing. "Where could she be?"

"I think she's here, somewhere." Annie told them about the dream she was having when Lucien's knock awakened her.

"I'm going to check the premises." Lucien removed his knife from its sheath. The blade flashing in the overhead lights was a cruel reminder that the danger foretold by their gifts was now upon them. "Sit tight and lock the door behind me."

He went back out the front door, and Jen locked it behind him. "Clothes," she said, and they took the stairs two at a time to throw on outdoor clothes and sturdy shoes. By the time they met downstairs, Jen was wearing a backpack with the other supplies they had picked up at the hardware store.

Rachel raced into the kitchen with her sisters right behind her. While she stuffed the pocket of her jacket with granola bars, Annie filled a thermos with water. Jen flipped on the outdoor lights then stood at the window overlooking the backyard.

"Lucien's at the gazebo," she said. "He's got something."

Annie joined her at the window, already knowing exactly what it was. "A voodoo doll," she said. "That's where the last one was."

She opened the back door and Lucien came in, holding a voodoo doll, green button eyes, red in the dark hair. Obviously meant to be Annie. There was a crude map attached to the leg along with a note.

If you want to see your grandmother alive again, come to Delphine's cottage. All three of you. Alone. No cops, or I slit her throat and take her boots as a souvenir.

Horror hit them like an avalanche in the Rockies. Annie and her sisters huddled together, taking strength from each other, holding back their horror by sharing it. Seeing Lucien's stricken look, Annie stretched one arm to include him, and he walked into their circle.

"I won't let him hurt you," he said. "*Any* of you."

"I know, Lucien." Annie squeezed his hand, her mind on fire with terror and uncertainty. "But, first, we've got to decide what to do."

"I might never have gotten out of the wilderness alive with those kidnapped children if the cops hadn't come," Rachel said.

"Agreed. I wouldn't have my children back, either." Jen stuck out her chin. "We're calling the cops. Period. But if anybody thinks we're going to sit here and wait while a depraved maniac kills Victoria and takes her boots, he's sadly mistaken. Who's with me?"

"All of us," Annie said, while Rachel and Lucien nodded their agreement. "I'll make the call."

"Hand me the map, first." Lucien studied the crude drawing while Annie told Sheriff Debeau about the evidence in Jacques' house and read the note regarding the kidnapping of Victoria Logan.

"Sheriff Debeau," she added, "if we didn't already know Jacques is the killer, that bit about taking Gran's boots as a souvenir gives him away. We want her back alive."

"I'm on it now." The sheriff barked a few orders to his deputies, which included the words SWAT team. "Miss Logan, I know you and your sisters grew up on a ranch and are tough as nails, but don't go all cowboy on me. Let us handle this."

"We'll wait for you at Delphine's shack," Annie told him.

"I can't stress to you enough how dangerous Jacques Morel is. We traced your John Davidson online stalker to him, and we never stopped investigating him, even after we arrested Pete Thibodeaux. Miss Logan, stay at Angel's tonight and let us do our job."

"Gran will disown us if we wait here like cowards."

He sighed. "Just keep out of Jacques' clutches and out of our way, then. Can you do that?"

"I promise we will." Annie added, "Barring the unforeseen."

As he was ending the call, she thought he said a word forbidden in the Logan household, but she couldn't be sure.

"You go, warrior woman!" Jen gave Annie a high-five, and Rachel saluted her with the cast iron skillet.

A sense of wonder burst through Lucien's worry, and he looked as if he had just stumbled into a candy store and been offered his pick of treats. "I know a back way to Delphine's that's a whole lot quicker than the route on this map."

"Then what are we waiting for?" Annie and her sisters trooped out the door and down the long pier to Lucien's boat. It was the picture of serenity, floating on the water, swaying gently in the breeze that stirred the mists surrounding them. If she didn't know better, she'd think they were going on a moonlight boat tour instead of a life-and-death mission to rescue Victoria Logan from the clutches of a butcher.

It was still dark when they arrived at the Swamp Witch's shack, the outline of it fading in and out of the mists, briefly illuminated by the pale moonlight. Annie was astonished at how closely the shack resembled her dream, right down to the two sightings they'd already had of deadly vipers hanging from trees and a fierce-looking alligator sliding in the water at the approach of Lucien's boat.

"The snakes and gators won't bother you unless they feel threatened." Lucien guided his boat into the deep shadow of trees and cast anchor. "If I need to take care of them, I have everything I need, right here on this boat."

"Can't we get closer to shore?" Jen spoke softly so her voice wouldn't carry. "We can't walk from here."

"We'll have to wade," he told her. "If I get any closer, Jacques will know we're here."

"Does he have X-ray vision?" Jen asked. The bossy one.

"He'll know." Lucien kept his voice soft. "Grow up in the swamp, and you develop a sixth sense."

"Jen, we're not going anywhere unless we have to. The sheriff's bringing a SWAT team." Rachel, the peacemaker. "Anyhow, you're not afraid of a little water. You'd swim the whole swamp if you had to."

"You're right. Alligators have never bothered me. It's the snakes."

"The cops will be here soon," Rachel told her. "We'll let them worry about the snakes."

Annie gave her sisters grace because this was their first experience being on the water in a swamp. After they finally settled down to focus on the problem, she listened for any sound coming from the direction of the shack.

"Do you think the kidnapper was telling the truth about Gran still being alive?" Rachel whispered.

"I don't know, but I don't trust a thing Jacques says," Annie told her. A man who would rape and murder was capable of any depravity. And her past two dreams about this shack had already shown her with her feet in the water.

There was no sign of life in the shack. No light, no sound that carried on the still air, no shadow glimpsed through the windows that glared into the night like evil eyes.

Swallowed by the swirling mists and swamped by a deepening sense of dread, Annie watched and listened.

SIXTY-TWO

Jacques slipped through the back door of the Swamp Witch's shack, congratulating himself on his cleverness. The voodoo doll he'd hung on Angel's gazebo would bring his quarry right to his door.

He had thought the killings would bring her to her knees and send her fleeing back to the other side of the world so he could go on living his life with Lucien. But, no, Annie had to be tough. Like her mama. She had to keep fighting back.

He'd show her. He had a new plan, now. The old lady asleep in the narrow bed along the back wall was his center-piece. He stomped across the floor to see if he could wake her. She just snored louder. He slapped his leg with glee. It didn't take many sleeping pills to keep her too woozy to run, but cognizant enough to eat and go to the bathroom. Most of the time, he kept her completely knocked out. Who needed chains with an ancient woman like that? He was twice her size, and ten times as mean.

He thought of the ways he was going to kill her. Snapping her neck would be easy, but he didn't want easy. He wanted brutal and bloody. He wanted a spectacle that would bring Annie to her knees, begging for mercy.

He'd have to kill the sisters first, of course. Especially Rachel. He knew what she'd done out in Colorado. For a while, she was a national hero, a role model for strong women everywhere in America. Her and that stupid cast iron skillet. Just let her try that silly trick on him. He'd gut her before she could lift a hand.

A burst of pleasure sizzled through him. He was going to enjoy killing Patrick Logan's girls. Annie would give him pause, but not enough to spare her. His own daughter had been his ruination, and she had to pay.

The only thing that would make his day of reckoning sweeter would be a witness. But he couldn't risk that, not yet. Maybe next time. He'd killed animals all his life, but killing a quarry who understood what was coming gave him a thrill unlike any he'd ever experienced. It was addictive. He needed the fix of power like he needed oxygen. He was already thinking ahead to his next game, his next targets. The Shadow would become a Creole legend far greater than the fearsome Rougarou.

He poked the old lady with the toe of his boot to see if she was playing possum, but she just snored louder.

"Enjoy your sweet dreams while you can, old woman. Soon enough, you'll be alligator bait."

All of them would. Including Annie. But not until she'd watched her entire family be murdered in front of her.

There would be no bodies this time. No evidence left behind. The alligators would take care of the bodies, and he'd torch the shack then watch it burn until every stick and board had turned to ash and cinders.

How long before Annie found the voodoo doll? She'd come after him like some modern-day Wonder Woman. Women like her didn't sit back and let others do their dirty work. If he didn't blame her for being the reason Delilah went back to that stupid ranch and never spoke to him again, he'd admire her. Like father, like daughter. She was every bit as tough as he was.

"You're going to get yours, girly." He stalked across the shack, popped a beer, and guzzled it down.

He was reaching into his ice chest for another when he noticed his rope missing. He was sure he'd left it coiled and hanging on a nail against the back wall. His hammer was still there, the head wedged between two nails, and so was his saw.

Jacques scratched his head. Maybe he'd left the rope in his boat. He'd have to figure out where he put it, but not until he had another beer. He crushed the can in his hand then had three more.

He was feeling invincible tonight. Why not celebrate? He had plenty to cheer about. The silver bracelet he'd planted in Pete's office would finally take down his lifelong rival.

Pete Thibodeaux had always stood between Jacques and everything he wanted, especially Delilah. He wouldn't have needed a date-rape drug if Pete hadn't been along that night. Delilah always had a soft spot for Jacques. All he needed was the right time and the right place to convince her she would have a happier life back in the bayou among her people. Jacques' life would have been wonderful instead of filled with empty years. He could have had a princess instead of a needy hag, whose only saving grace was her cruelty.

But, *no*, there was Pete, hanging around Delilah that night like a love-sick calf. Talking sweet talk. Making her feel special.

Memories of Delilah burned through him. Feeling sorry for himself, Jacques stumbled to his cooler for another drink. Suddenly, something whistled through the air behind him, and he turned to face the old lady, her boots planted wide, whirling a lasso with the ease of one born to the ranch.

"What the...?" The lasso fell around his chest, and Victoria

Logan cinched it tight, pinning his arms to his side. Shock immobilized him.

"I've got the constitution of a horse," she said. "It takes more than a little sleeping pill to put me down."

He lunged at her, and she sidestepped, nimble as a woman forty years younger. Before he could recover, she'd circled him, wrapping the lasso around his waist.

"You think you can mess with my granddaughters? I aim to take you down like a steer."

If he didn't do something fast, she was going to hobble him. He charged, roaring like a bull, and was gratified by her high-pitched scream.

## SIXTY-THREE

The scream pierced the night, galvanizing Annie and her sisters.

"*Gran!*" Rachel grabbed her skillet and bailed out of the boat with Annie right behind her.

"Wait for me!" With her backpack secure, Jen appeared beside them, fierce in the predawn.

"Be careful!" Lucien was suddenly in the water with them. "Be quiet and follow me. Jacques is less likely to spot us if we go through the back door."

Mud sucked at their shoes and green algae clung to their clothes as they made their way through the murky water. Something brushed against Annie's leg, and she leaped forward, tamping down her terror. Was that the scaly back of an alligator slithering away? Impossible to tell in the dark.

It was a relief to finally set foot on land. With her pants legs dripping wet and her shoes slick with mud, Annie stood on the bank, hidden from the shack by a thicket of bushes, and waited for her sisters.

Lucien took the lead and motioned for them to get down. They all hunkered over and crept toward the shack. Swamp creatures scurried away, and eyes peered at them from bushes and treetops.

"This is creepy," Rachel whispered, and Annie told her, "Try not to think about it."

There had been no more yells or screams from the shack. The lights were still off. Annie and her sisters had no idea what was happening.

Suddenly, there was a loud snap and Lucien cried out. Annie got to him first. His leg was caught in the teeth of the large metal trap, his jaw clenched in pain.

"It will take me a while to get out of it, Annie. Wait for the sheriff."

While she pondered the pros and cons, Victoria screamed again. "I can't wait. I'm sorry." Annie took off running with her sisters matching her, stride for stride. Rachel raised her skillet, while Jen held a hammer in one hand and the wasp spray in the other. The back door came in view, and with it, the loud sounds of a scuffle.

"He'll hear us coming," Annie said, "so don't hesitate. We're going in ready for battle."

Jen raised her hammer and destroyed the latch in one blow. Annie burst through the door first. Her grandmother had lassoed Jacques as if he were a steer at a rodeo. He bucked against the ropes while Victoria scrambled around him, trying to get close enough to secure his legs.

Jen aimed the hornet spray at his face. He screeched, "I'm on fire!" and then called her names that earned him another blast of the toxic spray.

"Bull's eye!" Jen said, while Rachel waded in with the skillet. Her bop to his skull could be heard clear out to the cougar trap where Lucien still struggled to free himself. Annie stormed in and delivered three perfectly placed karate kicks to the murderer's groin.

Jacques howled and spewed threats at Annie. "I'm going to

kill your stupid sisters then gut you like a wild hog. I'm going to slice you open and dance in your blood."

"Watch who you call stupid!" Jen shot another blast of hornet spray into his face.

Victoria screeched like a banshee and swooped in. "We'll see who does the victory dance."

The sisters stood back and let their grandmother have her moment of revenge and glory. Within minutes she had Jacques trussed up like a steer in a roping contest at a Colorado rodeo.

The front door burst open, and Sheriff Debeau swarmed through with his SWAT team. They came to a halt and took in the scene, their faces showing everything from astonishment to barely suppressed wicked glee.

Sheriff Debeau struggled to keep his expression neutral. "I see you've already done my job."

The knot on Jacques' head had grown to the size of a fist, his face was raw, and his eyes were swollen shut. If Victoria hadn't already had him bent double with rope, the pain where Annie had kicked him would have done the trick. He whimpered like a baby.

"Help me!" Jacques Morel turned to the sheriff with the desperation of his own victims, begging for their lives. "Get these women away!"

Early morning sunlight filtered into the den of Angel's house in the bayou. Annie and her sisters surrounded their grandmother, who sat on the sofa. Lucien leaned against the mantel, his foot bandaged, while Sheriff Debeau and Deputy Wanda Sparks sat opposite Victoria Logan, taking her statement. In spite of the fact that she had lassoed a killer and looked none the worse for wear in her cowboy shirt and boots, the sheriff had said he wanted to spare her having to go all the way to the St. Tammany Parish Sheriff's Department.

"Mrs. Logan," the sheriff said, "you said you were in the Marigny when Jacques Morel kidnapped you."

"That's what my GPS showed. I was up near a deserted park when this redhead ran into the street, waving her arms and screaming like the devil was after her. I stopped and got out to see if I could help. At first, she acted helpless and as sweet as could be, then this big man I later learned was Jacques came up behind me and wrapped a rag around my mouth. The next thing I know, I'm in the shack."

"Can you describe the redhead?"

"Short, not much taller than me. Mousy looking. Homely. Spoke with a Deep South accent."

"Jacques' girlfriend," Lucien said. "Helen Whitaker. She was at Pete's Place when somebody broke into Toni's car and left a rattlesnake. She's been snooping into my business since before Annie arrived."

"She's been spying on Angel in the Marigny, too, trying to find out my business. I have something for you." Annie went to the kitchen to bag the latest voodoo doll and bring it back to Sheriff Debeau. "Helen is making these with Molly Guidry in the cottage across from Angel in the Marigny. Jen gave photographic evidence to the New Orleans PD and the FBI."

"We'll pick her up. We've believed all along the killer had an accomplice. We'll likely find Mrs. Logan's pickup stashed at the big old Whitaker place outside of Pearl River with Helen's prints all over it." Debeau made the call then turned back to Victoria. "I know this is painful for you, but can you tell us exactly what happened in that shack?"

"When I came to in the shack, Jacques had my phone. He made me give him my password, and he sent texts to my granddaughters that I was sick and would be late arriving. He bragged that he planned on making Annie watch him kill me and her two older sisters before he finally put her out of her misery. He's evil to the bone."

"Other than keeping you captive, did he harm you in any way?

"I played the feeble old woman card." Victoria chuckled. "He thought I was so weak and pitiful he didn't even bother tying me up with that rope I stole. He thought a few sleeping pills would keep me under control. I spit most of them out. I could have walked out of there any time he left, but I've got more sense than to go wandering around lost in a strange swamp full of snakes and alligators without old Betsy."

"Old Betsy?"

"My shotgun. I just waited for my granddaughters to come get me."

"How did you know they would?"

"Because they're *Logans*. Our coat of arms bears the motto we live and die by—*Hoc Majorum Virtus*. 'This is the valor of my ancestors.' Hiram and I didn't produce any wimps."

"I'll vouch for that." Harold Debeau stood up to shake Victoria's hand. "Mrs. Logan, I promise you we'll put this killer away. I intend to make my parish a safe place, not only for you and your family, but for everybody who lives or visits here."

Annie walked with the sheriff and his deputy onto the front porch where early morning splendor made it impossible to dwell on the recent horror. Sheriff Debeau promised to call her as soon as they found Victoria's truck, and asked her to report if she had any more problems.

After he and his deputy left, Annie stood with her face turned up to the sun while the bayou whispered its story. There was nothing left of evil, no lingering horrors, no echoes of monsters, only the song of the water as it meandered through the wetlands.

By the time she got back inside, the front room was empty except for Jen.

"Everybody else is in the kitchen," Jen said. "While you were outside, we told Gran about Mom's letters."

"What was her response? Did she acknowledge Lucien as our brother?"

"You know Victoria. She just said she wanted breakfast."

When they walked into the kitchen, Victoria was already seated at the head of the table, looking every inch the tough matriarch of the family as well as the beloved grandmother who has helped raise Annie and her sisters. Lucien hovered near the coffee pot, looking uncomfortable and even slightly miserable.

Annie walked over and put her arm around his waist. "Nobody blames you for what Jacques did. You are our brother."

"And you're my grandson." Victoria dropped her bomb, and everybody crowded around her at the table except Rachel, who went to the coffee pot and brought back a cup for her grandmother.

"I thought Jacques was my father," Lucien said softly.

"When Delilah came back from the bayou carrying a newborn baby girl, I thought all kind of things." Victoria picked up her cup and took her time enjoying a bit of morning coffee. Her granddaughters gave her the dramatic moment she had more than earned. Finally, she continued her story. Her way. "Mostly, I was worried that my son Patrick might not be the father. I had a DNA test done for paternity without telling a soul. Patrick is Annie's father. I've got the proof in my safe at home." She smiled at Lucien. "That means he's yours, too."

"This is..." Lucien searched for words, overcome.

"A day for rejoicing, I'd say." Victoria patted the chair beside her. "Sit down, Lucien, I have a few things to tell you about being a Logan. The first thing is to forget that sorry skunk Jacques Morel ever existed. We're your family now. You got that?"

"Yes, ma'am." His smile was the most genuine one Annie had ever seen from her twin.

"That's settled, then," Victoria said. "Let's have breakfast."

"How do you like your eggs?" Lucien asked. "Fried or scrambled?"

"Fried, over easy."

Lucien nabbed a carton of eggs from the refrigerator, Rachel grabbed the bacon, and Annie got out the biscuit fixings. Jen poured herself a cup of coffee and tried to boss the whole thing.

Anyone looking in the window would have thought they

had been a family forever. But only Annie, observing with a twin's heart, could see the silver thread winding around them, stitching them back together, weaving a tapestry that could never again be ripped apart.

# SIXTY-FIVE

## THE MARIGNY



New Orleans was in a festive mood. Holiday decorations adorned the store fronts and balconies; Christmas tree lights glowed from every window, and holiday jazz played all over the Square and in the clubs of the French Quarter.

As Annie made her way to Green Oak Gallery with her two escorts, Victoria Logan and Angel Broussard, her own mood matched that of the city. Though she was dressed in the same white gown and cape she'd worn only weeks ago for her art show at the Galleria Le Logge, she felt as if she were an entirely different woman from the independent artist who had lived a bohemian life in Italy. She was more grounded now, more family-oriented, and more than a little enchanted by the man who met her at the gallery door. Paul Chenevert, resplendent in a tuxedo, smiling in a way that was meant only for her.

He greeted both women with a hug, but held onto Annie long enough to whisper, "You take my breath away. Save the last dance for me."

"I promise," she whispered back.

"Chenevert, if you try to hug me, I'll box your ears." Angel's broad smile belied his gruff manner.

"I'm quaking in my boots." Paul lifted a pant leg to display a pair of new cowboy boots.

"Me, too." Victoria lifted her green silk skirt to reveal the well-worn turquoise boots she wore everywhere, no matter the occasion. She had stayed in New Orleans since her kidnapping so she could get to know her grandson and make amends to Angel for keeping him away from his grandchildren. It took the two old curmudgeons only three days to discover how much they had in common. "I'm not buying a word of your bluster, Angel. Never did."

Rachel and her family—Hank Carson and her children, five-year-old Joey, and Susan, eight going-on eighteen—walked through the door in time to see the boots on display and burst into applause. Rachel had brought the boots from Colorado yesterday when she and her family flew in for the weekend in her husband's private jet. She'd said they were a gift to Paul for watching after Angel, but Annie knew better. The boots were a gift from a generous heart who always gave double what she received.

Jen and her family, who had driven from Gulf Breeze for the weekend, were right behind Rachel—Jen regal in her red caftan, gold bangles, and handcrafted necklace, and Benjamin clearly now at ease in his role of loving husband and doting father to their teenage twins, Tommy and Marianne.

Even their cousins, Dr. Richard Logan, a veterinarian, and his twin daughters, Alice, a search and rescue handler, and Jane, a doctor, had driven down from Tupelo for an impromptu family reunion.

Standing in the middle of her family, Annie knew she'd made the right decision to move back to the States. If she'd learned anything from the Honey Island Swamp murders, it was that family is everything. And so are good friends.

Toni arrived with Brick Beaufort and rushed over to join Annie. "The paintings are spectacular!" Toni said, and Brick agreed. Suddenly, Linda Holloway walked in, decked out in the same flowing red dress she had worn when she slandered Annie in her TV special. "Can you believe her?" Toni fumed. "The nerve."

"Nothing surprises me," Annie said.

Since Jacques Morel's arrest, Linda Holloway had become almost a permanent fixture on the news. She was still hashing over every detail of the Honey Island Swamp murders, the kidnapping of Annie Logan's grandmother, and the capture of the Shadow and his accomplice.

Because of Linda, the public knew that Jacques Morel was in jail awaiting trial for murder, kidnapping, and stalking, while his girlfriend, Helen Whitaker, awaited trial as an accessory on all counts. In addition to making the voodoo dolls Jacques used, Helen had not only helped break into Toni's car to plant the rattlesnake, but she had hidden Victoria's car in her barn and Evangeline's in the woods on Angel's property.

Evangeline's statement revealed that Helen had even wielded one of the knives that sliced her up and left her for dead. After Helen was brought in, she had confessed to knowledge—and fawning admiration—of the murders of Janine and Sylvie. Because of the brutal nature of their murderous crime spree, Jacques and Helen were called a modern-day Bonnie and Clyde. Neither of them showed remorse, and Helen was actively planning her wedding to Jacques.

Following Victoria's rescue from the Swamp Witch's shack, both Annie and Victoria had turned down Linda's plea for an interview. Linda stopped short when she saw Annie surrounded by family. Instead, she said to one of her gushing fans, "I just couldn't miss this chance to finally see the famous artist, face to face."

"Face to face, my hind foot," Victoria grumbled. "After the

way she slandered you, she'll be lucky if I don't take my shillelagh to her."

"Gran, behave!"

"I never have, and I'm too old to start now." The bells over the door played their song, and Vitoria beamed. Lucien walked in holding onto Evangeline, who wore a long blue velvet skirt to hide her bandaged stump. She was fragile-looking and still on crutches while she waited for her leg to heal enough so she could get a prosthetic foot. But she was smiling. She had survived.

"That's my grandson," Victoria added, as if she still couldn't believe it. She charged his way, every inch the indomitable matriarch. Her family followed while Paul lingered behind with Annie.

He leaned down to whisper, "Do I actually have you all to myself?"

It felt both exciting and intimate. But the moment was fleeting as Paul's clients began to flock in Annie's direction.

"Not yet. But soon."

"I'll hold you to that promise. Now, go wow your public."

He slipped away and left her to chat with art lovers about her watercolors. Spotlights spilled across her paintings, and the colors swirled around Annie, catching her up in one of her waking dreams. Her flat in Italy appeared, the pink stucco casting a glow on the two who walked in the garden—Paul and Annie, enjoying their summer place and each other. Stars fell from the painting of a meditation garden and lit the canopied bed in Paul's home in the Marigny where she lay in his arms, her sleep peaceful and her dreams of the beauty they would create together, both in art and in life.

Suddenly, there was Paul, standing in the swirl of color, reaching for her hand, not a dream but real, his smile a promise of their future.

Annie was finally home.

# A LETTER FROM PEGGY

Dear reader,

Thank you so much for reading *Without a Trace*. If you want to keep up to date with all my latest releases, just sign up at the following link. Your email address will never be shared and you can unsubscribe at any time.

*www.bookouture.com/peggy-webb*

Annie's story took me to New Orleans, a city in south Louisiana that I know and love. I so enjoyed bringing its rich history alive for you in *Without a Trace*! I hope you could see the beautiful French and Spanish architecture through my eyes, and hear the haunting strains of a blues lament wafting through the open doors on Bourbon Street. My own love of music flows through my veins like a river gone wild. I transferred it to Delilah, who gave it to you via the pages of the third Logan Sisters thriller.

The mist-shrouded bayous around New Orleans are a perfect hiding place for my villain, the Shadow. But Honey Island Swamp in the heart of nature is also a great setting to unveil the mystery behind Delilah Broussard Logan, mother to the Logan sisters.

I simply *love* Annie's story! And I hope you do, too. If so, I would be very grateful if you would write a review. I'd love to hear what you think. Your feedback means the world to me, and it helps new readers discover one of my books for the first time.

To loyal fans who have been with me through the years and to new fans who have joined me on this thrilling writing journey with Bookouture—my heartfelt thanks!

I love hearing from you! Do stay touch on my social media pages, my new You Tube channel, and my website. You'll find my blog with insider info on my website, and some surprises, too!

Thank you so much for being such amazing, supportive readers!

Peggy Webb

www.peggywebb.com

facebook.com/peggywebbauthor

instagram.com/peggy.webb.92

youtube.com/@PeggyWebbOnPageAndPiano

# ACKNOWLEDGMENTS

I am so blessed by the amazing team at Bookouture who *always* provide the best possible guidance and expertise. Your encouragement, support, and faith in me are the wind beneath my wings!

To Jess Whitlum-Cooper, my amazing editor, a heartfelt thank you for loving this book as much as I do and for helping turn it into the best possible version. Once again, you've proved to be worth your weight in gold. What a joy to work with you!

To the incredible Alba Proko, a big thank you for making the audio production such fun! To Noelle Holten, kudos and a big hug for great publicity. To Mandy Kullar and Jen Shannon for keeping me sane during production, a huge thank you. To Melanie Price and Occy Carr, kudos for fabulous marketing. To the terrific Jon Appleton, who gets the book last, navigates the murky waters between British vs American style, and finally whips it into tiptop shape, my deepest gratitude! To publishers Ruth Tross and Laura Deacon, who first loved the series, my eternal gratitude.

It takes a village. There are so many people I haven't named here. Behind the scenes, a huge team of experts at Bookouture worked hard to bring *Without a Trace* to bookshelves. To each one of you—thank you!

A special thanks to Elois Williams and Cindy Bowman for providing information and research materials on New Orleans.

On the home front I have the amazing support of my family and my friends. I don't want to ever know what it's like write a book without you! All of you are hereby instructed to stay safe and healthy!

To my readers, thank you for bringing my characters into your home, following their stories, writing reviews, and encouraging me on social media. You are *the best!* I'm so blessed by you!

Hugs to all!

Peggy

**Turning a manuscript into a book requires the efforts of many people. The publishing team at Bookouture would like to acknowledge everyone who contributed to this publication.**

### Audio
Alba Proko
Sinead O'Connor
Melissa Tran

### Commercial
Lauren Morrissette
Hannah Richmond
Imogen Allport

### Cover design
Eileen Carey

### Data and analysis
Mark Alder
Mohamed Bussuri

### Editorial
Jess Whitlum-Cooper
Imogen Allport

**Proofreader**
Jon Appleton

**Marketing**
Alex Crow
Melanie Price
Occy Carr
Cíara Rosney
Martyna Młynarska

**Operations and distribution**
Marina Valles
Stephanie Straub

**Production**
Hannah Snetsinger
Mandy Kullar
Jen Shannon
Ria Clare

**Publicity**
Kim Nash
Noelle Holten
Jess Readett
Sarah Hardy

**Rights and contracts**
Peta Nightingale
Richard King
Saidah Graham

9 781835 253984